Never stop creating!

Like a Mom

Raquel Drosos

ISBN-13: 979-8-9871597-2-9
E-book ISBN-13: 979-8-9871597-3-6

Cover design by Luísa Dias

First Edition: October 2024

Visit the author's website at www.raqueldrosos.com

To all the women who have been real with me
And to my husband and children

Chapter One

"It's time for drastic action," Lina says. It's Thursday morning, and the lawyers are gathered in the reception area. "This can't go on any longer."

"I know," Erica says.

"Put a finger splint on Chase's thumb," Lina says. "Or use that bitter nail polish. Then he'll stop sucking."

These are the kinds of conversations I overhear at Callahan & Ramos, the boutique law firm where I work. We're all women at the office—Erica, Lina, and Jasmine are lawyers, and Bree and I are legal assistants. On my first day, I was surprised to find it was just the five of us and no men. I've been working here for a month now, and I still find the office dynamic fascinating.

Erica and Lina founded Callahan & Ramos a year and a half ago using both of their last names. Prior to that, they worked at a large law firm together for six years. "Lina and I go way back," Erica said on my first day. "We were best friends in law school. We met when we were young, hot, and single and now we're moms of third graders…"

"And still hot," Bree said.

"Aww, thanks, Bree."

Callahan & Ramos focuses exclusively on estate planning law. The lawyers spend most of their time behind closed doors, working or meeting with clients, but when they get together, they act more like friends than coworkers. Erica, Lina, Jasmine, and Bree have a million inside jokes; they're constantly reliving stories from Jasmine's wedding, which took place the week before I was hired, and they know everything about each other's families. The four of them have the closest bond I've ever seen in a work environment.

Lina and Jasmine's clients arrive, bringing the thumb-sucking discussion to an end. Bree, whose desk is next to mine in the reception area, calls out to Erica. "The website was updated. Looks great!"

"Let me see," Erica says.

Erica leans over Bree's computer, and I open the firm's website on my computer too. The layout is cleaner and more modern than it was this morning, and the images on the homepage are new. I click on the "Meet the Team" tab and find the picture of the five of us that was taken last week. We're standing near the couches in the reception area; the hallway leading to Erica, Lina, and Jasmine's offices stretches out behind us. Everyone is smiling and looks put together—we're an attractive group. I close the website again.

The women I work with know how to dress for their body types and wear the right amount of makeup, skills that I admire because they don't come naturally to me. I spent my teenage years in ponytails and sweatpants and only learned how to dress nicely and style my wavy brown hair in college. I still don't wear makeup, and I feel more comfortable in hockey skates than high heels. My looks are okay; I'm thin and fit with long, strong legs, but my butt is flat and my torso is shaped like a V from my narrow hips to my broad shoulders. I do, however, have the large breasts that are the trademark of the women in my family. While it's annoying to wear three sports bras when I run, I've grown to love my breasts as one of my best features. My face is nice too, though it's more sweet than sexy—it's oval-shaped and olive-skinned, with big hazel eyes. I think men find me attractive, but I don't have as much fashion sense as the women at the office.

They're all pretty in different ways. Erica has a pear-shaped body, a round, cheerful face, and the most beautiful hair I've ever seen. It's not so much blonde as it is gold, falling in shining layers to her waist. "It's my natural color," she said when I complimented her on it. "I haven't had a single gray hair yet."

"I don't know how that's possible," Lina said. "Four kids and no grays. I only have two kids and I yank out a gray hair every day."

"But you have Ethan as a son," Erica said. "He'd turn anybody gray."

Lina sighed. "Three trips to the ER so far this year. I have to get rid of that skateboard..."

Lina is slim and toned with short brown hair, dark eyes, and glasses. She and Erica are both in their thirties and have children ranging in age from eight to three. I hope to have kids myself one day, so I enjoy hearing stories about their families.

Jasmine doesn't have kids. She's twenty-seven, a year older than me. She's the firm's only associate, and she started working here exactly a year ago; we're supposed to go out for happy hour today to celebrate her anniversary. Jasmine is the daughter of Filipino immigrants, speaks four languages, and has a loud, carrying voice you can hear from a block away. She's five feet tall, if that, with a curvy body, flawless brown skin, and black hair. I consider her the warmest person at work, though Lina and Erica are friendly too.

Bree is different. She laughs and chats along with the others, but she doesn't let her guard down; I can never tell what she's thinking. She's twenty-four and has silky brown hair, green eyes, a tiny waist, and slender legs. She walks in heels as if they were her bare feet and is elegant and poised at all times. Though her name is Brielle, she insists on being called Bree, which I think is strange; she seems too serious to go by a nickname. Bree has been working for Callahan & Ramos since its inception and will be starting law school part-time this summer. Like me, Bree is single, but we don't have much else in common. Though we share responsibilities at work, she remains aloof toward me, and I find her more intimidating than the other women at the office.

"Gemma." Erica looks up from Bree's computer and addresses me. "I'm going to send you an email about the Bianchi couple I just met with. Could you open up a matter for them?"

"Sure," I say.

I get to work. Being a legal assistant was never my dream job, but at least Callahan & Ramos is a nice place to work; it's better than the intense, fast-paced law firm where I had my first job after college. I ended up as a secretary at that large firm after spending six months finishing my novel—a novel that was rejected by every agent and publisher who read it—and failing to start a career in writing or editing. I worked at that first firm for a year, then spent two years as an assistant editor for a literary journal in Arizona. Now that I've moved back to New Jersey, I miss the literary journal sometimes; the job fueled my creativity. The landscape out West also provided inspiration for the novel I'm currently writing, which I continue to work on though it will likely be garbage like my previous book.

At the end of the work day, I head out the door with Erica, Lina, Jasmine, and Bree. Our firm is on the first floor of a small office building on Bloomfield Avenue, the main street in Verona. We walk to an Irish pub called Finn's, get a round of drinks, and raise a toast to Jasmine. Then we sit at one of the tables and start talking.

"They finally fixed my name on the website," Jasmine says. "Took them long enough—my clients kept getting confused. I can see why you guys kept your maiden names when you got married."

"I would have taken Roger's name, but it's too hard to spell," Lina says. "So many consonants in a row...everyone messes it up."

"Artie was mad I didn't take his, remember?" Erica says.

"That was funny—you were such a snob about it. You were like..." Lina sticks her nose in the air and adopts a snooty tone that sounds nothing like Erica. "'The Callahans are a family of lawyers. I can't give up my name.'"

"Eww, did I say that?" Erica says.

"Kinda, yeah."

The topic shifts to the house Jasmine and her husband just bought and how she plans to decorate it. Everyone shares design ideas and looks at pictures of paint colors and furniture on Jasmine's phone. I observe the conversation around me without contributing much. I like and respect all these women, but I get the feeling I'm on the outside of their clique; it's not my place to offer an opinion.

"You're so quiet, Gemma," Jasmine says to me a while later, while the other girls are chatting. "Is there anything you want to talk about?"

"I like to listen mostly," I tell her. "I've learned a lot by listening."

"Fair enough."

We stay at the bar for an hour, and then I head home. I live in Oakfield, the small town where I grew up. Oakfield is nestled between the more affluent and more exciting towns of Verona and Montclair; it lacks the bustling downtown and thriving restaurant scene of its neighbors, but it's less expensive. Its affordability, low crime rate, and decent schools attract a mix of blue-collar and white-collar families of various ethnicities. Oakfield's streets consist of small, aging colonial and Cape Cod-style houses anchored by corner stores and delis. Main Avenue has no nightlife, just a supermarket, a library, and several pizzerias. Though Oakfield is a boring place to live, it's home to me. I pull into my driveway, then head inside to have dinner with my dad. Hopefully I can squeeze in some writing after we eat.

***

The next morning is bright and sunny; by noon, it's seventy degrees. New Jersey rarely has nice weather in early April, and I keep looking out the window while I'm at work, wishing I could be outside. Bree stops by my desk on her way out of Erica's office. "Time for a coffee break," she says.

I point to my thermos. "I have a coffee."

"No, a coffee break is when we all get together. You'll see."

Bree turns on the coffee maker, and I join Erica, Lina, and Jasmine on the couches. Everyone turns toward Erica, who seems preoccupied.

"Mackenzie was crying after school yesterday," Erica says, referring to her daughter. "My mom picked her up and asked her what was wrong, but Mackenzie wouldn't tell her. It took me until bedtime to get the story out of her. Apparently, the popular girls ganged up on her and told her she was fat."

A collective groan goes around the group. "Those fucking bitches," Jasmine says.

"I know," Erica says. "I told her that she's beautiful and that everyone has different body types. I said she should never listen to mean girls—they act mean because they're insecure about themselves. But I know what they said is bothering her. She kept looking in the mirror this morning, tugging on her clothes, and it broke my heart. She's only seven! I didn't think this body image shit would start so early."

"It's sickening," Jasmine says. "Kids deserve time to be kids. Mackenzie should be playing with dolls and running around the playground, not worrying about how she looks."

"It's too late for that," Erica says. "Now that she's aware of her appearance, I can't stop her from criticizing herself. And it's going to get worse the older she gets..."

"Try to build her confidence in other ways," Lina says. "If she feels good about who she is as a person, she can shrug off comments about her looks. That's one of the reasons I pushed Cristina into soccer—sports give you a sense of achievement, and they make you appreciate what your body can do. It's good to feel strong before you feel pretty."

"Mackenzie isn't the type for sports," Erica says. "She hates conflict and competition. She just wants to draw and make up stories and live in her fantasy world where it's all sunshine and rainbows. She's so nice to everyone; she can't understand why people aren't nice to her."

Everyone goes on talking about Mackenzie, letting Erica share her feelings and offering advice. I don't say anything, but I pay close attention. This coffee break feels familiar; it reminds me of the time I've spent with my aunts over the years, listening to their problems and absorbing their wisdom. After a while, the group breaks up and we go back to work.

When I leave the office, I head to get Michela from her preschool. Michela is my youngest cousin and my aunt Soph's only child; I babysit her a lot, and we have a close relationship. Aunt Soph isn't expecting me to pick up Michela today, but it's perfect weather to take her to the park. Aunt Soph won't be home until seven, and I'm sure Michela will be happy to get out of after care early. As soon as Michela sees me, she runs up to me and throws her arms around my legs. "Aunt Gemma!" she yells.

"Do you want to go to the park?" I ask her.

"Yeah!"

We head to Oakfield Park, the only park in town, with its sprawling playground. As we drive, Michela tells me about her day.

"Andrew dumped all the crayons on the floor," she says. "And he threw his pillow at naptime. He's not nice."

"That doesn't sound nice," I say.

"And Caroline said a bad word and had to go in time out!"

We reach the playground, which is packed with parents and kids. Michela, who was shy as a baby and a younger toddler, is now friendly to everyone. I never have to entertain her at the park; she runs up to random kids and says, "Want to play?" Today is no different. After five minutes she's weaseled her way into a game of tag with a bunch of older girls. I'm not sure if Michela grasps the concept of the game, but she's running and laughing and that's what's important. She tends to be cautious, and I like seeing her let go and enjoy herself.

Michela follows the girls up and down the jungle gym and over to a tunnel on the ground shaped like a log. The girls climb on top of the tunnel, but Michela crawls inside instead. As I'm waiting for her to come out, I notice a man nearby who is playing with his son. The little boy, who is around Michela's age, keeps popping out of the tunnel on one side or the other; every time his dad spots him, he scoops him up and tickles him. The kid shrieks with delight until his dad puts him down, and then he races into the tunnel to start the game again. The dad is attractive; he has vibrant blue eyes, curly hair so dark it's nearly black, and a short beard. The tattoos on his arms stand out against his pale skin.

He's wearing a plain black t-shirt and jeans, and his sneakers are as beat-up and muddy as a little kid's. He doesn't look like a dad, but it's clear from the way he's snatching up that boy and kissing his belly that the kid is his. The dad has a second kid with him, too; every few minutes, he checks on the sleeping baby in the double stroller next to him. "Aunt Gemma," Michela says, poking her head out of the tunnel. "There's a spider in here!"

"Spiders belong outside," I say. "It's not going to hurt you."

Michela goes back into the tunnel, and the boy's dad comes closer to me to stage his next attack. I glance at his tattoos. There's a tiger and a ferocious bird and something that looks like a comet but I can't make out the details because he's moving again, grabbing his son as he runs out of the tunnel. "Got you!" he says. "You'll never escape!"

"Daddy!" the boy squeals.

The dad throws his son into the air, then puts him down and lets him run back to the tunnel. The boy crashes into Michela, who is coming out at the same time. Both kids are unfazed by the collision. "Hi!" Michela says. "Want to play?"

"Yeah!" the boy says. "You be the princess and I'll be the monster."

"Okay!"

They take off running. An elaborate plot begins to unfold, a plot only the two of them understand; there are monster noises and magic spells and dramatic falls to the ground. The dad smiles as he watches his son and Michela rolling around. "God knows what they're doing," he says to me. "He has the wildest imagination."

"Imagination is good," I say. "He'll never get bored."

"True." The dad checks his stroller again. The baby sleeping there has a mass of dark curls like his father and brother. "I should wake Scotty up. He passed out in the swing before, but now it's getting close to bedtime. Still, he looks so relaxed..."

"He's adorable," I say. "How old is he?"

"Eleven months; he's turning one next week. How old is yours?"

"She's not mine—she's my cousin. And she'll be four in June."

"Cool, same as Nate. He turns four in May."

8

I smile at the name, because it seems to fit his kid. I like meeting people whose names suit them. "That's a nice name."

"Thanks. What's her name?"

"Michela." As we're talking, Nate starts climbing up a rock wall that looks like it was meant for a twelve-year-old; it stretches high into the air, to the tallest part of the jungle gym. "Woah," I say. "That's some climb..."

"I know, right?" his dad says. "I used to tell him not to do it but he insisted..."

"It's great that he's brave. Michela is afraid of everything."

"I don't blame her. I was afraid of everything too when I was a kid." He laughs. "Still am, actually."

This is an odd thing for a man to say, especially to someone he doesn't know; I study his face, but he doesn't seem embarrassed. Then I see Michela following Nate up the rock wall. My heart races—she's never climbed so high before—but she scrambles to the top with ease. The kids run back and forth until Nate disappears into a steep tunnel slide.

"Shit, he always falls off that slide," his dad says. "Watch Scotty for a second?" He dashes to the other side of the jungle gym.

Nate's dad gets there just in time; Nate shoots out of the slide and he catches him. Michela comes flying out behind Nate and he catches her too. The kids run off in different directions. I glance into the stroller at Scotty, who has woken up and is blinking at me with big brown eyes. "Hi, cutie!" I say.

Nate's dad jogs over to me and takes the handlebar of the stroller. "Thank you."

"You're welcome."

He chases Nate, and I follow Michela to the swings. After a few minutes, I get a text from Aunt Soph saying she's on her way home. "Time to go home and see Mommy," I tell Michela.

Aunt Soph arrives at the apartment at the same time as we do. Aunt Soph is a single mom and an OB-GYN, and as usual, she looks exhausted. She gives Michela a kiss. "How was your day, my love?"

"So many people got in trouble, Mommy!" Michela says. "Caroline was in time out for the whole playtime..."

Michela launches into the stories she told me earlier. Aunt Soph is nodding, but I know she's only half-listening. She sends Michela to the bathroom and sinks down onto one of the kitchen chairs. "Thank you for picking her up, Gems," she says.

"No problem!"

"You want something to eat? I know your dad is probably cooking something amazing..."

"I'll wait until I get home," I say.

We chat for a few minutes. "I wanted to ask you a favor," Aunt Soph says. "They canceled my Wednesday yoga class, and now the only class that's available is Sunday mornings at eleven. Do you think some Sundays you might be able to..."

"Sure, I can watch Michela," I say.

"It's only an hour," Aunt Soph says. "And if you're busy certain weeks, I'll skip it. I already signed Michela up for a toddler arts and crafts class on the library lawn on Sunday mornings, so you can take her to that if you want."

"That sounds fun!"

"Mommy!" Michela whines from the bathroom. "The floor is wet!"

"Oh God, what did she do?" Aunt Soph says.

"I'm going to head home," I say. "I'll be over on Sunday."

I drive to my house, which is five minutes away. When I get into the kitchen, I find my dad at the stove, stirring a pot of broccoli rabe. "Hey Gems," he says. "Long day at work?"

"No, I took Michela to the park." I glance at the oven. "What are we having? Salmon?"

"Yeah, I made it with a pesto glaze this time."

"Ooh, sounds good!"

My dad loves to cook; he makes dinner for the two of us every night. He gets home from work by four most days, so that gives him plenty of time to prepare meals. As always, his glass of scotch is on the counter next to him; he takes a gulp of it. "There's a tray of roasted potatoes too," he says.

"Awesome—I'm starving."

He smiles. My dad is in his fifties, but he's still a handsome man—his dark Italian skin complements his gray hair, and his brown eyes are warm and intelligent in his tired face. He's in good shape because he exercises and eats a healthy diet, apart from the scotch. "Food is ready when you are," he says.

"Let me put on pajamas and I'll be right back."

I head upstairs. We have an old, creaky house; the stairs make noise when you step on them and the rooms are small and narrow. Yet I adore my house. The kitchen may be tiny, but it's filled with delicious smells and the cabinets are jammed with pots and pans and plates that we use every day. Years ago, my parents made the rooms bright and cheery by painting the walls light colors and picking out nice furniture, and the house feels cozy in spite of its flaws. I go to my room to change. We have three bedrooms, but mine is the only one that is used as a bedroom. My dad doesn't sleep in his bed; he passes out reading in his armchair every night. The last bedroom, the one at the end of the hallway, aspired to be a second child's room, but my parents never got to make a second child because my mom died. We use that spare bedroom for storage; there are shelves teeming with books, rows of hockey trophies, and childhood toys I can't bear to throw away. My mom's journals are there too, in a box under the desk. I've read each of the journals many times and I cherish them more than the pictures I have of her. I grab paper from the spare room and leave it on my nightstand; I always keep paper and a pen next to my bed, so I can write down ideas in the middle of the night. Then I go back downstairs.

My dad has set the table for dinner, and his glass of scotch is filled to the top again. I sit down and pour myself some wine. "How did the kids' presentations go?" I ask.

He laughs. "They were hilarious. One group did a sketch where Shakespeare was a rapper, and the whole class was hysterical..."

My dad goes on to explain his students' projects. He's a high school English teacher in a small town forty minutes from where we live. He's been teaching there for over thirty years and directing the school play every spring, and his students love him. It must be exhausting to corral teenagers, but my dad is in his element. "I'd rather work with teenagers than adults," he said to me once. "Teenagers are so present...they live every moment as if it were the most important moment in the world. They're figuring out who they are, and things that seem small to us— that concert or that girlfriend or that book you made them read and actually understand—shape their identities. And they make you laugh! Most adults have forgotten how to laugh." People usually call my dad Gio; pronounced like the English name "Joe," it's the nickname for his full name, Giordano. At work, though, he's Mr. Cimino, one of the most popular teachers in school.

My dad and I finish dinner and go into the living room to relax. I was planning to work on my novel tonight, but I'm exhausted; I'll get to it tomorrow. After half an hour, my dad is asleep, and the book he was reading has slipped to the floor. I take the empty glass out of his hand and bring it to the sink. My dad has been drinking scotch every night for as long as I can remember. My aunts say the habit started after my mom died, and they're always trying to get him to stop.

"You have to take it easy, Gio," Aunt Soph said last week, after seeing my dad toss another bottle of Johnnie Walker into our recycling bin. "You're ruining your liver."

My dad shrugged. "Everybody's gotta die of something."

My dad drinks because he misses my mom; that's the same reason he sleeps in the living room instead of in his bed. His drinking gets him through the night, and because he's a happy, functional drunk, it doesn't bother me. When I was little, he would start drinking after dinner, right before my bedtime; as I got older and more independent, he would crack the bottle open at dinner. Eventually, when I lived in Arizona, he settled on four P.M. as a start time. It's not healthy, but I don't expect my dad to change his routine after all these years. Tomorrow morning, like every morning, he'll wake up at five thirty, take two Advil for his headache, and head to the gym before he goes to school. He'll put his heart into teaching all day, and when he gets home, the cycle will start again.

I wash and dry the empty glass by hand, because the dishwasher is already running. Then I go to my room and fall asleep.

Chapter Two

New Jersey never makes up its mind about the spring. It dangles a warm day in our faces, then follows that up with weeks of cold and rain. Sunday is windy and damp; I put on my winter coat, pick up Michela, and drive to the library for art class. There are groups of parents and kids sitting on blankets on the lawn, and a teacher is organizing her cart full of supplies. "What are we going to make, Aunt Gemma?" Michela asks. "Do we get to use paint?"

"I hope so! I'm excited, too."

Out of the corner of my eye, I notice the family we met at the park on Friday walking across the lawn. Nate's dad has Scotty in one arm and a blanket in the other, and Nate is next to him. "There's your friend from the park," Nate's dad says to him. "Michela, right?"

"Hi!" Michela says.

Nate runs to Michela, leaving a trail of muddy footprints across our blanket. "Want to race up the hill?" he says.

"No, buddy, we have to stay here for class," Nate's dad says. "Help me with this blanket."

They sit down next to us. Scotty leans forward and starts batting at the blanket with his hands. "The blanket is soft," his dad says. "And it's blue."

"Boo," Scotty repeats.

"Blue is my favorite color!" Michela says.

"Mine too," Nate's dad says.

I notice that Nate's dad is shivering. He's wearing a short-sleeved t-shirt, even though his kids are in heavy coats. "Aren't you cold?" I ask him.

He shrugs. "I always remember to bundle them up, but I forget about me."

"Do you want a sweatshirt?" I say. "I have one in my car."

"It's all right."

"You sure? It's big on me—it'll fit you."

"I'm fine."

I look at the goosebumps on his arms and I can't let him suffer. "Be right back," I say. I take Michela's hand; we walk to my Honda Civic, which is parked alongside the lawn, and I grab my sweatshirt out of the back seat. It's the faded red University of Arizona sweatshirt that I've worn all over the country, and I've been leaving it in my car because the weather is unpredictable. I bring it to Nate's dad.

He laughs when he sees it. "Perfect—pink has always been my color."

"It's not pink," I say. "It's red."

"It's pink. Give it to me, though—I'm freezing."

Nate's dad puts the sweatshirt on, leaving the hood up. A few of his curls escape from the hood, and the red material makes his blue eyes pop. "Looks good, Daddy," Nate says.

"Yeah? You think?"

"Yeah!"

"He's the expert," I say to Nate's dad.

"Of course." He ruffles Nate's hair, then grins at me. He's so cute; it's inconvenient, really. I steal a glance at his hand. No ring. He could still be married, though. My uncles are loyal to their wives and they don't wear their rings; they've gained so much weight over the years that the bands no longer fit. My dad, by contrast, wears his ring even though my mom has been dead for over twenty-five years. A ring doesn't always tell the whole story.

"I wonder what the craft is going to be," Nate's dad says to the kids. "I see a bag of pom-poms over there..."

"Pom-poms!" Michela says.

"We have to make sure Scotty doesn't eat one."

The teacher introduces herself and passes out supplies. We're making animals out of cardboard tubes, and the kids get glue, paint, googly eyes, and pom-poms. Michela is disappointed at the sight of her paintbrush. "I don't want this one," she pouts. "I want blue."

"You can't always get blue," I say.

"Switch with Nate," Nate's dad says. "Orange is his favorite."

Nate and Michela trade paintbrushes, and Nate plops down next to her on our blanket. They start playing with the art supplies; before long, there are googly eyes and pom-poms everywhere. The two of them are ignoring the teacher's instructions and shooting pom-poms through tunnels they've made out of cardboard tubes. Scotty is busy dipping his fingers in different colors of paint. "No mouth," his dad says, pulling Scotty's hand away from his face. Scotty grabs his dad's arm, leaving a streak of paint on the sweatshirt. "Oh man, I'm sorry," his dad says to me. "It's probably washable..."

"It's okay," I say. "Art is supposed to be messy."

We smile at each other. "Is this where you went to college?" he asks, glancing at the logo on his chest.

"No, I went to Seton Hall. But I worked at the University of Arizona for two years, as an assistant editor for one of their literary journals."

"That sounds awesome."

"It was fun." I think back to my office in Tucson—my desk covered in papers and the glimpse of mountains outside my window. "One of my old professors was the editor-in-chief and she offered me the job. I love reading and writing so it was perfect for me."

"Why did you leave?"

"I missed my family," I say. I enjoyed my job in Arizona, but I was lonely; I remember worrying about my dad, and being brought to tears every time Aunt Soph sent me a picture of Michela looking more grown up than the last time I'd seen her. "Everybody I love lives here in New Jersey, and I didn't like being out West by myself."

"It's nice to have family close by," Nate's dad says.

"Daddy, look!" Nate holds up a cardboard tube, which is covered in googly eyes and glue. "It's a monster!"

"Looks great, buddy!"

"I made one too," Michela says. She bounces the monster up my arm. "Roar! I'm going to eat you!"

"Roar!" Nate says.

Suddenly I find myself attacked on both sides by cardboard tubes. Nate and Michela are laughing and so am I, but I can hear Nate's dad's voice above the chaos. "Take it easy, Nate...leave her alone..."

"Roar!" Nate dives on his dad. Nate and Michela attack him for a while, until Nate bumps into Scotty and knocks him down. "That's enough," Nate's dad says, picking Scotty up. "We're supposed to be making crafts."

"But the monsters are hungry," Nate says.

"Let them eat pom-poms or something."

Nate and Michela line up pom-poms to feed to the monsters, and Nate's dad cleans the paint off Scotty's hands with a baby wipe. "What do you do now?" he asks me. "Do you work for a journal around here?"

"No, I'm a legal assistant at a law firm."

"Really? That's a completely different job."

"I studied creative writing and there's no money in that, so I have to make a living somehow."

"I get it," he says. "I went to music school and now I work in customer service."

"Where do you work?"

"It's a logistics company that distributes imported foods to retailers," he says. "It's a boring job and the money isn't great, but it's all remote; I can keep the kids home with me instead of putting them in daycare. I

17

get a lot done at night and when Scotty is napping, so I can give them some attention during the day. It's not perfect, but it works." Scotty grabs his dad's shirt and pulls himself up to a standing position. "Right, Scotty?"

"Dada," Scotty says.

"Go ahead—tell me."

"Dada. Dada."

"That's me."

Scotty grabs his dad's face with both hands, and his dad kisses his nose. The baby laughs. It's adorable to watch but I feel like an intruder, enjoying this display of affection in a family that's not mine. I turn to Nate and Michela instead.

"Ow," I hear Nate's dad say. "That's my eye. Here, play with this."

I glance back at him and see Scotty yanking on the strings of the sweatshirt. I want to keep talking, but I'm starting to feel weird; this guy is probably married and I shouldn't be too friendly. Then again, we're just talking—not flirting—and he's been asking me plenty of questions, too. "What do you play?" I ask. "You said you went to music school."

"I sing and play guitar. I write music too—that's what I studied, songwriting. But I don't have much time for that now that I have the kids..."

"I can imagine."

"What do you write?"

I feel my face flush. I'm always embarrassed when people ask about my writing. "Novels," I say. "I'm working on a fantasy novel now...a fantasy trilogy, actually. But I don't know if it'll be any good."

"Don't think about if it's good—just write it," he says. "You shouldn't be a critic too early in the process."

"Oops," Nate says, and Michela lets out a shriek. The cup of water Nate was using to rinse his paintbrush has tipped over, soaking Michela's shoes and leaving a puddle on our blanket. "Sorry, Michela."

"Get it off!" Michela screams.

"It's just water," I say. "Relax."

"Get it off!"

By the time we calm Michela down and clean up the mess, the class is breaking up. "Bye, guys," Nate's dad says.

"Bye," I say.

I strap Michela into her car seat and watch Nate's dad put his kids in the small gray Toyota across the street. He's just finished buckling Nate when he glances down at my sweatshirt. "Oh shit," he says. "This is yours…"

"That's not a nice word, Daddy," Nate says.

"Sorry buddy." He pulls off the sweatshirt, then hesitates. "Um…do you want me to wash this and give it to you at the next class?"

"I'll wash it," I say. "I'm sure the kids give you enough laundry to do."

"That's for sure." He tosses the sweatshirt to me. It brushes against my face as I catch it and I notice its male scent—nothing overpowering like Axe or cologne, just the smell of his skin mixed with whatever shampoo he uses. A thrill goes through my stomach. "Thanks," he says. "I'm Luke, by the way."

"I'm Gemma."

"Cool. See you next week, Gemma."

"Aunt Gemma!" Michela wails. "My feet!"

"Okay, okay," I say. "We're leaving." I turn away from Luke and get into the car.

Chapter Three

My dad is one of five kids. He has three older sisters—Rosalba, Domenica, and Giovanna—and one younger sister, Sophia. General family wisdom says that my grandparents wanted a son and kept trying until they got one, and Aunt Soph was an accident ten years later. My grandma always denied this, but she's not alive anymore and Grandpa doesn't bother to lie about it. Aunt Ro, Aunt Dee, and Aunt Vanna are all close in age and happily married, and they're best friends. Aunt Soph is different; she's the driven, serious one, the most educated person in our family and the most self-critical. Yet her sisters love her, and they love my dad though he doesn't have much in common with them or with my uncles. My dad's sisters and Grandpa all live in Oakfield; the extended family gets together for dinner most Sundays, and we spend every holiday together.

My uncles are Italian-American as well, and they're loud and warm-hearted like their wives. At family parties, male conversations revolve around sports, leaving my dad a mostly silent observer; he understands hockey because he watched me play for years, but nobody is fooled by his attempts to feign interest in baseball, football, or basketball. He would rather talk about the books he's been reading, but that's a discussion he can only have with me or Aunt Soph. Still, my dad likes to drink and cook and talk about food, and he speaks with the same Jersey accent my uncles have, so he fits in.

My first cousins are all boys, except for Michela. Aunt Ro, Aunt Dee, and Aunt Vanna had their sons around the same time I was born. The eight of us went to the same schools—Louie and Ant were in my grade—and played on the same sports teams. My cousins have always been my friends, but I was never as close with them as they were with each other. Maybe it was because I was the only girl, or because I was more interested in writing stories than playing wiffle ball or video games, but I never fully integrated into their group. At times I envied the boys' automatic friendship, which started at birth and continues to this day. Yet I had discovered at a young age where I belonged at family parties, and it wasn't with my cousins—it was with my aunts.

Aunt Ro, Aunt Dee, Aunt Vanna, and Aunt Soph were the most important women in my life while I was growing up. They bought me my first bra, gave me the talk about periods and sex, took me shopping for my prom dress, and tried, unsuccessfully, to get me interested in makeup. I spent countless hours in my childhood and adolescence sitting at the table with them, listening to them talk. I heard about every one of their breast lumps and uterine fibroids and surgeries and invasive tests; I learned how to treat menstrual cramps and yeast infections and UTIs. They shared the neighborhood gossip—who was dating and who was cheating and whose kids were in trouble, a litany of scandals that inspired my early writing. I used to jot the stories down on a napkin, changing the people's names, so I could use them later. I loved hearing my aunts argue and tell stories and give advice; they taught me about relationships and about being a woman. When Aunt Soph decided to become an OB-GYN, the talk frequently turned to pregnancy and birth.

"I tore so bad with Louie," Aunt Ro said, in a conversation I remember vividly. "That huge head of his...I had to do Kegels for months..."

"Remember when Vanna's water broke on Easter?" Aunt Dee added. "All over my new couch!"

"They say it never happens in public—it happened to me," Aunt Vanna said.

"But you had an easy labor with that baby," Aunt Ro said. "Tommy was out in three pushes, before the doctor walked through the door..."

My aunts' wisdom came in handy when Aunt Soph ended up pregnant by accident. She broke the news to everyone at Thanksgiving dinner in 2010. She'd had a one-night stand with Donovan Braun, a neurosurgeon who practices at the hospital where she delivers babies. Aunt Soph had first met Donovan in medical school when she was doing her neurology rotation. Though he was only a resident in neurosurgery at the time, he had already gained a reputation for his exceptional talent—and for sleeping with every female doctor and nurse who crossed his path. He hit on Aunt Soph during the rotation, but she rejected him; several other girls in her class had sex with him. Years later, when Aunt Soph was in private practice and Donovan had become the most renowned neurosurgeon in the state, they ran into each other at a bar. A few drinks later and she was in his Mercedes doing what she swore she'd never do back in medical school. Aunt Soph was mortified by the incident; she wanted to move past it, but a broken condom and the luck of the draw left her carrying Michela along with her shame. Plan B doesn't always work, as it turns out.

I'm not sure why Aunt Soph was attracted to Donovan—Aunt Soph, who swore her career was more important than any man, who was always too busy working to bother with a boyfriend. I saw Donovan in an interview on TV once and I'll admit he was handsome, but his eyes were cold. "He's a genius," Aunt Soph said once. "Smartest person I've ever met. But he's evil." I guess some women fantasize about sleeping with a brilliant madman—the dangerous one nobody can figure out, who combines superior intellect with animal impulses—but I don't get it. I want a guy who is nice to me. Aunt Soph never explained why she slept with him; maybe she was just drunk, or lonely. When she decided to keep the baby and not tell Donovan that it was his, my aunts were up in arms.

"You can't let him off the hook, Soph!" Aunt Dee said. "He has to take responsibility for his kid."

"He's better off not knowing," Aunt Soph said. "He doesn't want to be anyone's father."

"But he is your baby's father," Aunt Ro said.

"My baby doesn't need a father—especially not a father like that," Aunt Soph said. "I don't want to look the man in the eye anymore, let alone share my kid with him. And I don't need to chase him for child support; I make plenty of money on my own."

"But what if he wanted to be in the baby's life?" Aunt Vanna said. "He has a right to that."

Aunt Soph laughed—a hard, mirthless laugh I'd never heard before. "Oh, you don't know him. The things I've heard...I'm sure he's fathered plenty of kids he wants nothing to do with. He just likes to fuck and let women deal with the consequences. I'm not telling anybody the truth—my name will be the only one on the birth certificate, and the baby will be a Cimino. I can raise my kid by myself."

"You won't be by yourself," Aunt Ro said. "We'll help you."

"Every step of the way," Aunt Dee said.

Aunt Soph's eyes filled with tears. "I know."

"Don't cry, Little Soph!" Aunt Vanna hugged her. "There's nothing better than a baby!"

"You'll be a great mom," Aunt Ro said.

Witnessing Aunt Soph's pregnancy was a pivotal experience in my life. I was a senior in college, and though I was still living at home, I was starting to feel like an adult. At the same time, my favorite aunt—the one who seemed perpetually young and single, the one who was the most like me—was becoming a mom. I had never been so close to someone who was pregnant, and it was fascinating—watching her run to the bathroom to puke every day for months, putting my hands on her belly to feel the baby kick, going to the ultrasound that revealed Michela was a girl. Actually, my aunts had guessed Michela was a girl back in the first trimester. Aunt Soph was ten weeks pregnant at the time, and everyone was at my house for Sunday dinner. Aunt Soph got up from the table to grab a plate of food.

"You're having a girl, Soph," Aunt Ro said. "I can see it in your ass."

My other aunts burst into laughter. "Check out the big booty on Soph!" Aunt Vanna said.

"You can't tell this early," Aunt Soph said.

"Sure you can," Aunt Ro said. "You think you know everything because you're a doctor, but we're the ones who have been through it and watched our friends go through it. As sure as I'm sitting here, you're having a girl."

My aunts were right about Michela being a girl, just like they were right about many of the things Aunt Soph experienced during her pregnancy. They said she was carrying low and would deliver a few weeks before her due date, which she did. But they didn't predict that after twenty-six hours of labor, she would have a C-section due to failure to progress. Both Michela and Aunt Soph were physically healthy after the surgery, but Aunt Soph didn't heal psychologically for a long time.

"I feel like something was taken from me," she said to me once, months after Michela's birth. We were alone on the porch at Aunt Ro's house, drinking wine and watching the kids across the street chase fireflies on their lawn. "I went through this whole pregnancy and labor and in the end they had to cut her out of me. It's like running a marathon and being pulled out of the race before the finish line."

"But Michela is here, and she's perfect," I said. "You created her, and you did birth her—it's just a different kind of birth. That's what you tell your patients."

"It wasn't different—it was embarrassing! I didn't have a good reason for a C-section, like a breech baby or placenta previa. Just failure to progress. 'Failure to progress...' what a horrible, demeaning phrase. Why would we tell a mom-to-be that she's failing at anything? I'll never use that term with my patients again." Aunt Soph shook her head. "I've spent my whole career delivering babies and I couldn't deliver my own. I'll never get over that."

Early on, Aunt Soph struggled with her new identity as a mom. She is an organized, diligent person who likes to get tasks accomplished, and the chaos and monotony of parenthood took a toll on her. She couldn't stand the ruined clothes and ruined plans and lack of sleep and endless schedule of feedings and diaper changes. Everyone else in the family was delighted with Michela; when Aunt Soph showed up to Sunday dinners with the baby, my aunts flocked around her. They clamored to hold Michela and told Aunt Soph how lucky she was to have her. Aunt Soph would stand there looking lost and helpless until, inevitably, Michela had to eat and someone would hand the baby back to her. One evening, when Michela was about two months old, my dad pushed past the crowd and put his hand on Aunt Soph's shoulder. "You okay?" he asked her.

At that moment, it struck me that this was my dad's little sister—that he had memories of Aunt Soph in diapers, sucking her thumb and following him around the house. She looked into his eyes. "No."

"Let's talk about it. The others will watch the baby for a bit."

My dad led Aunt Soph to the couch, where she burst into tears. He hugged her as she rambled about how depressed and guilty and exhausted she felt. "It's tough," my dad kept saying. "It's okay to feel how you feel. It's really tough."

Later that night, when Aunt Soph had composed herself and seemed almost normal, she took Michela into Aunt Vanna's bedroom to feed her. My other aunts went with her, and I trailed along behind them. Aunt Soph unbuttoned her shirt and struggled to get the wailing Michela to latch onto her cracked and bleeding nipples.

"Fuck it, Soph," Aunt Dee said. Aunt Dee was the only one in the family who had breastfed her kids; my other aunts and my mom had used formula. "Give that baby a bottle."

"Don't discourage me," Aunt Soph said. "Breast milk is the best thing for a baby."

"The best thing for a baby is to have a happy mama," Aunt Dee said. "Don't you ever forget that."

"Ever," Aunt Ro said.

Aunt Soph shook her head and put Michela back on her breast. She winced as Michela latched on, ate for a minute, then let go and started crying again. "Don't look at me like that," Aunt Soph snapped at her sisters. "There's no formula to give her anyway."

"I have formula in the house," Aunt Vanna said. "I bought it. Bottles too."

"You knew I was going to fail?" Aunt Soph said.

"No. I know babies are unpredictable," Aunt Vanna said.

Aunt Soph looked down at Michela with disappointment in her face. Then she held the baby out to her sisters. "Do what you want. Just get her away from me."

Aunt Dee and Aunt Ro comforted Michela while Aunt Vanna went to get the bottle. I followed Aunt Soph to the living room, where the men were watching sports. She filled a glass of wine nearly to the top and sat down next to my dad. They leaned against each other, sipping their drinks, looking at the TV with glassy eyes. As I watched them, I tried to process everything—to incorporate the harsh realities I'd seen into my previously rosy view of parenthood. I hadn't realized how much misery was involved in raising kids.

Over the years, Aunt Soph has become more confident as a mother. She adores Michela; she teaches her and disciplines her and tries to make her happy. Aunt Soph still has moments of insecurity, especially when she compares herself to other moms, but she's doing better now than when Michela was a baby.

"Michela said you took her to an art class this morning," Aunt Dee says to me. It's Sunday night, and we're standing around Aunt Ro's kitchen counter, snacking on appetizers before dinner. "Where was that?"

"At the library," I say. "It was cute." I start describing the class, but I'm interrupted by the arrival of my cousin Ant and his fiancée, who got engaged this past Friday. It's the first time we've seen them since the proposal, and everyone starts cheering and exclaiming over the ring.

"This is so exciting!" Aunt Vanna says to Aunt Dee. "I'm happy to see the family getting bigger." She throws a pointed glance at Tommy and his wife. "Now we just need some babies..."

"Stop it, Mom," Tommy rolls his eyes. "We're not ready yet."

Ant and Lauren start talking about the venues they're considering for the wedding. They're planning to invite close to two hundred people. The number sounds overwhelming to me; if I get married someday, I'd rather have a smaller wedding. I guess it will depend on my husband's side of the family too, but the guest list shouldn't be huge on my end. The people I care about are the family members I see at Sunday dinners; I don't have close relationships with second or third cousins, and I drifted away from my friends after I moved to Arizona. On my mom's side of the family, I have one living relative—Aunt Cara, my mom's sister, who has been living in Sweden with her wife for the past twenty years. My mom's parents both passed away before she graduated from college, and she and her sister were best friends. Aunt Cara was with my mom the night she died. Over the years, I've heard the story of my mom's death in bits and pieces.

I was nine months old at the time, and my mom left me home with my dad and went out to dinner with Aunt Cara. After the meal, they were walking to their cars when an SUV came barreling down the street in the wrong direction and hit my mom. The driver had a mix of three different drugs in his system and didn't bother to stop to see what he'd done. Aunt Cara ran to my mom, who was lying in the street, and held her hand as she bled out. My mom was conscious for a few minutes, and she asked for my dad over and over. "He'll be here," Aunt Cara told her. "Gio will be here. He's on his way." But my mom was dead before she saw the paramedics, let alone my dad.

I once overheard Aunt Dee saying she wished Aunt Cara had skipped that part of the story, because what traumatized my dad the most was that my mom called for him in her last moments and he wasn't there. He was a mess for a year after she died; my aunts, including Aunt Cara, and my grandma were at my house every day, helping him take care of me. I don't recall any of this. My earliest memories, from when I was four or five, are of playing with my dad in the backyard, or standing on a kitchen chair to help him make pizza, or reading books with him. He was happy and fun and gave no indication of the grief that had consumed him. When I asked about my mom, he answered my questions and told me stories about her; he was sad sometimes, but he spoke with such fondness and enthusiasm that I longed to know the person he described. "She loved you very much," he always said. "I wish she could see you now." The anniversary of my mom's death is hard for him every year, and he still refuses to drive past the place where she was killed. When he has strong feelings of sorrow, he tends to withdraw instead of talking to me, and I only saw him cry over my mom once— the day he showed me her journals.

I was twelve, and I told my dad that I wanted to become a writer. My mom was a playwright; she and my dad met in college when he directed one of her plays. After college, my mom got a job as a personal assistant to a theater producer in New York—a job she eventually left to stay home full-time with me—but she continued to write on the side. A few of her plays were produced by local theater companies long before I was born. My strength was in writing novels and short stories, not plays, but I felt that my love of writing connected me to my mom. When I shared my dreams with my dad, he led me into the spare room and took out a stack of sketch pads.

"These were your mom's journals," he said. "She liked to write the first draft of her plays by hand, while she was brainstorming; once she had most of the dialogue down she'd start typing. She would write her thoughts in her journals too—descriptions of what was going on in her life, or how she felt...and the pieces of her novel are in here."

"I didn't know she wrote a novel," I said.

"She never finished it; it was in the early stages when she died. I wanted to finish it and publish it for her, but the scenes were scattered...I couldn't figure out where she was going with it." He opened one of the journals. "I'll look through them to make sure everything is appropriate for you to read, and then you can have them. Your mom wrote on sketch pads because she said lined paper restricted her thoughts...oh." He paused with his fingers over the page. "I forgot she used to make her *G*'s like that."

We were quiet for a moment; I watched his hands trembling. When he looked up at me, there were tears in his eyes. "I'll give the journals to you tomorrow, all right?" he said.

"All right."

"Go back to working on your story."

My dad went down the hallway to the bathroom, closed the door, and ran water in the sink. Though the water was loud, I could hear that he was crying. I sat outside the door, trying to figure out what to do. He didn't want me to see him like this. The only other time I'd heard him cry had been in secret—I was supposed to be sleeping, but instead I was hiding at the top of the stairs, listening to Aunt Ro tell him that my grandma had died. I was ten at the time and I was scared; I loved my grandma too, and the sight of my dad and Aunt Ro crying left me feeling helpless. A few days after my grandma's funeral, I got up the courage to ask my dad about death.

"I'm sorry," he said. "I don't have the answers. I don't believe in an afterlife, if that's what you mean. Some people do; you can believe in it if you want. All I can say for sure is that when someone dies, his or her body stops working and you don't get to see that person again. It's not fair and I'll never make sense of it." He squeezed my hand. "I love you, Gems. We're going to get through this together, one day at a time. As long as I've got you, I have to keep moving forward no matter what."

I leaned my head against the bathroom door, wondering how to comfort my dad. He was my best friend; I wanted to help him. "Dad?" I called. "Are you okay?" He didn't answer. I went downstairs, curled up in his armchair with my notebook and my teddy bear, and focused on the enchanted palace in my story. When my dad came downstairs later, he acted like everything was fine, though he started drinking earlier than usual. I woke up the next morning to find my mom's journals stacked at the foot of my bed.

At times, my aunts have told my dad that he should try dating again, but he refuses. He had one girlfriend after my mom died, back when I was three; they were together for six months. According to my aunts, the woman was sweet and attractive, but my dad couldn't bring himself to fall in love with her. Since then he's been alone.

Ant and Lauren's wedding is the main topic of conversation at dinner tonight. Ant seems bored after a few minutes, but Lauren is glowing from the attention. When the meal is over, Aunt Ro brings out coffee and dessert. I grab a few napkins and a pen and slip away to the living room by myself. I was working on my novel all afternoon, and ideas were swirling in my head during dinner; I want to write them down while they're fresh. I've built my fantasy world based on the natural features of Arizona along with some elements of the fairy tales my grandma told me when I was little. The rules are set and I've written drafts of key moments in the first book, so it's time to start with chapter one and see where it takes me. I picture the opening scene of the novel— the sky glittering with stars as Alana sneaks out of her house to meet with her fellow rebels—and start scribbling. Nobody needs me in the dining room now, and if I could get a few sentences down...

Chapter Four

It's a busy week at work. The lawyers have several new clients, and one of the couples is my high school guidance counselor and her husband; they chat with me after their meeting with Jasmine. They ask if I'm still writing—I say, "Yeah, kinda," and quickly change the subject—and tell me about the traveling they've been doing since they retired. We also have another coffee break on Thursday. Lina calls us together to tell us how she gave her eight-year-old daughter the sex talk.

"Kids were talking about it at school," Lina says. "With the wrong information, of course. Cristina asked me questions and I told her the truth." Lina tells us how she explained the mechanics of sex and where babies come from. She also told Cristina that she's in charge of her body and that no matter what other kids are doing, she can say no to anything that feels wrong. Erica watches her with wide eyes.

"Damn," Erica says. "You're brave! I expect to have that conversation with my kids someday, but at age eight..."

"You think I gave her too much detail?" Lina asks.

"No, it's good that you told her," Erica says. "Most moms would have panicked."

"You did the right thing," I say to Lina. I don't speak up much at work, but this is a topic I feel strongly about. When I was growing up, I could ask my aunts—or my dad—anything and get an honest answer. No topic was taboo. Because my family was open with me, I was comfortable in my body and didn't feel pressured to do things I wasn't ready to do. "Now Cristina will always turn to you for advice. If you had avoided the question, she would get her information from someone else next time—someone who might not have her best interests at heart."

"Thanks, Gemma," Lina says. "I hope she'll always talk to me. I wish I had been able to talk to my mom! She never taught me anything; I had to get a half-assed story from the kids in the neighborhood..."

The rest of the week passes by quickly. On Sunday morning, I spend longer than usual deciding what to wear. I want to look cute when I see Luke, but I can't wear something sexy to a kids' art class. Plus he's probably in a relationship and I'm not going to flirt with a guy who's taken. I settle on jeans and a teal top with a knot in front that Aunt Soph always borrows from me. The shirt flatters my chest without revealing too much skin, and if Aunt Soph wears it, it must stand up to the rigor of toddler activities. Then I head out to pick up Michela.

We're early for class, and most of the other families aren't there yet. Michela looks adorable in a flowered dress with leggings; she keeps doing twirls to show me how the skirt spins, then throwing herself into the grass and laughing. "You're crazy," I say, tickling her neck.

I look up and see Luke, Nate, and Scotty approaching. Luke smiles when he sees me. "Hey, Gemma."

"Hey, what's up?"

He spreads out his blanket so it overlaps with mine and sits down next to me, while Nate joins Michela in the spinning and falling game. "Nate is driving me crazy," Luke says in a low voice. "So many tantrums. I can't take it anymore."

"Oh no," I say. "What's he freaking out about?"

Quietly, so the kids can't hear, Luke explains Nate's recent meltdowns. Nate is diving into the grass with Michela and paying no attention to us. As we're talking, Scotty uses Luke's shirt to pull himself up to standing, turns, and starts walking toward Nate and Michela. He takes two steps, claps in excitement, and falls on his butt. "Great job, Scotty!" Luke says.

"He's walking now?" I ask.

"He does a few steps at a time. He crossed the living room on his birthday yesterday, so that was exciting."

"Aww—happy birthday, Scotty!" I say.

Scotty toddles back to me and Luke. The baby studies me for a moment, then lunges forward and grabs a fistful of my hair. "Let go," Luke tells him.

"It's okay," I say, though I'm in pain. I try to get my hair free, but Scotty has an iron grip. "I don't want to hurt him..."

"Here." Luke starts untangling my hair from Scotty's fingers. Luke's face is close to mine, and I can see how worn out he looks—there are deep lines between his eyebrows and dark circles under his eyes. Then his hand brushes my cheek and my only thought is how I'd like him to kiss me. "Got it," he says, releasing the last piece of hair. "Sorry about that."

"No worries."

We lock eyes, and my heart skips a beat. Then Luke turns back to Scotty. "No hair, buddy."

The teacher arrives and addresses the class. "Before we start today's project, I have two announcements to make," she says. "First, I want to remind you that the library is holding our annual festival and used book sale this weekend, from Thursday through Saturday. We'll have plenty of activities for kids, including story times, a magic show, and crafts."

"Can we go to that?" Nate asks Luke.

"We'll go Friday or Saturday; I have my show on Thursday," Luke says.

"The full schedule of events is on our website," the teacher says. "Also, the library has an urn of coffee left over from a fundraising event this morning; it's on the table across the lawn. Help yourselves to some free coffee before we start class."

"Oh sweet, coffee," I say to Luke. "Watch Michela and I'll grab some for us."

"You don't have to get one for me. I don't drink coffee."

I stare at him. "You have two kids under five and you don't drink coffee?"

"Sounds crazy, right? But I can't have it; it makes me anxious."

"Anxious about what?"

"Nothing in particular," he says. "Just gets my mind racing. You go—I've got Michela."

I turn this over in my head as I walk across the lawn. Luke doesn't strike me as an anxious person, and I wonder why coffee would have that effect on him. Then I remember something else he said—something at the park, about being afraid of everything. That doesn't seem to fit him, either. I approach the table and recognize my hockey coach from high school, who volunteers at the library sometimes. "Cimino!" he says. "How's it going?" We chat for a minute, and then I take my coffee back to the blanket, which is covered in art supplies. "I just saw my old hockey coach," I say to Luke and the kids. "Apparently he's retired now..."

Luke raises his eyebrows. "You played hockey? Ice hockey?"

"Yeah! I started in kindergarten, and I was on the varsity team in high school. I played right wing."

"What's right wing?" he says.

"It's one of the forwards...you don't know hockey?"

"I don't know anything about sports. In high school I was a nerd with a guitar."

"Did you say you're playing a show on Thursday?" I ask.

"Yeah, at this bar called The Garage in Montclair. We go on at nine..."

"Aunt Gemma," Michela says. "Can you help me fold this?"

Luke and I focus on getting the kids' craft started. We follow the teacher's instructions and show Nate and Michela how to fold construction paper into a puppet. Once the kids get the hang of it, I turn to Luke again. "What were you saying about the show?"

"Oh, it's with my friend from college—we were in a rock band together a while back. He and his brothers own The Garage so he plays there all the time, and he's been nagging me to do a show with him. I haven't performed in years but I figured I could do one gig."

"That sounds fun."

"Daddy." Nate shoves his puppet into Luke's face. "I made this for you."

"Thank you, buddy. It's awesome!"

"I'm making the next one for Mama."

I zone in on Nate's words. I'm about to get some information.

"Sounds great," Luke says. "You can send it to her."

"I want to give it to her today," Nate says.

"You know you won't see her today."

Nate kicks his feet against the blanket. "I want to see Mama!"

"You can call her later," Luke says. "Why don't you work on your craft, so it'll be ready when you talk to her?"

"I need more paper," Nate grumbles.

"I need more paper too," Michela says. "Let's ask the teacher!"

The two of them bolt across the lawn toward the teacher. Luke and I share a moment of awkward silence, watching Scotty roll a marker around in the grass. "Your wife's on a trip?" I ask.

"My ex-wife," he says. "She lives in L.A. now; she's trying to do the music thing. I have physical custody of the kids but she's been FaceTiming with them, so they ask about her...Nate does, anyway. I don't think Scotty understands who she is; he was only eight weeks old when she left."

"Eight weeks?" I'm shocked. "She hasn't seen them since then?"

"She was here for a week in November, when the divorce went through, but other than that she's been gone. She's supposed to take them to L.A. with her for the month of August and every other Christmas—that's what we agreed to. The rest of the time they're with me."

"Wow." I watch as he pulls the marker away from Scotty's mouth, brushes some dirt off his shirt. "Must be tough."

"I'm glad they're with me." He meets my eyes. "That's what I wanted. But yeah, it's tough, especially with Scotty crying all night—"

"He doesn't sleep?"

"It's his teeth—teething is torture. Still, things are better than when Sylvie was here and we were fighting. Fighting with her took everything out of me; I couldn't be the parent I wanted to be."

"You seem to be doing a good job with your kids."

"I don't know about that," he says. "You can't tell if you did a good job until years later, right?"

"Scotty!" Nate and Michela are back, and Nate is livid. "That's my marker!"

"You weren't using it," Luke says. "Let him have it for a minute." Nate yanks the marker out of Scotty's hand, and the baby starts to cry. "I said let him have it—"

"It's my favorite color!" Nate says.

"You'll get it back. Give your brother a turn."

"No."

"No?" Luke sets his jaw. "Give it back now or we're going home."

Nate turns and flings the marker across the lawn. In an instant, Luke is on his feet with Nate's wrist in his hand. "That's it. We're leaving."

"No!" Nate whines.

"You didn't listen, so now we have to leave. Bring that marker back and pick up your crafts."

Nate stomps and scowls, but he follows Luke's orders. The three of them head toward their car. "Bye, Gemma," Luke calls over his shoulder. "Bye, Michela."

"Bye," I say. I'm sad to see them go, especially because I was learning more about Luke. Yet it's good to see that he disciplines his kids. I've watched so many parents at the park make empty threats and then let their kids do whatever they want.

"Nate wasn't acting right," Michela whispers.

"I know," I say. "That's why he got punished."

"Can you open this marker for me?"

We spend the rest of the class working on the craft and go home with a pile of construction paper puppets.

Chapter Five

I find my mind returning to Luke a lot over the next few days. I feel less guilty thinking about him now that I know he's not married. Still, his circumstances aren't ideal. He's only been divorced for five months and it seems like he didn't have a healthy relationship with his ex. I try to imagine what it would be like to be married, and a parent, and then divorced. I've never had a real adult relationship, let alone been through the end of a marriage. Maybe it's naive of me to think anything good could happen between me and Luke.

The truth is I've had little experience with men and some of that is my fault. I'm picky. I find plenty of guys attractive from an objective standpoint, but if I don't feel a spark when I'm talking to someone, I lose interest right away. On the other hand, when I do like a guy, he takes up a ton of space in my brain; no other man, no matter how interesting or good-looking, can catch my attention. I'm loyal to the point of foolishness. This makes me a good person to date because I would never cheat, but it also means I take too long to get over people. I probably would have ended up married to my high school boyfriend if he hadn't moved away early in our relationship. His name was Nico, and we had been playing hockey together since we were kids; we were close friends when he asked me out. We were sixteen—he was my first kiss and my first love and we were happy together. Looking back, I wish I had slept with him because it would have been a beautiful experience, but we were both virgins and extremely cautious and never went past second base. We dated for a year, until his family decided to move to New Zealand. We couldn't stay together given the distance and the time difference, and I spent many sleepless nights crying into my pillow and writing bad poetry before I was able to move on. I'm friends with Nico on social media; he's married now and has a toddler and a dog. I'm glad my first romantic experience was with him, because the two guys I've slept with since then were assholes and I would hate to have only bad memories of men.

I lost my virginity to a guy named Dario when I studied in Rome for a year in college. He was in one of my classes, and he grew up in a small town outside of Rome. Dario was devastatingly handsome and a smooth talker who knew how to turn me on. My infatuation with him was fed by the excitement of being in a new culture, surrounded by the language I had always wanted to speak; after years of struggling in Italian classes, I was finally in Italy and I found the language flowing out of me unimpeded, as if a floodgate had been released. I only spoke Italian with Dario and that was part of the appeal. Dario and I were friends and were always flirting, and after a while I started having sex with him. He made me feel amazing, but he was also a womanizer who was sleeping with other girls behind my back. I wasn't fooled by his lies and I never called him my boyfriend, but I convinced myself that he would fall in love with me and he would change. Eventually I had to admit he was playing with me and I stopped seeing him. I hated men for a while after that, partly because of Dario but also because I was living in a country where I couldn't walk down the street without getting hit on, a country where male infidelity is expected and many mothers encourage their sons to sleep around. It wasn't a pleasant place to be a woman and that made me angry. I read every piece of feminist literature I could get my hands on and refused to let another man into my heart for the rest of my life.

Then I went back home to the United States and spent time with my dad and my cousins and my uncles and was forced to accept that there are good men in the world, and that those men are worth loving. So I took up my search for a relationship again.

I didn't have much success. When I was living in Tucson, I went on four dates with a guy named Justin; he was smart and we had great conversations, but I didn't like how roughly he touched me the one time we had sex, and I didn't like how he checked out other women when he thought I wasn't looking. I stopped going out with him, and I went on a few other first dates, none of which progressed to sex or a second date. Since moving back to New Jersey I haven't been involved with anyone.

Luke is the first guy who has interested me in a long time. I know divorce is a red flag, but he didn't sound bitter or depressed when he talked about it; maybe he's moved on. Plus he's an artist like me and so sweet with his kids and I got such a rush when he touched me and fuck it, I'm going to his show on Thursday night. Why not? It'll be fun to see him perform, even if we only end up being friends. Music is, in my opinion, the greatest of all the arts—it expresses the human condition better than literature, painting, or any other form. I love music and I can't imagine living without it, even though I don't understand it. I can't play an instrument or sing in tune, but I find music to be a comfort in tough times, and a source of motivation when I exercise, and an inspiration for my writing. I like rock music the most, and I want to hear what Luke has created.

Thursday is a long day at work. Every few months, the firm holds events at our office to attract new clients, and this evening is the first one I've attended. We have a free workshop about estate planning that is open to anyone in the community, followed by tapas-style refreshments and the chance for people to chat with the lawyers. The event runs from six to eight and by the end I'm exhausted, but the prospect of seeing Luke gives me a second wind. "Should we cap off the night with a drink at Finn's?" Bree asks the rest of us when we finish cleaning. None of the lawyers are interested.

"Not tonight, Bree—"

"Have to get home to the kids—"

"I haven't seen Mark since yesterday—"

"Gemma?" Bree says to me.

"I'm going to see a band in Montclair now," I say.

"Oh yeah?" Bree says. "You're going with friends?"

"By myself."

"Can I come?"

I'm surprised; I thought Bree didn't like me. "Sure, why not?"

"Awesome. What's the address?"

I give Bree the address and then head down Bloomfield Avenue from Verona into Montclair. As usual, it takes me forever to find parking; Bree is already waiting on the sidewalk when I arrive. The Garage is sandwiched between a French bakery and a smoke shop; the dim windows, hand-painted sign, and black wooden door don't attract attention, and I've never noticed it before. "This is the first time I've been to this place," I tell Bree. "Just so you know..."

"It'll be cool." She links her arm through mine and pushes open the door.

In the small, dingy entryway, we pay a cover charge and have our hands stamped by a bouncer with a mohawk. From there, we walk into the main room—an open space with hubcaps and license plates hanging on the walls and a bar running along one side. There are a few tables with mismatched chairs and a stage at the far end of the room. No bands are playing at the moment, but the dance floor is full of people drinking and chatting. "Mirror first," Bree says, leading me to the bathroom.

The ladies' room is run down and covered in graffiti; there is only one toilet and a sink, and it's a tight squeeze for the two of us. I wonder what Bree is thinking as she fixes her hair in the grimy mirror. Does she want to hang out with me? Or was she desperate to have something to do? This doesn't seem like her kind of bar. "You should have told me we were going out," she says. "I would have brought something to wear. I guess I could go for the sexy secretary look." She opens the top few buttons of her blouse, revealing a dainty gold necklace and a glimpse of her cleavage. "That's better."

"Bree, you're gorgeous," I say. "It doesn't matter what you wear."

She laughs. "Shut up. I wish I had your boobs! I have to buy mine at Victoria's Secret."

"Mine are too big, honestly. They're annoying."

"I bet the boys don't mind them."

We leave the bathroom together. I look at the people around us; the crowd is mostly our age and dressed in a mix of styles. There are some people with piercings and colorful hair and some people in flannels and black pants and some people wearing simple t-shirts and jeans. The room is buzzing with anticipation, and I feel hyped for the show. Luke and his bandmates are setting up their instruments, so Bree and I push through the crowd to get closer. The other guys in the band have cooler clothes and newer shoes than Luke, but he still seems to belong with them; he's plugging in his guitar and laughing at something the drummer said. Luke glances at the crowd and sees me, and his face lights up. He jumps down from the stage.

"Gemma!" he says. "I didn't expect you to be here."

"I want to hear you play," I say.

"Yeah? Pressure's on, then. We're on for an hour—you'll hang around after the set?"

"Definitely," I say. "Oh—this is my friend, Bree..."

"Hey, I'm Luke." Luke turns back to me. "See you soon."

He stops to talk to the bartender, then gets onstage again. "What are you having, ladies?" the bartender asks me and Bree. "It's on the band."

Bree wiggles her eyebrows at me. "Ooh, we're with the band." We order drinks and take a seat at the bar. "So," Bree says. "Are you and Luke a thing?"

"Not yet," I say. "I want to be, but for now we're just friends."

"He's not looking at you like a friend."

I glance at the stage and see Luke's eyes moving over my body. We catch each other's gaze and we both look away. "We'll see," I say.

"He's cute. How do you know him?"

"My cousin's art class, and the playground."

"The playground?" Bree's eyes are wide. "You pick up men at the playground? Is he somebody's dad?"

"Yeah, but he's divorced—he's available."

She laughs. "You're hilarious. Hook me up with the drummer—he's got sick abs."

I look at the drummer, a shirtless guy with a shaved head and a ripped physique covered in tattoos. "I didn't think he'd be your type," I say.

"Totally my type. My first kiss was with a guy who looked like that. I was thirteen—same day I got this." Bree shows me the scar on her forearm. "I was crowd-surfing at Warped Tour and got dropped onto the asphalt. Six stitches."

"Damn."

"Those were my wild younger days."

"Who was the guy?"

"Some guy in the crowd I was dancing with. He had a lip ring—I remember that."

A guitar riff bursts from the speakers, and Bree and I turn to the stage. "What's up? It's Carter," the blonde guitarist says. There are a few whoops of recognition from the crowd. "Some of you know me from my band High Velocity, but tonight I'm doing something different, handing over lead vocals to my old friend Luke Reddin..."

Luke Reddin. This is the first time I've heard Luke's full name; it's not extraordinary, but there's a simple music in it. I tune back into Carter's talking.

"Back in Boston we called ourselves Orange Line, after the subway we used to take to this punk house with live music," Carter says.

"That place was fucking foul," Luke says.

"Yeah, roaches everywhere. But we played some great gigs there—it was always packed. Anyway, this song is called 'Break Your Fall.'"

The song is loud and catchy, and the crowd starts dancing. Bree and I stay at the bar because we still have our drinks. I like the rhythm of the song and the whole band seems talented, but what stands out to me is Luke's raspy voice. It's both gritty and melodic, heartfelt and unashamed; it reminds me of parking lots and traffic and rain and music blasting in basements and all the gray features of New Jersey, of home. I could listen to him sing for hours. "They're really good," Bree says.

"I know."

"Finish that beer so we can dance."

I down the rest of my drink and follow her to the dance floor. Before long we're jumping around with the mass of strangers. Most of Orange Line's songs are fast-paced and good for dancing, but there are also some darker, slower ones. From what I can make out of the lyrics, I like the band's writing. There are plenty of the standard songs about girls but also one about the creative process and one called "Astrophysics" that I think is about death; it starts out quiet and sad and explodes into anger after the first verse. Luke and Carter banter between songs, and the audience seems hooked on their words. It's the most fun I've had in a long time, dancing with Bree and letting the gravel in Luke's voice seep into my skin. I'm disappointed when the set is over.

After Luke and his bandmates clear their instruments off the stage, they show up on the dance floor and start chatting with a group of people. They drag some tables and chairs together, and Luke motions for me and Bree to join them. He introduces us to the rest of the band. "Carter is my main man from Berklee," Luke says. "We played together for years. Matt is on bass; he used to play with us in college too. He came out from New York tonight for old times' sake. And this is Eddie—we go way back to Verona High." He claps the drummer on the back. "This motherfucker is the reason I had to get a ride here—"

"You gotta tell everybody that story?" Eddie grumbles.

"I go to your house to rehearse and you back your fucking pickup truck into my car..."

The conversation continues that way for a few minutes, with the boys making fun of each other, and we do a round of whiskey shots. Luke sits down next to me. His face is bathed in sweat and his eyes seem unnaturally bright, almost manic with enthusiasm. "What did you think of the show?" he asks.

"It was awesome," I say. "Your voice has so many layers—I hear parking lots in it and traffic and rain..."

"In my voice?"

"Never mind." My face gets hot. "I mean you sounded great. I like your voice."

"I like your voice too," he says. "I haven't heard you sing..."

"Trust me, you don't want to."

"But I like the way you talk. I like your *O*'s and your *A*'s...living in Arizona didn't take the Jersey accent out of you. And your speech is straightforward—you don't drag out your words like girls sometimes do, or lift your voice at the end of your sentences like everything you say is a question. You just say it."

I had no idea he was paying such close attention. "You notice a lot."

"People's voices make an impression on me."

We start talking about the lyrics to one of the songs, and my mind races, trying to figure out what's happening between us. Most of my friendships with guys have involved some flirtation, but this feels different; Luke isn't teasing me or touching me, just listening intently like I'm the only person in the room. His eyes haven't left my face except for the one time they flicked down to my chest. He's attracted to me, I know he is, but he isn't making any moves so I'm confused. Maybe he's still in love with his ex. Or maybe he's interested in another girl, someone I haven't met. I glance at his hand, which is lying on the table next to mine, and notice that the skin around his fingernails is frayed and bloody. "What happened to you?" I ask, stroking his fingers.

"That's nothing." He pulls his hand away. "Bad habit."

That settles things. Luke doesn't want to flirt with me, not if he rejected a signal like that. I'm disappointed, but at least I know how to treat him —like a friend and nothing more. "We're going out for a smoke," Eddie says to Luke.

"Want to go?" Luke asks me.

"Sure," I say. A new band is setting up onstage, and soon it'll be too loud for us to hear each other. "I don't smoke, but..."

"Me either," Luke says. "Fucks my voice. But it'll be good to get some air."

Luke is right—the bar was hot and stuffy, and it's a relief to be outside. The night is chilly; a pleasant shiver runs through me as I lean against the stone wall of the building, with Luke next to me. We watch the headlights of cars passing by on Bloomfield Avenue while the air around us grows dense with cigarette smoke. A Jeep pulls up to the red light in front of us; I can hear its radio playing an emo song that was popular ten years ago. Luke and I nod along to the music. "Great song," I say.

"I listened to this nonstop in sophomore year of high school," he says.

This doesn't make sense; I do some calculations in my head. "How old are you?"

"Twenty-five."

No way. I figured he was in his thirties! The lines in his face... "I'm twenty-six," I say. "So Nate was born when you were..."

"Twenty-one. It was the week before I turned twenty-two and the week after I finished college. Sylvie was a year younger than me and she never got to graduate; that's something she always held over my head."

"She went to Berklee too?"

"Yeah. We'd been dating for almost a year when she got pregnant. We were usually careful but one time we were at a concert and we were wasted...anyway. Sylvie was on the fence about what to do, but I wanted to keep the baby. Once she saw I was on board, that she wouldn't have to go through anything alone, she wanted him too. We figured we were old enough to handle a kid...we had no idea what we were getting into."

I think back to how immature my friends and I were in college. It would have been a rough transition, learning how to raise a child at that age. "That sounds overwhelming."

"It was. We weren't ready to be adults, let alone parents. But I got a job and Sylvie stayed home with Nate, and we moved to Verona to be near my mom and stepdad. It was a good thing we had their help because we didn't know anything about babies at the beginning."

"Sylvie's parents didn't help?" I ask.

"Hell no. They're in Vermont and they're a mess, alcoholics and always at each other's throats...Sylvie hadn't spoken to them since she left for college. They don't even know the kids exist. Sylvie had a lot of demons, growing up the way she did...I thought if I loved her enough I could take that pain away." He shrugs. "Stupid, really."

The others have gone inside, Eddie with his arm around Bree's waist, and Luke and I are alone on the sidewalk. His breath forms little clouds in the air. "You weren't happy together?" I ask.

"We were happy sometimes. But things were always turbulent, and once we had Nate the problems got more intense. Sylvie could be so cruel—there was no line she wouldn't cross when she was angry. Still, some of it was my fault; I didn't understand how hard it was for her to be home all day with a baby, with none of her friends around...I get it now. We tried to make it work—I switched to the job I have now, so I could work from home and she could get out of the house and work too. Then Scotty came along and everything went to hell again. That sounds horrible." He gives me a guilty look. "I love Scotty. I love both my kids."

"I know you do."

"But those weeks after he was born were a nightmare. Nate was jealous and acting out, and Scotty had this terrible colic—he would scream nonstop from four to seven every night. Sylvie was losing her shit and lashing out at everybody...this is weird, though." He pauses. "Should we be talking about this?"

"I don't mind," I say. He seems uneasy, so I change the subject. "The crowd was into your band. Are you going to play any more shows?"

"I can't; it's too much of a commitment. It was hard enough getting ready for this show. My mom and stepdad helped with babysitting—they knew I needed the break—but they're not available all the time."

"Are they with your kids now?"

"Yeah, they're watching them at my place. Feels strange...it's the first night in a year I haven't put the boys to bed. I hope they fell asleep all right."

I look into Luke's eyes, thinking of the devoted dad I knew before tonight and the musician I saw onstage. Both sides of him exist at the same time and with equal intensity. "You must miss performing," I say.

"I do. The release of it, the adrenaline...and feeling connected to the people you're playing with. But mostly I miss writing music. Gemma, I have this much creativity..." He spreads his arms wide. "And this much time to use it." He brings his thumb and forefinger together. "I get inspiration for songs constantly—I'll hear a melody in my head, and as soon as I start to record myself or mess around on my guitar someone cries or something breaks or Scotty shits his pants and everything gets thrown off. I never get to complete a thought. It's maddening."

"I can imagine."

"I could ignore my ideas, and I do that a lot because I don't have the time or mental space for them. But it's depressing, spending all day doing everything other than the one thing you were born to do. And suppressing the music doesn't last long, anyway...it finds its way back."

"No way to stop the flood," I say.

"That's the perfect word—it's a flood! A deluge of ideas. But to turn those ideas into songs I have to work, I have to try things over and over until I get it right and I don't have the chance to work...listen, I was reading this essay about Michelangelo—"

"How did you find time to read that?"

"I don't sleep. Scotty cries every night because of his teeth and it takes me forever to fall asleep once I've been woken up. I have to read and read to quiet my mind and by the time I drift off, Scotty wakes up again and I'm back in his room. I barely got two hours of sleep last night."

"You should let Scotty cry it out for a few nights," I say. "Don't comfort him—see if you can break the habit."

"No. I want him to know I'm always there for him, whenever he needs me."

Luke's eyes are blazing, and I know there's more to this than a bad sleeping pattern. "Got it," I say.

"I've tried writing songs in the middle of the night but my brain is so fried by that point that everything comes out like shit...anyway...what was I saying?"

"Michelangelo."

"Right. In the British Museum they have a drawing by one of Michelangelo's students, with feedback written on it. This is what Michelangelo wrote: 'Draw Antonio, draw Antonio, draw and don't waste time.' I wish someone had said that to me years ago, before I had kids...I wish I had spent every free moment writing and playing music. Maybe I could have made something great. You could do it though." He leans closer to me. "You still have time to yourself and you could use it to write an amazing novel. When do you write?"

"I try to get in an hour after work," I say. "But sometimes I'm too tired. And I write on the weekends."

"That's a start, but you should make it a daily routine. Maybe you can wake up early and write before work."

"Some days I run before work."

"Then on the days you don't run—or on the days you run, you can wake up even earlier and do both. The more time you spend on your book, the better it's going to be."

I'm not sure how to respond to this. Luke's advice would be useful if I were talented, but who's to say I'm talented? For every great artist, there are thousands of unsuccessful artists whose life's work goes unnoticed. I could indulge in my passion only to find that my writing doesn't matter to anyone but me; I'm better off doing something practical with my time. "Is it worth it, though?" I say.

"What do you mean?"

"Never mind."

"Will you let me read some of your book?"

"Hell no."

"Why not? You heard my music."

"That's different," I say. "Those songs are finished—they're ready for people to hear them. My work is still in progress, and writing should be private until it's done."

"Fair enough. Tell me what it's about, then."

"You'll be bored."

"No I won't."

I start explaining my story—slowly at first, then with more enthusiasm once I see that he's interested. "Here's the premise: Fairies are human-sized magical beings whose job is to protect nature. They coexisted peacefully with humans for centuries, but as humans began taking more and more from the Earth, fairies all over the world started to fight back. Wars erupted between the two species and most of the fairies were wiped out; the last remaining fairy colony, which was eliminated a decade ago, was in Sedona, Arizona. My novel starts when Alana, one of the surviving Sedona fairies, starts planning a revolt against the humans who killed her family. She's joined by other fairies as well as some humans who are on her side..."

I go on to tell him the basics of the plot. It's the first time I've talked about my book with anyone, and Luke is an avid listener. "What if humans find out which stones are powerful?" he asks. "Can they use them against the fairies?"

"That's exactly what happens because—"

A car horn startles both of us. I look up to see a white Audi making its way over to the curb. "My stepdad," Luke says. The driver, a man with gray hair and glasses, rolls down his window. "I have to get my guitar," Luke tells him.

"I can't park here, so I'll drive around the block again," his stepdad says.

"All right."

Luke goes into the bar, but I don't follow him; I noticed an inconsistency in my story while I was talking, and I have to make note of it. I type my thoughts into my phone. When I'm finished, I see that the Audi has parked in an open spot down the block. Luke comes back outside; he's carrying an amp and wearing his guitar and an extra bag. "Your stepdad is parked over there," I tell him.

"Thanks." Luke hesitates, then puts his free hand on my shoulder. "I'm glad you were here tonight. I'm glad we got to talk."

"Oh—me too!"

"Do you want to meet at that library festival on Saturday? I was planning to take the kids."

"I'm having a yard sale with my dad on Saturday," I say. "But depending on the time..."

"We could go tomorrow night instead—around seven?"

"That sounds good."

"Okay." He gives my shoulder a squeeze before he lets go. "See you then."

I watch him walk down the block toward his stepdad's car. Now I'm totally lost. Does he like me? If he does, he should have kissed me—he was standing close enough. And he wants to see me tomorrow but it's not a date...I guess we're friends. I go back into the bar, thinking I'll ask Bree for advice, but she's deep in conversation with Eddie and I don't want to throw off her game. I tell her I'm going home and head out to my car.

Before I fall asleep, I stick a post-it to my laptop that says: "Draw, Antonio." I set my alarm for six A.M.

Chapter Six

Luke gave me good advice about waking up early. I made progress on my novel this morning—my mind was clearer than it is at night—and I arrive at work already feeling accomplished. Bree is much warmer towards me than she's been in the past, but she doesn't mention last night, so I don't either. I'd like to know if she hooked up with Eddie, but I get the vibe that she doesn't want to talk about it at the office. It's nice to work with her now that she's being friendly, though.

After work, I have an early dinner with my dad and stop at Aunt Soph's place to pick up the stuff she wants us to sell at tomorrow's yard sale. Then I drive to the library. Though it's after seven, Luke isn't there yet; I walk through the book sale and buy two books. It's nearly seven thirty when Luke and the kids show up. "I'm sorry," he says, looking flustered. "We had a diaper explosion."

"No worries."

Nate tugs on my arm. "Where's Michela?"

Now I feel stupid. Of course I should have brought Michela. Maybe that's why Luke wanted to meet me in the first place, so his kids would have someone to play with. "She goes to sleep early," I tell Nate. "I'll bring her next time. There's a magic show starting in a minute—do you want to see it?"

"Yeah!" Nate says.

We head to the kids' section of the library, where a magician is about to perform. Nate joins a group of kids on the rug in front of the magician, and Scotty toddles after him. "Nay!" Scotty calls. "Nay!" He tries to walk faster and nearly crashes into a book cart; Luke pulls him back at the last minute.

"Let's sit for a while," Luke says. He scoops up Scotty and a book, and I join them on the folding chairs near the rug. Scotty is absorbed by the book, which has buttons that make animal sounds. "What did you buy?" Luke asks, glancing at the books in my hand.

I show him the first book, *A Tree Grows in Brooklyn*. "This is my favorite novel," I say. "I lent my copy to a friend in Tucson and never got it back, so I bought a new one."

"No shit! I'm reading that right now."

"Really?" I say. "I bet you relate to Johnny, the singer tied down by family responsibilities."

"Nah, he's useless. The best character in the story is Katie. She does what needs to be done no matter what—no matter how much it hurts."

This is an interesting perspective, one I didn't expect to hear from Luke. "Good point."

"Although I don't agree with everything Katie says—like when she tells Francie no love will ever matter as much as her first love. I think she's wrong about that." He looks at my other book. "What else did you get?"

"*Leaves of Grass*, by Walt Whitman. I have a copy, but mine is old and falling apart, and it doesn't include the preface like this version does."

"I haven't read that."

"You haven't read Walt Whitman? He seems like your kind of poet. The first quote I ever read by him was taken from the preface...let me see..." I flip through the pages until I find the right lines. "Start here, with 'This is what you shall do...'"

Luke leans over to read the passage. I remind myself that we're friends, that it doesn't matter that his shoulder is pressed against mine or that the slightest movement would bring our heads together... "I like this part," he says. "'Your very flesh shall be a great poem and have the richest fluency—'"

"Dada." Scotty smacks Luke in the face, then jabs his finger at the animal book. "Dis. Dis."

"You want me to read this?" Luke turns from me to Scotty. "Okay, buddy. 'Welcome to the farm. The sheep says: baa baa!'"

"Baa," Scotty says.

"'The cow says: moo moo!'" Luke nudges me. "Your turn."

I point to the pig. "'The pig says: oink oink!'"

For some reason, Scotty finds this hysterical. He bursts into delighted giggles, revealing his little teeth—two on the bottom and four on top. I oink a few more times to keep him laughing, and Luke laughs too and kisses him on the forehead. "You can do the duck too, Gemma," he says.

We entertain Scotty with the book until the magic show is over. Nate runs up to us. "Can we go to the rainbow cave?" he asks.

"I thought you wanted to buy books," Luke says.

"Rainbow cave first." Nate turns to me and lowers his voice. "Do you know about the rainbow cave?"

"No," I say. "Is it a secret?"

"I'll show you."

We head to the other side of the kids' section, where there is a display of picture books on a table with a rainbow tablecloth. The tablecloth is so long that it nearly touches the floor. "Dragons live in the rainbow cave," Nate explains. "They hide here so people in the library don't see them." He gets down on his hands and knees and crawls under the table. "Come on!"

I follow him. It does seem like a magical world under the table, with colorful curtains on all sides. "What are the dragons' names?" I ask.

"This one is Orangey." Nate points to an empty space between us. "He's in charge. He has a baby brother named Indigo who is sometimes annoying. And Greenie and Bluey live over there."

"That's so cool!"

Luke lifts up one side of the tablecloth and smiles at me. "You comfortable under there?"

"I'm meeting the dragons," I tell him.

"Of course. Just watch out for Spiky—he might invade again."

"Not Spiky!" Nate says.

"I heard he came up with some new spells..."

"We need new spells too!" Nate says to me.

Luke, Nate, and I play the dragon game while Scotty crawls in and out from under the table. Then we go to the book sale so the kids can pick out books. Scotty keeps rubbing his eyes; I check my phone and see that it's eight thirty. "We have to go home after I buy these," Luke tells the kids. "It's getting late."

"I want to go back to the rainbow cave!" Nate says.

"Next time. We can talk about dragons while you're in the stroller."

"Stroller?" I ask Luke. "Are you walking home?"

"Yeah, we've been walking everywhere since Eddie banged up my car. It should be out of the shop in a few days."

"Where do you live?"

"The apartments on Chestnut Street."

They're a mile away. "That's a long walk," I say. "And it's dark! Do you want a ride?"

"We're okay."

"You sure? Nate can sit in Michela's car seat, and I have her old infant seat in the trunk that Scotty can use. I'll drive carefully."

Luke thinks about it. "If you don't mind..."

"It's no problem."

We head out to my car. The kids sit in the stroller while I dig through the mountain of stuff in my trunk, looking for the car seat. "My car doesn't usually look like this," I tell Luke. "It's because of the yard sale..." I pull out the seat and close the trunk. "Here we go."

Luke is looking at the back of my car, at the lone bumper sticker depicting Cathedral Rock in Sedona, Arizona. "The place from your story," he says. "Is that where you used to live?"

"No, I lived in Tucson, in southern Arizona. But I visited Sedona with my dad on our road trip. After I left my job, he flew to Arizona to meet me and we drove back to New Jersey together. We saw a dozen cities and national parks across the country but Sedona made the biggest impression on me."

"Why?"

"The scenery is breathtaking," I say. "Sedona has massive rock formations that seem to challenge the sky—rocks in rich shades of red and orange. Even the dirt under your feet is orange. And there are endless canyons dotted with trees and steep cliffs with layers of rock in different colors...it makes you feel small, being surrounded by natural beauty."

"Damn."

"It was my dad's favorite place, too—he liked it even more than the Grand Canyon, which he'd always wanted to see."

"It's cool that you took a trip like that with your dad," Luke says. "You must be close."

"We're super close. My mom died when I was a baby, so it's always been him and me."

"Oh." Luke's face is solemn. "I'm sorry."

"It's okay. I wish I could have known her, but I had my dad and my aunts...mostly I feel sorry for my dad." I pause. I usually avoid the topic of my mom's death because it makes people uncomfortable, but it's easy to talk to Luke; I feel like I can tell him anything. "He really loved my mom, and he still really misses her. That's the saddest part, I think."

"Must be awful."

"It is." I notice Nate trying to wriggle out of the stroller. "Anyway, your kids are getting antsy—let's set up this car seat."

We put the kids in the car and set off toward Chestnut Street. Within minutes, both boys are asleep; the car seems oddly quiet. "Listen to that," Luke says. "The sacred sound of nobody saying 'Daddy.'" He sinks down into the passenger seat and closes his eyes. For a moment I think he's asleep too, until he opens his eyes and looks at me. "You think I complain too much."

"I think you like to hear yourself talk," I say. We both grin. "But seriously, all parents complain about their kids sometimes. You have to; you'll go crazy otherwise."

"I agree, but nobody in my life wants to hear that. I don't have friends who are parents, and forget about my mom—she thinks my kids are angels and that it's my fault when they misbehave. If I try to talk about how I feel, her attitude is 'you've made your bed, now lie in it.' I get that, but I should still be allowed to vent. I'm constantly under pressure...constantly exhausted..."

"Especially because you're alone," I say, thinking of Aunt Soph.

"I'm not going to get any sympathy there—my mom was alone with me most of the time for ten years, and that was by choice. She never married or dated my father and they get along to this day. Back when Sylvie got pregnant my mom said not to marry her, to share custody and see how things turned out, but I didn't listen. I wanted to marry Sylvie; I was in love with her."

"Do you still love her?"

We pull up to a red light, and I turn to see Luke's reaction to my question. Maybe I'm overstepping a boundary, but I want to know, and I figure this friendship has gotten so weird that there are no rules anymore. Luke doesn't seem offended; he shakes his head. "No. The longer she's been gone, the more I can see we were wrong for each other. And the way she left...she walked out after one of our fights and I didn't hear from her for a month, other than one text saying she was safe and she was never coming home. Imagine, a whole month without asking how the kids were doing. They could have been dead for all she cared. I could never love somebody like that again. Why?" He searches my face. "Why do you ask?"

"Just curious." The light changes, and we drive on again.

"Did you wake up early to write today?" he asks.

"I did, and I got a lot done. Not that it matters...nobody is going to care about this story..."

"I care about it."

"So the book has an audience of two—you and me," I say. "I've been through this before; I wrote a novel a few years ago that was a failure. It was a coming-of-age story about a girl who moves to Italy, and I was proud of it. I spent my senior year of college and the six months after I graduated working on it; I barely saw my friends because all I wanted to do was write. Once the novel was finished, I queried a million agents and small publishers and even sent some excerpts to literary journals, and I kept getting rejected. I wasted so much time and effort making something no one liked."

"Did you ever think about self-publishing the book?" he asks.

"For what? It obviously wasn't good enough to be published. My aunts and their friends would've been the only ones buying it, and that's embarrassing. The whole thing was embarrassing—pouring my soul into my work and finding out that it sucked."

"Just because your book wasn't published doesn't mean it sucked," he says. "Maybe you didn't get it in front of the right person, someone who understood your vision and knew how to market it. Maybe it was bad timing based on what kinds of books were selling at the time. Or maybe it did suck."

"Thanks a lot."

"Most of what I make sucks too, but you have to make the stuff that sucks because it's part of the process, part of practice. You got that story out of you, so it served its purpose—it cleared the way for the story you're writing now, and the one after that, and the one after that. One of those stories will make an impact. If you hadn't written that book, you'd still be stuck in the mud of your old ideas; instead you grew. Nothing you create is a waste."

I think through his words. Luke touched on something I've always felt but never trusted—that being compelled to write is enough justification to write. I've spent many years searching for validation of my talent; I entered writing competitions when I was younger and won many of them, and I longed to have a book published as the ultimate achievement. But maybe those accomplishments don't equate to progress. Maybe progress comes from working and failing and working and failing and working some more... "Do you really believe that?" I ask Luke.

"Of course. A hundred percent."

"Daddy," Nate whines from the back seat. "Are we home yet?"

"Almost, buddy."

A moment later, I pull up to the curb outside Luke's apartment building. He takes his backpack and stroller out of the trunk, then leans into the back seat to unclip Nate. "Wait on the sidewalk while I get your brother," Luke says to him.

"Do you need help?" I ask. "You have a lot of stuff..."

"Sure, if you could get Scotty, I'll take Nate and the stroller...thanks."

I open the back door and find that Scotty is still asleep. I unbuckle him as gently as I can, lift him into my arms, and let his head fall onto my chest. He stirs, then sticks his thumb in his mouth and goes back to sleep. I follow Luke into the building, up to the second floor, and through his apartment door. There are toys everywhere—on the couch, on the floor, on the dining room table. A mattress with crumpled sheets is lying in the middle of the living room, and the hamper in one corner is overflowing with laundry. Nate, who is yawning, sits down and takes off his shoes. "Go pee," Luke tells him. "I'll meet you in the bathroom in a minute." He holds out his arms for Scotty. "Give me the baby—I'll get his bottle—"

"He's asleep," I say.

"Yeah?" Luke peers at Scotty's face. "Wow, he's out! Let him sleep, then. I'll feed him when he gets up later—"

"Daddy!" Nate calls from the bathroom. "I need help!"

"Could you put Scotty in his crib?" Luke points me toward one of the bedrooms. "If he wakes up, I'll grab him when I'm done with Nate."

I push open the bedroom door. It's a small room with a crib and a changing pad on the floor. I take a second to enjoy holding Scotty; I notice his puffy cheeks, his long black eyelashes, his soft breath on my neck. It's cozy and warm to have him in my arms. I pull off his shoes and lay him down in his crib.

I go back to the living room, and Luke comes out of the other bedroom a few minutes later. "Nate is passed out," he says. "I didn't even have to tell him a story."

"That's good. Scotty's fast asleep, too."

We walk toward each other, stopping just short of touching. I look around for something to say and my gaze falls on the mattress on the floor. "Classy, right?" Luke says, nudging the mattress with his foot. "When we moved to this place, with the two bedrooms, I figured I'd get one and the boys could share the other. But every time Scotty cried, he woke Nate up, so I had to separate them. I can't sleep in Nate's room because he keeps talking to me and he won't go to sleep, and my bed doesn't fit in Scotty's room, so I ended up here. I didn't bother moving the bed frame because someday I'll go back to my bedroom. Hopefully."

"Makes sense."

We fall silent. Luke starts chewing on the skin around his fingernails. "Anyway," he says. "I think you should leave because you're making me nervous."

"Really?"

A scream makes us both jump. Scotty is crying. "Shit," Luke says. "I knew he'd need the bottle. Diaper is probably soaked, too." I follow him into the kitchen. Every inch of the fridge is covered in little kid artwork, and to me this makes up for the dirty dishes in the sink. Luke fills a glass with hot water and drops the bottle in. Then he meets my eyes. "I'll be honest," he says. "I like you. I like you a lot. But it's risky for me to get involved with anyone right now, and you don't want to date a dysfunctional fuck like me."

My heart leaps. "I don't think you're dysfunctional."

"No? Twenty-five and divorced, with two toddlers up my ass? You don't consider that dysfunctional?"

"I don't mind the divorce as long as you're over her. And I like hanging out with your kids."

"You like them now. Wait until you see how much work they are, and how we'll never have a minute to ourselves—you'll want to cut and run. And that won't be good for me or the kids." Scotty's cries get louder and more desperate; Luke tests the bottle on his arm, shakes his head, and runs hot water in the glass again. I'm trying to figure out what to say, but Scotty's crying makes my thoughts feel scattered. There's so much restraint in Luke's body, so much tension in his jaw and his shoulders and his hands and maybe if I throw my arms around his neck... "I didn't mean for this to happen," he says. "I was trying to put my life back together and take care of the kids—I wasn't looking for someone new."

"So you're not ready for a relationship," I say.

"It's not only about me. I have to think about the kids, too. Nate and Scotty depend on me for everything they need every single day; I can't afford to be unstable. They've been through enough already, and if I start something with you and it crashes and burns...forget it. It's a bad idea." Luke tests the bottle on his arm again, finds it satisfactory, and heads toward Scotty's room. "Lock the door when you leave, okay?"

I stand in the kitchen alone, my heart racing. Luke told me to leave but I can't leave, not when I know he's aching for me too. Any moment now I could be intertwined with him, running my hands over his skin...but I can't think like that. I have to stay rational. I go to the living room. On the floor near the mattress is a battered copy of *A Tree Grows in Brooklyn*, lying upside down and open to mark the page. I pick it up, thinking that reading will calm me down, but I stare at the words in the book without seeing them. There's only one sentence in my brain and it's *I like you a lot*. Luke is mine if I want him and I want him with every nerve in my body...

It's simple. I take off my clothes.

My underwear has just hit the floor when Luke walks out of Scotty's room alone. His eyes widen and he runs to me and grabs me. "What are you thinking—"

I'm not thinking, I'm feeling his beard scraping my lips and his hands on my breasts and the heat of his body as his clothes come off too. No tattoos on his chest, only his arms, and I like that. The kisses get more insistent and my hand is between his legs... "I don't have condoms," he says.

"I'm on the pill—I don't care."

These are words I never say but without them he'll stop and I don't want him to stop, I want to follow this feeling wherever it takes me, to the mattress on the floor and Luke inside me. It's the first time I've had sex without a condom and it's exhilarating, his bare warm skin melting with mine until he feels like part of me, inextricable from me. The climax hits me in waves and he comes after me with a moan and clutches me to his chest. We both catch our breaths. "Gemma," he says. "That was—"

He can't finish his sentence because I'm kissing him, kissing his lips and his cheeks and his eyes with a swell of affection I can't contain, he's the most beautiful man I've ever seen and I love the taste of his mouth and his skin and the way his laugh ripples through his body and mine... "You're a sweetheart," he says. "This feels so good..."

Then we hear it—the wail. Scotty is crying again. His voice is so shrill I want to cover my ears. "Maybe he'll go back to sleep," Luke says, stroking my face. We wait several minutes but the crying doesn't stop.

"Dada!" Scotty sobs. "Dada! Dada!"

Luke sighs. "See what I mean? I never get a break." He kisses me, then gets out from inside me, out of bed, and puts on his pants. "Be right back."

The door to Scotty's room closes, but I can hear Luke singing him a lullaby. The sound fills me with shame. How could I have seduced Luke steps away from his innocent boys? What if Nate had walked in on us? And we weren't quiet so who knows what the kids heard...the thought makes me want to puke. I didn't consider the kids at all, I didn't listen when Luke said his life was complicated, and now the connection we shared feels tainted. I'm disgusted with myself; I get out of bed to look for my clothes.

When Luke comes back, I'm near the front door putting on the shirt I threw across the room. He pulls me close to him. "Where are you going?"

He sounds vulnerable and this deepens my guilt. I thought he'd be cool; men always act like sex is no big deal. Instead his arms are tight around my waist and his eyes are filled with hurt and longing. "I don't know," I say. "I...I wasn't leaving—I was—"

"You just wanted to hook up, right?"

"No, no, I like you. I just feel overwhelmed." Scotty starts crying again, and we both wince. "Listen to this..."

"It's fine." He lets go of me. "You can leave."

"Luke—"

"Nah, it's been fun. See you around."

I reach out to touch his face, but he turns and goes back to Scotty's room. I wait outside the door for a while; Scotty keeps crying and I feel like I'm about to cry, too. I put on my shoes and go out to my car.

As I drive home, I replay everything in my head. I shouldn't have left Luke's place. I made it seem like I was only interested in sex, when really I'm crazy about Luke and I wish I were still in his arms. Hearing the baby cry was strange, though—how do parents have sex without feeling gross? I wonder if Luke thinks I'm a slut or if he'll hold me again the way he did a few minutes ago...I'm an idiot. Why did I leave? I could go back, but I'm an emotional wreck and I'll probably do more harm than good. I'll explain everything to him on Sunday.

Saturday seems to last for years; I can't focus on the yard sale because I'm thinking about Luke. On Sunday, I pick Michela up for art class. I'm on edge the whole drive, while Michela chatters away in my ear. Luke and the kids aren't there when we arrive. My heart is hammering, anticipating the moment when I'll see him, but he never shows up.

Michela hands me a pack of rhinestones to open for her. "Where's Nate?" she asks.

"I don't know," I say. "I was wondering the same thing."

I feel hollow, looking at the empty space on the lawn where Luke usually puts his blanket. There could be some other reason he's not here, but it's likely that he's avoiding me. The situation has turned out worse than I thought.

Chapter Seven

Erica calls a coffee break as soon as we arrive at the office on Monday. "Five minutes," she says. "I need to vent about something."

"I love when you get pissed off," Lina says.

We gather on the couches. I've been sick to my stomach since yesterday's art class, but writing this morning helped me feel better. I'm interested to hear what Erica has to say.

"I went to Zoe's Little League game yesterday," Erica says. "Artie was home with the rest of our kids, so I sat with a group of moms who were chatting. They were ripping apart this other mom, Sheryl, who has a son on the team. 'Sheryl isn't here again,' one of the moms said. 'She misses half the games. And she never volunteers to bring snacks for the kids.' Then another mom was like, 'She thinks Little League is her babysitter. I asked her to help us plan the end of season pizza party, and she said no.' They went on like this for half an hour, bashing Sheryl for not participating in Little League."

"Because Little League should be everyone's top priority," Jasmine says, rolling her eyes.

"Obviously," Erica says. "It made me so angry. Sheryl is nice to everyone, and her son is a good kid—he's been in Zoe's class the past few years. I see Sheryl hugging him when she drops him off at the field, and when she does stay for games, she pays attention instead of socializing or scrolling through her phone. Just because she doesn't volunteer doesn't mean she doesn't care. Maybe she doesn't have time—maybe she has a sick parent or a sick child or she's starting her own business, or any one of a million other things that are more important than Little League. How can other moms judge her when they know nothing about her life?"

"I can't stand when moms are cruel to other moms," Lina says. "We're supposed to be in this together—we're all going through the same struggles. But instead of supporting each other, we ostracize anyone who doesn't do things our way."

"I've been putting up with bullshit like this since the moment I had Zoe," Erica says. "Who cares if you breastfeed or bottle feed? Who cares if you don't show up to every school event or every damn classmate's birthday party? Who cares if you stay home full time or work full time or anything in between? We're all trying to do what's best for our families, and parenting is hard enough without everybody criticizing you. I wanted to turn to these moms at the field and say, 'Ladies, shut the fuck up!'"

"You should have said it," Jasmine says.

"But then I'd be an outcast, and so would my kid," Erica says. "At least I can share my feelings with you guys. Lina gets it because she's in the trenches with me, and you three might learn something from us that will help when you have kids. If you have kids."

"I'll be asking you for advice about everything when I'm a mom," Jasmine says.

"Are you and Mark going to start trying?" Erica asks.

"Pretty soon. We want to get this house in order first..."

We chat for a little longer, and then the lawyers head to their offices. I feel depressed, staring at my computer. The coffee break was a welcome distraction, but now my mind is back on Luke. I don't know how to make things right with him. I wish I could text him, but I don't have his number. Maybe I should stop by his apartment after work...but that seems desperate. Am I desperate? I'm used to being pursued by the guys I like, not the other way around, so I'm not sure how to act; I don't want to look like a stalker. It's probably better if I run into him by accident. I take Michela to the park that evening, and for the next two evenings in a row, but we never see Luke.

On Saturday, I get a call from Aunt Soph. "Michela is sick," she says. "Sore throat and a fever."

I bite my lip to keep from shouting every expletive I know. "That's terrible," I say. "Is she okay?"

"She's all right. It was bound to happen—it's been going around her school. No art class for her tomorrow."

The universe hates me. Now I can't talk to Luke. Then again, if he doesn't want to see me, he might skip class like he did last week. It won't matter if I'm there or not.

By Wednesday, how Luke feels about me is no longer my most pressing concern. I haven't gotten my period. It usually comes once I get to the sugar pills in my pack, but I started those three days ago and I'm not bleeding. I can't be pregnant—that's nearly impossible—but it's disturbing. I buy a box of pregnancy tests and wait to take one until the morning; my aunts taught me that it's best to use first morning urine.

I head to the bathroom as soon as I wake up on Thursday. I had a bad night's sleep, and I feel cold and jittery. It'll be negative, I tell myself. I'm on the pill—it has to be negative. I pee on the test and watch pink creeping across the white screen. One line shows up—the control line. I wait three minutes, my eyes on the empty space next to the first line, but nothing else appears. That's a relief. I wash my hands and brush my teeth, and then I realize I left the test lying on the floor. I pick it up.

There's a second line. A faint line, barely noticeable, but a line. I turn the test different ways; the line is lighter from certain angles, but it never disappears. A second line means I'm pregnant.

Panic seizes my body. My heart pounds out of rhythm; my chest gets tight. This can't be happening. Not to me. Not from one mistake. Why did I have sex without a condom? And how am I going to tell Luke? He thought dating would make him unstable—imagine having another baby. Because I will have this baby, even though I'm terrified, even though it's bad timing; I've always wanted to be a mom. A mom...I think about Aunt Soph and Michela and grab the edge of the sink to steady myself. I'm not ready for this. I'm not ready to dedicate my life to someone else. And who knows what pregnancy will do to my body and then I have to give birth and I've been drinking too much wine lately and that can't be healthy...

Then logic comes to my defense. I read the test after the time window—that means it's not accurate. I'm on the pill, and I take it every day; the odds of getting pregnant are less than one percent. Still, one percent isn't zero percent, and sometimes I forget my pill in the morning and take it after work instead...I'm screwed. I have to take another test. There's one more test in the box; I'll take it tomorrow morning, and then I'll decide what to do.

I wrap the test in a million layers of toilet paper so my dad won't see it and I throw it in the trash. I go back to my room and try to concentrate on writing, but instead I spend the time googling what a positive test looks like and what happens if you read your results too late. I feel nauseous all day at the office and during dinner with my dad; this could be my first pregnancy symptom or a sign of how nervous I am. I go to bed early, but I don't fall asleep for hours.

I take the second test on Friday at four A.M. Negative. That's reassuring, but there's still no sign of my period. By the time I get to work, I'm exhausted from running and writing and worrying; I'm nearly falling asleep at my desk. Around lunchtime, I head to the bathroom to pee and I see blood.

Blood—bright red splats of blood and I'm sobbing, sobbing and shaking with relief. I'm not pregnant. I'm not pregnant! Someone knocks on the door. "Gemma?" It's Jasmine's voice. "What's wrong?"

"I'm fine," I say. It takes me a while to compose myself; when my tears slow down, I grab a tampon from the box we keep under the sink.

I leave the bathroom and find Jasmine waiting for me in the hallway. "I got my period," I tell her. "I was afraid I wouldn't get it this month."

"Oh girl, I've been there." She puts her arms around me. "It's okay now. Everything is okay."

I hug her back; it's a comfort to be held, to feel less alone. "Can we have a coffee break?" I ask.

Erica, Lina, and Bree join us on the couches. They're watching me with interest; I'm sure they didn't expect me to call a coffee break. I hadn't planned on it, but after seeing Jasmine react with compassion, I decided I want to talk to these women. They've shared so much of their lives with me; I can trust them. "I like this guy," I tell them. "But things are complicated because he's divorced and has two kids."

"That sounds like bad news," Lina says.

"I know. Maybe I'm crazy for wanting to date him..."

"But you slept with him," Jasmine says.

"Well...yeah," I say. We all laugh. "It's not my proudest moment, but..."

"He's hot—I met him," Bree says.

"Back up," Lina says. "Who is this guy? How do you know him?"

I tell the girls everything that has happened between me and Luke. I expected to feel embarrassed, but they listen without judgment. When I get to the part about Scotty crying while I was in bed with Luke, Lina and Erica groan.

"Babies love to kill the mood," Erica says.

"It's happened to you before?" I ask.

"A million times," Erica says. "You get used to it."

"You learn to finish quick," Lina says.

I tell them the rest of the story, up until the moment in the bathroom. "Thankfully, I'm not pregnant," I say. "But I don't know what to do about Luke. What do you guys think?"

"You already got your answer," Lina says. "Luke said it was risky to start a relationship, and I agree—it's too soon after his divorce. Five months is not enough time to get over your ex-wife."

"But they haven't been living together for almost a year," Erica says. "So they've essentially been divorced for longer. And it's not like he bitches about her all the time—he seems to have moved on."

"I think it's unhealthy," Lina says.

"I'm with Lina," Jasmine says. "If Luke couldn't make his marriage work, he's probably screwed up. Then again, people warned me Mark was screwed up and we have a great relationship."

"What's wrong with Mark?" Bree asks.

"A bunch of stuff from his past...plus he works twelve hours a day and his mother drives me insane..."

"We remember that part," Erica says.

"The point is, I knew about his issues when we started dating and I accepted them," Jasmine says. "I didn't fool myself that he was perfect, or hope that his problems would go away. Because problems don't go away. If you want to date Luke, be ready to deal with drama from his ex-wife. Be ready to help him take care of his kids."

"He'll put his kids ahead of you," Lina says.

"And we don't know if he wants to date you," Bree says. "Clearly he's into you, but if you want to be his girlfriend and he would rather stay friends with benefits, that's not going to work. Don't throw yourself at his feet."

"I won't," I say.

"It's going to be rocky at times," Jasmine says. "But everybody has flaws, and for you, maybe the good things about Luke outweigh the bad."

"What is it that you like about him?" Erica asks. "If you like that he's cute and a musician, you shouldn't date him. You'll find plenty of guys like him without the baggage. But if it goes deeper than that..."

"I do like that he's a musician," I say. "He understands the creative process better than anyone I know, and he's a passionate person, always brimming over with things to talk about. But I also like that he's a dad. He has responsibilities instead of being self-absorbed, and he gives his kids so much love and attention."

"Just because he's good with kids doesn't mean he's good with women," Lina says.

"That's a valid point," Erica says. "A very valid point, and we shouldn't confuse the two. Still, I think it's a plus for Luke's character. Anyone who willingly spends that much time with two toddlers can't be a selfish asshole."

"I know he's a good guy," I say. "He's earnest with his kids, and with me. He doesn't play games—he shows what he feels."

"Oh honey," Erica says. "He means a lot to you."

"He does."

"Then go for it," Erica says. "It's worth the risk if you feel a strong connection. Sometimes you have to take a leap and trust the magic."

"You're kidding, right?" Lina says. "We're adults and we're supposed to give her good advice! Gemma, I'm sure he's special but this sounds like a bucket of heartache. I wouldn't get involved."

"You have to say that—you're our resident cynic," Erica says. "Anyone else?"

"As long as Luke wants to be your boyfriend, I don't see a problem with it," Bree says. "If things get too intense, you can just break up with him."

"I don't want to start a relationship with one eye on the exit," I say.

Bree shrugs. "I always do."

"I think you know, deep down, what you need to do," Jasmine says. "In these situations, talking to other people is a way of clarifying what we already feel. It doesn't matter what the rest of us say, because you know in your gut if this is a pipe dream that you need to give up, or if you and Luke could be good for each other. Be honest with yourself and go with your gut."

"Your gut, though—not your libido," Lina says.

Bree is doubled over with laughter. "This is the best workplace ever."

"Speaking of work," Erica says. "I have a client coming in any minute and I don't want him overhearing this..."

"Back to your desks, ladies," Lina says. "Gemma, let us know what happens."

We all return to our computers. I feel lighter now that I've shared my problems with the girls. Even if things don't work out with Luke, I'm glad to have these women as friends; they're smart and kind and I feel like part of their group for the first time.

Bree rolls her chair back from her desk and nudges me with her foot. "I guess Luke was better in bed than Eddie?"

"You slept with him that night?" I say.

"He was wasted—it was awful."

We're still giggling when Erica's client, a frowning older man in a suit and tie, walks through the door.

After work, I drive to Luke's apartment building. Now that I've gotten past the pregnancy scare, my drama with him seems small; I want to have a relationship with him, so I should tell him that upfront. I'm going to talk to him now instead of waiting until Sunday. If he thinks I'm crazy or he doesn't want to be with me, I'll move on.

Luke answers the door with Scotty in his arms. His eyebrows go up when he sees me, but he drops his gaze right away and his tone is cold. "Gemma. What's up?"

"Can we talk?" I say. "I know this is out of the blue, but I don't have your number and I don't know how else to find you...and I want to talk."

Luke thinks for a moment; Scotty starts tugging on his hair. "Okay." He pushes open the door to let me in. "Let's talk."

I follow him into the apartment. Nate is on the floor surrounded by blocks and plastic dinosaurs. "Hi!" he says. "Is Michela here?"

"No, it's just me," I say.

"Oh. Want to see my dino land?"

"Sure!"

I sit on the floor next to Nate while he describes each of his towers and dinosaurs. Luke watches us, silently gnawing on the skin around his fingernails, while Scotty bangs blocks together and puts them in his mouth. When there's finally a break in Nate's chatter, Luke addresses me. "What did you want to say?"

I take a deep breath. "Luke, I'm sorry I messed this up. I really like you. You're sincere and interesting and I feel inspired every time I talk to you and I wasn't only looking for, um..." I glance at the kids. "Um...a physical thing."

"What's a physical thing?" Nate asks.

"Don't worry about it, Nate," Luke says.

"I know I sent the wrong message that night," I say. "I panicked. I've never been in that situation before, with the baby crying."

"It's weird." Luke nods. "I know. It's weird for me, too."

"But I shouldn't have left and I've been regretting that ever since. Then all this time went by when we didn't get a chance to talk and I thought you were avoiding me..."

"I wasn't," he says. "I thought you were avoiding me. When I didn't see you in class on Sunday—"

"I couldn't go because Michela was sick."

"Really? My kids were sick the Sunday before that. Fever and a sore throat?"

"Yeah."

"Maybe they had the same thing." His eyes are fixed on mine. "Look, I'm glad you're telling me the truth, but if you're not ready to be serious..."

"I want to be serious. I want to be your girlfriend. I know the kids are your top priority and I respect that; the fact that you put them first is one of the reasons I like you. And I'm not expecting fancy dates or vacations or any of the extraneous stuff people look for in relationships. I just want to be with you...talking to you, holding you..." My voice is wavering, but I press on. "But if you don't want to take that chance, I get it—we can keep our distance. At least you know that I was never playing with you...that I care."

Luke takes my hand. He runs his thumb over my fingers—over my short, unpainted nails, over the garnet ring that used to belong to my mom. His touch is gentle and I feel like my heart is expanding, taking up all the room in my chest. "I want to have a relationship with you," he says. "We can try it. I don't know how it goes from here..."

"Let's get dinner tonight," I say.

"I don't have anyone to watch the kids. My mom and stepdad went away for the weekend."

"We'll bring them with us."

"Bring them?"

"Yeah, of course."

He grins. "All right."

We get out the stroller and walk to the Mexican restaurant down the block. There's an outdoor patio with multicolored tables and chairs, and Nate makes us drag all the orange chairs together at one table. We order a bunch of tacos and a bottle of wine and Nate eats plate after plate of chips and Luke and I take turns holding Scotty on our laps because he refuses to sit in the high chair. There are crumbs and globs of guacamole everywhere, but Luke and I are talking and laughing and there's nowhere I'd rather be than across the table from him. When the meal is over, we put the kids back in the stroller. My shirt is covered in stains because Scotty was using me as a napkin and Nate is complaining that his straps are too tight. "Come here," Luke says, tugging on my arm.

"What's up?" I say.

"Just come here."

He kisses me. It's so nice to kiss him, to feel his soft lips along with the prickle of his beard, to let my mouth fall into a rhythm with his. "What are you doing?" Nate asks.

"Kissing my girl," Luke says. "You'll get used to it."

Chapter Eight

Luke and I have been dating for a little over a month, and we're happy together. Still, our relationship is unlike anything I've experienced before.

We spend a lot of time with the kids. Sometimes Luke's mom and stepdad will babysit for a few hours on the weekend or give us a date night, but for the most part, the kids are with us. Though Nate and Scotty are a handful, I adore them. I love teaching Scotty new things and I love the way Nate's eyes sparkle when he's playing one of his pretend games. The four of us can usually be found at the park or the library or the supermarket or on the floor at Luke's place surrounded by toys. On Saturday mornings, we take Nate to soccer class; Luke and I play with Scotty in the dewy grass and watch Nate run around with a pack of toddlers. Art class is over, so I bring Michela to Luke's place on Sundays to play with Nate. Days with the kids are full of diaper changes—Luke's responsibility, but an essential part of our schedule—as well as crayons, cartoons, bottles, and piles of laundry.

At night, Luke and I have time to ourselves. We push the armchair in front of Nate's door when we're having sex, and now that Scotty has gotten his molars, he rarely wakes up at night. Even when he interrupts us, it doesn't freak me out—I've grown accustomed to the idea that couples have sex while there are kids in the house. Luke and I love to lie in bed, cuddling and talking; though he talks a lot, he's a good listener, too. He can always tell if something is bothering me, if my legs or sore or my eyes or dry or I had a bad day, and he'll give me a massage or let me vent until I feel better. I like that he's in tune to my emotions; I want him to understand me, and I want to know everything about him.

"Show me a picture of you when you were younger," I said one night early on. I find it easier to get inside people's heads if I can imagine their childhoods.

"When I was a kid?" Luke asked.

"A kid, a teenager—sometime before I knew you."

"My cousin sent me an old picture yesterday." He picked up his phone and found the picture. "That's me...and those are my cousins, Bella and Marisa. Bella is my age and Marisa is two years younger."

I studied the photo. Luke was on a crowded beach next to two girls with curly hair. He was an awkwardly skinny teenager, all arms and legs without a toned muscle in sight. He had no beard or tattoos but it was easy to recognize him; my heart warmed at the sight of his face. "You look just like Nate," I said. "How old were you?"

"Maybe fourteen, fifteen? I'm not smiling with my teeth, so it's back when I had braces. And that was when my grandparents used to rent that house on LBI. We always went on vacation with my cousins; Bella and Marisa are my only first cousins, my mom's sister's kids, and we were together almost every day growing up. I don't get to see them as often now that they moved to Morristown."

I peered at his cousins. Bella and Marisa resembled Luke, but they had dark eyes and tan skin. Luke, by contrast, had patches of red on his chest and shoulders. "Looks like you had a sunburn going," I said.

"I always burn. Greek and Italian on my mom's side and I got stuck with my father's skin. I must have missed some spots on my shoulders...man, I look terrible."

"You were cute." I kissed him. "You're cuter now, though."

"I should hope so! Let me see one of you."

"I have a bunch."

I showed him my phone. I had several old photos from family parties, as well as a picture of me with the hockey team. "Gemma, you were such a tomboy." Luke grabbed my breasts. "Why were you hiding these under those baggy t-shirts?"

"I hated tight clothes," I said. "And I didn't care about looking attractive back then. I started paying attention to how I dressed in college."

"So college is when you went wild?"

"I was never wild! Why would you say that?"

"Just the way you got naked in my living room..."

"I like you a lot," I said. "And a girl can be sexually confident without sleeping around. You want to know how many guys I've been with?"

"Yeah, I do."

"I had a boyfriend in high school but we never had sex. I slept with an Italian asshole when I was studying abroad, a guy I went on a few dates with in Tucson, and you. You're the third one."

His face was glowing. "And hopefully the last...if you don't get tired of me..."

"I can't imagine getting tired of you. Give me your list."

"You already know it."

"Really?" I was floored. "Only me and Sylvie?"

"You're surprised?"

"I thought...musicians..."

"Daddy," Nate whimpered from his room. "I can't open the door."

"What's the matter, buddy?" Luke asked.

"I had a bad dream."

"Be right there." Luke put on his clothes and tossed mine to me. "Give me a minute, baby."

Comforting Nate took longer than a minute, and by the time Luke got back, I was asleep. I find it hard to stay up late these days, since I wake up earlier than I used to. When I spend weeknights at Luke's place, I set my morning alarm for five thirty so I can drive back to my house to write and get ready for work. On Fridays and Saturdays, I sleep in Luke's arms until the kids wake us up. I love staying with him, but I don't get any more sleep than I do on weeknights.

The first night I slept over, I was woken by the feeling of small feet climbing over my legs. "Daddy!" I heard Nate's voice say. "Daddy! Wake up!"

"I'm not Daddy yet," Luke said. "I'm sleeping."

"I want breakfast!"

I opened my eyes to see Luke checking the time on his phone. "Nate, it's five fifteen! Go back to sleep."

"But I'm hungry."

Luke groaned and buried his face in my neck. "Five more minutes."

"Why is Gemma here?" Nate asked.

"I'm Daddy's girlfriend," I said. "Sometimes boyfriends and girlfriends sleep in the same bed."

"That's weird."

Nate's little jaw was set, and I knew I'd have to do something to win him over. "I'll make breakfast for you," I said. I got up and followed him to the kitchen. When I looked through the cabinets for cereal, I noticed a box of pancake mix. "Want to make pancakes?" I asked Nate.

"Really? Chocolate chip?"

"Sure!"

There were no chocolate chips, so we threw M&Ms into the batter instead. Nate was delighted by the way the colors bled into the pancakes as the candy melted. "Can we make one with all orange M&Ms?" he asked.

"Of course! That's your favorite color, right?"

"Yeah! And we'll make a blue one for Daddy. And..." He thought for a moment. "What's your favorite color?"

"I like green."

A few minutes later, Luke joined us in the kitchen. His hair and clothes were disheveled, and he was squinting in the bright light. He kissed me. "Thank you. I needed that time..."

"We made you a blue pancake, Daddy!" Nate said.

77

"Pancakes before six A.M.?" Luke said to me. "You have a lot of patience."

"I'm not working off four years of sleep deprivation like you are."

After that morning, I made it a point to include Nate in the kitchen. I like to cook—I learned from my dad—and though I can't make elaborate meals with the kids around, I know plenty of simple recipes. Luke's idea of cooking is microwaving chicken nuggets, so he's pleased with everything I make. Nate loves to help me wash vegetables or pour broth into a pot of soup or spread cheese on pizza, and he's always proud of our meals. "I cooked this," he tells Luke.

"It's delicious, buddy!" Luke says.

Luke eats every meal with his kids. Though this is a good routine for the boys, it's a lot of work for us. Meals used to be my time to unwind but now they're stressful. Nate and Scotty make an unbelievable mess—if Scotty gets one cracker with peanut butter, he'll smear peanut butter on every inch of his high chair and cover the floor in crumbs. "It's impossible," Luke said the other day as he was sweeping. "How does he multiply food? You can't make this many crumbs with one cracker."

"And presumably some of the cracker made it into his mouth," I said.

"Presumably."

At mealtimes, Luke and I have to play characters in Nate's fantasy games and convince Scotty to eat instead of smashing his food, so we don't get much time to talk. The nights I eat at home with my dad are always a relief. Still, I miss Luke and the kids when they're not around, and the joy of being with them is worth a little madness.

***

Now that we're always together, I've seen more of Luke's anxiety. He's okay most of the time, but he has his moments. Some days he'll check the front door a million times to make sure it's locked, or he'll have the kids wash their hands if they touched the bottom of their shoes or went too close to the garbage can or picked something off the ground that was probably a stick but might have been poop. I know Luke is overreacting, but I usually don't interfere. His worries only caused conflict between us once—yesterday, when we were having lunch with the kids.

We stopped at a diner after Nate's soccer class, and Nate was interested in the burger I was eating. "Can I try that?" he asked me.

"Sure!"

"You can't have the burger, Nate," Luke said. "It's undercooked."

"No it's not," I said. "It tastes well done to me."

"It looks pink," Luke said.

"Gemma said it was okay," Nate said.

"It's totally okay," I said.

"Let me handle this!" Luke snapped.

I was taken aback; Luke never talks to me like that. "All right."

We were all quiet for a minute. "I'm sorry," Luke said. "That came out really harsh."

"It's fine," I said. "You shouldn't get so worked up over nothing."

"It's not nothing in my brain—that's the problem." Luke looked at Nate. "You want the burger, buddy? Go ahead."

I gave Nate a few bites of my burger. He enjoyed it, while Luke mutilated his thumb with his teeth. I tried to stroke Luke's hair and he flinched. "Don't worry, baby," I said, though his behavior was making me worry, too.

Luke took my outstretched hand and kissed it. We both went back to our food.

Later that night, we were in the kitchen making pasta for dinner. Scotty was stacking Tupperware containers and Nate was rolling his cars across the floor; I had already stepped on a car and my foot was throbbing. "Throw a quote at me," Luke said to me.

"A quote?"

"I like inspirational quotes from artists and leaders—things that make me think. You've read more books than I have so you probably know some good quotes. Throw something at me."

I thought for a while. "'Don't run around this world looking for a hole to hide in,'" I said. "'There are wild beasts in every cave.'"

Luke grinned. "That's directed right at me, isn't it?"

"Yup."

"I like it. Where's it from?"

"Rumi."

"What's Rumi?"

"Oh honey, I have so much to teach you."

I have so much to learn from him too. Luke weaves music into his life, and the kids' lives, every day. Sometimes he'll sit on the floor playing his acoustic guitar, and he'll let the boys bang on the body of the guitar and strum the strings. "It's good for them to get used to the instrument," he says. "How it feels, how it sounds. Then if they want to play someday, it'll feel natural to them." Both of his kids love music; they play with tambourines and egg shakers and turn pots and pans and boxes into drums. Scotty is always dancing, and music is the only thing that soothes him when he's having a tantrum. Nate sings his way through daily activities, making up songs to narrate what he's doing. "Puttin' on my shoes, puttin' on my shoes," he'll sing as he slides his feet into his sneakers. "Peas, peas, peas," he sang the other night at dinner, tapping his hand on the table next to his plate. "I don't want to eat these peas..."

"But they're good," Luke sang back, matching his melody. "They're good, they're good for you." Nate smiled.

Luke puts music on when we're driving or cooking or making crafts, and I've discovered several new songs I like. He mostly plays rock, but he mixes in pop and jazz and classical music and even the annoying kiddie stuff Nate requests. This afternoon, we're at the table playing with Play Doh and listening to a piano composition that stirs my emotions. "I love this," I say to Luke. "What is it?"

"It's a piece by Einaudi, a contemporary composer. It's called 'Nuvole Bianche,' which means—well, you speak Italian..."

"White clouds," I say. I'm quiet for the rest of the piece, letting my mind soak in the music. "That was amazing," I tell Luke when it's over. "How the piece is sad and uplifting at the same time. You feel the weight and sorrow of life along with the beauty. Especially that part in the middle, where the music builds to a peak and that other melody comes in...is it a melody? Whatever it's called, it's high-pitched like the voice of a kid and it fights to be heard, fights to have hope in spite of the darkness. Anyway..." I cut myself off, embarrassed by my lack of eloquence. "I'm not making sense—I don't know the terms to talk about music."

"Don't worry about the terms," he says. "Music is for everyone, not just experts. Art is for everyone. If you feel it, you get it."

His face is serious, without a hint of mockery, and this makes me less insecure. "It's giving me an idea," I say. "Put it on again."

Luke starts the piece over, and I grab a pencil and some construction paper out of Nate's art box. I sit on the couch, using a picture book as a base, and write everything that's brewing in my head. A character is taking shape, a character named Linus; his name arrives along with his image. He's my main character's little brother, the brother she's been taking care of since their parents died in the Sedona massacre. I've struggled with Alana recently because she's too cold, too ruthless, and here comes her brother with his optimism and innocence and imagine how it would feel to have him battling alongside her...I write through "Nuvole Bianche" and a few more instrumental pieces, outlining several scenes between the siblings. I could keep going, but I want to be with Luke and the kids; it's Sunday, and we won't get to spend as much time together once the work week starts. I put the papers into my purse and go back to the table.

Luke is watching me with interest. Scotty is on his lap, smashing the colorful snowmen Luke built for him, and Nate is rolling balls of Play Doh across the table. "Something for your story?" Luke asks.

"Yeah, just brainstorming a new character."

"When are you going to let me read this book?"

"I don't know...when the writing isn't bad. If it's ever not bad."

"Don't be so hard on yourself."

I study Luke—his unruly hair, the line of his jaw, the Play Doh under his fingernails. I trust him, but the idea of showing him my unfinished work makes me cringe. What if he thinks it's terrible? It is terrible. He could give me feedback to make it better...but I'm not ready to have someone else's hands in my writing this early in the process. My story is too new and unstable and sensitive to change—I need to establish my voice before I let him in. I will let him in, I decide, once I'm further along; if I can share my work with anybody, it's Luke. "When the story gets more solid," I say, nuzzling my head against his shoulder. "And I know where I'm going. Then you can read it."

"Awesome."

A new song shuffles on, a classic rock song this time, and both Luke and Nate nod their heads to the beat. "I never asked you," I say to Luke. "What's your favorite song?"

"That's impossible—it's impossible to pick. I have twenty different choices in my head, from 'Jungleland' to 'Like a Stone' to multiple songs by Muse..."

"Your favorite love song, then."

"I'm not a big fan of love songs," he says. "Most of them aren't about love—they're about conquest or lust or infatuation. They don't say what it means to be devoted to someone for the long term, to share your life with another person."

"That's true," I say.

"When I think of love stories, I think about my mom's parents," he says. "They were married for sixty years—sixty years! Plenty of people don't get to live that long, let alone love someone for that long. But they got it right. There was harmony between them, in spite of their flaws; they enjoyed being together. I'm glad I grew up seeing that kind of love...I wish they were still around."

"They passed away?"

"In my junior year of high school—my grandma two weeks after my grandpa. She didn't want to stay here without him; she always said he held her world together."

"That's so sad," I say.

"It was sad, at the end. But everything up until the end was happy."

"Daddy," Nate says. "Put on the song that goes, 'DA! Da-da-DA-da! Da-da-DA-da!'"

"That Vivaldi concerto?" Luke grins. "See, Gemma? Art is for everyone."

Later that night, I stretch out on the mattress to read while Luke puts Nate and Scotty to bed. Once they're asleep, Luke lies down next to me and we start kissing. Making love to him has lost none of the beauty and excitement of the first time; the feelings keep getting stronger. Sex gives us pleasure but it's also an act of closeness, a way for us to climb into each other's skin. My body belongs with his and I can feel with every touch that he adores me.

After we have sex, we cuddle for a while. "This is one of my favorite parts of you," Luke says, kissing the mole on my side, to the left of my breasts. I used to hate this mole and always made sure my bathing suits were positioned to cover it. "And here..." He kisses the beauty marks on the inside of my thigh. "I love these little guys..."

He takes a bite of the beauty marks and looks up at me, his soft curls tickling my skin, and I feel a rush of tenderness so powerful it makes me dizzy. It's too early for me to feel this way, like I love him and I'll always love him and I'll spend the rest of my life tangled up with him. "Guess what?" I say, playing with his hair. "You can keep them."

"Yeah?"

"Yeah."

He kisses the beauty marks one more time, then leans into my arms. "I'll try my best to deserve them..."

I run my hands over his back, his arms, his shoulders. He's not very built; when he works out, he does it using an app on his phone, while the kids pretend to do pushups next to him. Still, his arms are toned, and I like the shape his tattoos take over his muscles. "Tell me about your tattoos," I say. "What's the story behind them?"

"I'll start with the first one." He points to a pair of dice on his upper arm, close to his shoulder. It's a simple design, all in black; the front of one die shows a four and the other shows a three. "This was the symbol of the first band I ever played in, Don't Say Seven. One of the guys suggested that name based on some gambling superstition, and it stuck. We formed the band when I was fourteen and played together for two years, until the drummer and the bassist went away to college. We had a decent following in high school, and we put these dice on everything—

on stickers, on pins, on the cover of the horrible EP we recorded in one guy's basement. I used to tell people that when I turned eighteen, I was going to get a dice tattoo on my arm. Fast forward to prom weekend in senior year—I went down the shore after the dance with a bunch of friends. My buddy Brandon was there, and Eddie, the drummer you met; Eddie and I had formed a new band by then. We went to Seaside for three days, and it rained the whole time. I'm not talking drizzle—it was a nonstop downpour."

"I remember that weekend!" I say. "My prom was the week after that, and we went to Seaside too. It was sunny, and we kept saying we were lucky not to have the weather of the previous week."

"Good for Oakfield."

I marvel at how Luke and I once lived parallel lives—we were the same age, in the same grade, growing up in towns next to each other, visiting the same places—and we never crossed paths. Or maybe we did cross paths and we didn't notice each other. Maybe I never would have met him if it hadn't been for Nate and Michela. "So," I say. "It rained..."

"And we were bored to death. The last night we were having some drinks, and Eddie decided to get another tattoo; he had several already. He said, 'Luke is coming with me—he's getting those dice he always talked about.' Everybody remembered..." Luke gives me a sheepish grin. "So I couldn't back down, obviously."

"Obviously."

"My mom was pissed. It's not a bad tattoo, though—could have been worse. Nate likes counting the dots on the dice."

"Your tiger tattoo is for Nate, right?" I point to the name on the tiger's paw.

"Yeah. When he was born, he had the sharpest fingernails—like daggers. Sylvie and I were scared we'd hurt him if we cut them, so we left them alone for weeks. Most of the time he wore mittens, but when we took them off he gave us brutal scratches—slashed me across the face once. Sylvie said he had the claws of a tiger, and that became his nickname—we called him our Little Tiger the whole first year." He smiles at the tattoo. "Now his favorite color is orange so the tiger still fits."

"I like it."

"And the phoenix is for Scotty." I look closer and see Scotty's name on the bird's wing. "I picked that image because it felt like he was born from the ashes of my marriage. Sylvie and I made each other miserable, yet Scotty rose from the wreckage—this beautiful person who grew in spite of everything. At least we made him, him and Nate...that's all we did right."

"Do you have Sylvie's name anywhere?" I ask.

"She used to be on the back of the tiger, but I got it covered up after she left, when I got the phoenix. The tattoo artist made it look like a shadow. It felt final, getting rid of her name—even more than when I sold my ring. It helped me move on."

I peer at the tiger and I can't see a trace of Sylvie's name. Still, it's odd to know that it's there—invisible yet irreversible. Luke may not love her anymore, but her presence in bed with us makes me feel small. Sylvie is the mother of his kids, the wife he might have spent his life with if she hadn't left him. I don't know if he'll ever feel for me what he felt for her. "What's the matter?" he asks, stroking my hair. "Did that upset you, about Sylvie?"

"It's okay. Tell me about the last tattoo—the comet."

"I got this for my friend Brandon, who died when we were nineteen. He had a grade four brain tumor—gone within a year of the diagnosis."

"Oh my God."

"It was fucked up," Luke says. "Brandon was a great guy, and ridiculously smart—valedictorian of our high school class. He went to Stanford to study astrophysics but halfway through freshman year he was back in Verona and dying. I would visit him when I came home for breaks—his family lived next door to us—and it was sickening, seeing him so weak, seeing him deteriorate. His older brother, Ollie, kept saying not to give up hope; Ollie was my friend too, the drummer who asked me to join Don't Say Seven. When Brandon died, Ollie and I got these tattoos, with Brandon's initials on the tail of the comet. Ollie said seeing a comet is a rare, awe-inspiring experience; once a comet passes you by, it won't return in your lifetime. He said he liked to picture Brandon's soul traveling through space. I don't believe in that stuff." Luke shrugs, but his voice is thick. "I think when people are gone, they're gone...but the idea is nice."

"I'm sorry, Luke." I put my arms around him. For a while we hold each other without speaking. The word "astrophysics" jogged something in my memory; it takes me several minutes to make the connection. "You wrote a song about Brandon," I say.

"I did. My writing changed after he died...my perspective on life changed. Brandon had so much to offer the world, so much he could have accomplished, and it disappeared with him. Losing him made me realize there's no escaping death; no matter how careful I am, it'll find me when it's my time. The only thing I can do is give all of myself to every moment I have left—all of my love to the people I care about, all of my truth to the things I write and say. There's no time to be indifferent, no time to pretend you're tougher than you are because the only way to connect with anyone is to be vulnerable. The same goes for art—you get it." He laces his fingers through mine. "When you write you have to dig deep, you have to go to the dark places, you have to expose some of your soul if you want to make anything that's authentic...anything that's...that's..."

"That's worth remembering," I say.

"Being remembered is part of it—leaving your voice behind after you're gone. But I'm not talking about immortality, I'm talking about reaching out into the void, about knowing that somebody else—maybe somebody you've never met—suffered less because of what you made. That can only happen if you're willing to share what's inside you and that's what I want to do. Maybe it'll never be worth much to anybody, but...I'm going to have nothing left to say when they bury me."

I trace the initials on his arm. This is a beautiful philosophy, and I understand Luke better now that I've heard it. Still I feel shaky, thinking of my mom and the stories she never got to write, thinking of what life would be like if Luke were dead. I'm so attached to him already...and what would happen to his kids? He's their whole world. "What you say is worth a lot to me," I tell him. "So is everything you do. Everything you are."

"I'm glad."

"And I hate the idea of someone burying you. You'd better stick around for a while."

He kisses me. "I'm staying here with you for as long as I can."

We talk for a few more minutes, and then we snuggle under the covers. I used to have a hard time sleeping next to someone else; I disliked sharing a bed with friends at sleepovers, and I always went back to my place to sleep after sex with Dario or Justin. But I've been comfortable in Luke's bed since the beginning. I curl up in his arms, listen to his heart, feel his body relax against mine...and drift off.

Chapter Nine

The next day at work, I get a text from Aunt Soph: *What kinds of toys does Nate like? I have to get him a present.*

I pick up my phone to respond. Nate turned four a few weeks ago, and his birthday party is this Saturday. Luke's mom and stepdad are hosting the party; they couldn't have it last month because they were remodeling their kitchen, but now their house is ready for guests. I'm glad Aunt Soph and Michela are coming to the party—it will make things less awkward for me.

This party will be my first time meeting most of Luke's family, and I'm apprehensive about it. I only know his mom and stepdad so far. They're both accountants; his stepdad, Harry, is friendly and nerdy, and I have no trouble making small talk with him. Luke's mom is another story. Nora is polite to me, but I can tell, from the look in her dark eyes, that I'm being evaluated. I don't have anything to hide but being watched puts me on edge. The situation is new to me; Nico's mom adored me, and I never met Dario or Justin's mothers. I'm careful around Nora and I'm trying to understand her. She has nervous hands, hands that are always fidgeting with something, and her house is immaculately clean. She's patient and generous with the kids but often snippy with Luke, which bothers me. I'm never at ease in her house the way Luke is at ease in mine. Luke was worried about meeting my dad, but my dad just introduced himself, shook Luke's hand, and offered him a drink. The two of them get along well and my dad likes having Nate and Scotty around. As I explained to Luke, my dad has always trusted my judgment when it comes to guys; he gives me honest advice, but he's not overprotective. My aunts, on the other hand, have voiced their disapproval of Luke many times, though they've never met him. I'm sure Aunt Soph will change her mind once she meets him on Saturday.

As the party gets closer, I ask Luke about the guests. His relatives on his mom's side are going to be there, including Bella and Marisa, but his father is on tour in Europe and won't be attending. Luke's father is the lead guitarist in a rock band that was popular back in the '90s. Their fan base is smaller these days, but they're still making music. During his childhood, Luke spent a weekend every month with his father, unless he was on tour; they see each other less often now. From what I can tell, their relationship isn't close, but it isn't strained either. Luke accepts him from a distance, expects little of him, and isn't concerned that I haven't met him.

On Saturday at noon, I head to Nora and Harry's house with Michela and Aunt Soph. Harry answers the door and invites us inside. There are trays of food laid out on the granite kitchen counters, and the living room is beautifully decorated as always. Through the sliding glass door, I see groups of people on the deck, enjoying the sunshine. Nate is running around the backyard with somebody's dog, and balloons bob up and down in the breeze. Everyone seems to be outside; the living room is empty except for Luke and Scotty. Scotty is in Luke's arms, hiding his face in Luke's neck.

"Hey guys!" Luke says. He reaches out to shake Aunt Soph's hand. "You must be Sophia—nice to meet you—" Scotty notices Aunt Soph and bursts into tears. "It's okay," Luke tells him. "This is Michela's mommy! She's nice!" Scotty keeps wailing. "I'm sorry—he has a little stranger anxiety..."

"Poor baby," Aunt Soph says.

"It's nothing personal—he freaked out earlier when my aunt tried to hold him."

"I don't want to scare him," Aunt Soph says. "Um...I could go outside..."

"Is Nate outside?" Michela asks.

"He is! He's been waiting for you to get here," Luke says. "I'll be out in a minute."

Aunt Soph and Michela head outside, and I start rubbing Scotty's back. Over the past few weeks, Scotty's fear of strangers has gotten more intense. He used to be fine around new people as long as he was with Luke, but now he screams if random adults get too close to him at the grocery store or the park. He likes being out in public, but he doesn't like crowded places and he doesn't like strangers intruding on his space. Luke says this is a normal part of development, but I feel bad every time he cries. "I wonder how long this phase is going to last," I say to Luke.

"Who knows. Nate got over it in a few months but he was never this extreme."

Scotty lifts his head and bats at my arm with his hand. "Hemma," he says. This is what he calls me, since he can't pronounce the soft *G* sound yet. "Hemma."

"Want me to hold him so you can talk to people?" I ask Luke.

"I'll take him," Harry says, walking over to us. "You guys go outside and have fun. Come here, Scotty—Grandpa bought you some new toys..." The two of them disappear down the hallway. Luke and I go out to the deck together.

Luke introduces me to his relatives. Everyone is welcoming, and I feel more relaxed. The guests are mostly adults; Luke has a few second cousins with babies, but the only kid Nate's age is Michela. I meet Bella, Marisa, and Marisa's boyfriend, and we chat with Bella for a while. When she and Luke are talking, the conversation moves at a hundred miles an hour; they use the same gestures and finish each other's sentences. "Bella is an English teacher like your dad," Luke tells me. "She's the one who made me read *A Tree Grows in Brooklyn*."

"That's my favorite novel," I say.

"Mine too!" Bella says. "Have you read anything else by Betty Smith?"

We talk about books, and then Bella brings up the kids. "I can't believe Nate is four!" she says. "Time flies. Is he starting preschool in the fall?"

"I haven't decided yet," Luke says.

"Haven't decided?" Bella says. "You can't wait until the last minute! Most of the preschools have probably filled up already."

"He doesn't need to go to school. I'm home all the time," Luke says.

"But school would be good for him," Bella says. "To build social skills more than anything."

"Yeah, he should have more friends his own age," I say.

"And kindergarten is going to come as a shock if he's never been in school before," Bella says.

"It's full day kindergarten in Oakfield—they don't offer half days anymore," I tell Luke. "It'll be a rough transition, going from being home with you to school all day every day..."

"Okay, okay." Luke attempts a smile. "If you two are going to gang up on me..."

"I can ask Aunt Soph if there's any room in Michela's class," I say. "It'll be easier for Nate if he already has a friend at school."

The hours pass by smoothly; we eat and talk and sing "Happy Birthday" to Nate. At one point, I end up inside the house, hanging out with Aunt Soph and Michela. "Mommy," Michela says. "I have to pee."

"Where's the bathroom?" Aunt Soph asks me.

"Bella just went in the downstairs one, but there's another bathroom upstairs," I say. "It's the first door on the left..."

The moment they're out of sight, Nora walks into the house alone. I give her a vague smile and pretend to be interested in the food on the counter. She knocks on the bathroom door, and Bella says she'll be out in a minute. Nora heads toward the stairs. "Michela is in the upstairs bathroom," I say. "Sorry—she should be quick—"

"No problem."

Nora and I stand next to each other, trying to make conversation. I can tell she feels as awkward as I do, but that doesn't make things easier. Finally, Bella comes into the kitchen, and Nora leaves for the bathroom. "You look tense, Gemma," Bella says. "Have a glass of wine."

"I can't," I say. "I might spill it on the white couch or something."

Bella laughs. "Aunt Nora isn't so bad," she says in an undertone. "She's just nervous. Throwing parties gives her anxiety."

"I think I give her anxiety."

"Maybe. She's always suspicious of new people. But she'll warm up to you; give it time." Bella hands me a glass. "For now, let's have some wine."

I enjoy talking to Bella; when the party is over, Luke and I make plans to visit her and Marisa. I say goodbye to everyone and give Luke a kiss. "I asked my mom to watch the kids tomorrow night," he says. "Want to go to that Italian restaurant you mentioned?"

"Sure!"

On the drive home, I turn to Aunt Soph. "What did you think of Luke?"

"He's a sweet guy," she says. "Very sweet. And he's head over heels for you! I don't know what happened with his ex and you should keep that in mind...but I can see why you like him."

"Is Nate coming to my birthday party?" Michela asks.

"Of course, my love," Aunt Soph says. "Two more weeks!"

"Speaking of Nate," I say. "Do you think there will be a spot for him in Michela's preschool this fall? It'll be his first time in school, and he'll feel more comfortable if he's with Michela."

"Nate has never been to school?" Aunt Soph says. "But he's so smart! He speaks like an adult."

"Luke talks to him like an adult," I say.

"I'll ask the head teacher. She's one of my patients; maybe she'll do me a favor..."

By the time I sit down to dinner with my dad, Aunt Soph has sent me the link to sign Nate up for Michela's preschool. Now it'll be up to Luke to decide if he wants to enroll Nate. I'll talk to him about it tomorrow.

Chapter Ten

It's Tuesday morning, and I'm on three hours of sleep. Nate and Scotty have the same summer cold and they were coughing all night. I didn't get up early to write; I barely woke up in time to get to my house and get ready for work. When I arrive at the office, I find Bree and the lawyers gathered on the couches. "Is everything okay?" I ask.

"Jasmine has some news," Erica says. "She wanted to tell all of us at the same time."

I grab a coffee, which I desperately need, and sit down next to Jasmine. She has the hint of a smile on her face, so I figure it must be good news. "I know I'm supposed to go to that conference with Lina in January," she says. "But I have to cancel my ticket. The doctor says I shouldn't be traveling at that time."

"Why? What's wrong?" Lina says.

"It's too close to my due date." Jasmine pulls an ultrasound photo out of her pocket. Erica and Lina scream.

"I knew it!" Erica says. "Yesterday when we were driving back from the courthouse and you were nauseous—"

"Congratulations! How many weeks?" Lina says.

"Eight." Jasmine is beaming. "I wanted to tell you guys as soon as I found out, but Mark wanted me to wait until the end of the first trimester. Finally we compromised and said as soon as I heard the heartbeat..."

"Isn't that the most beautiful sound?" Lina says.

"We're so happy for you!" Erica hugs Jasmine. "How's Mark? Is he excited? Is he freaking out?"

"I think he's in shock." Jasmine passes around the ultrasound photo. "We're both in shock...we didn't expect it to happen so fast. It was my first month off the pill!"

"You're lucky. Sometimes it takes forever to get pregnant with the first one," Erica says.

The ultrasound photo comes around to me, and I smile at it. The baby looks like a little bean; I remember these kinds of photos from when Aunt Soph was pregnant. "This is amazing, Jazz!" I say.

"I can't believe it's real," Jasmine says. "I feel blessed and thrilled...and also worried. Is it normal to be so worried?"

"Oh yeah. You'll be worried for the rest of your life," Lina says.

"It's a jumble of emotions," Jasmine says. "And Mark is no help. He wants to be a dad, but he's a pessimist...he says it's too early to get our hopes up."

"Roger was like that too," Lina says.

"Not Artie," Erica says. "He was giddy like a little kid."

"Really?" I say.

"He thought he was the king of the universe for knocking me up," Erica says. "Especially the first time. It took us almost a year to get pregnant with Zoe; we were charting my cycle and using ovulation kits and all that shit that drives you crazy. Finally we said fuck it, we're just going to have unprotected sex whenever we feel like it and see what happens. One month my period was late, and I took a test without telling Artie. I remember I came out of the bathroom, and he was getting ready for work in front of the mirror. I handed him the test and I said, 'Honey, here we go.'" She grins. "I'll never forget the look on his face."

"I'll never forget the look on Roger's face when I told him I was pregnant again two months after Cristina was born," Lina says. "Once Ethan was out, it was time to tie those tubes..."

"I didn't know you got your tubes tied," Jasmine says.

"I can't be on the pill and Roger wasn't getting anything snipped, so..."

"I heard that's a bigger surgery than people realize," Jasmine says. "Was the recovery tough?"

"Nah," Lina says. "I was sore for about a week."

"I'm terrified of having surgery," Jasmine says. "I've never even gotten stitches! What if I need a C-section?"

"It'll be fine," Erica says. "Doctors do them all the time and they're safe. I had a C-section with Chase—placenta previa, no way to avoid it. The recovery takes longer than a vaginal birth, but you bounce back. Our bodies know how to bounce back. And I had A.J. vaginally two years later."

"Erica went natural with all three of her vaginal births," Lina says.

"You mean no epidural?" Jasmine says. "You're a superhero!"

"You could do it too, if you wanted," Erica says. "It's all about knowing the right techniques. I'll teach you some strategies when you get closer to your due date. It's good to be prepared, no matter what your birth plan is; you should try to make it to five or six centimeters before you get an epidural."

"I asked for an epidural the second I got to the hospital," Lina says.

Erica and Lina go on talking about their births, and Jasmine asks them a million questions. They don't shy away from the intimate details, but I've heard similar stories from my aunts, so none of it comes as a shock to me. Bree, however, stays silent and looks appalled. She's the first person off the couch when Lina says it's time to go back to work.

"We have to do something later to celebrate!" Erica says. "I would suggest going to Finn's after work, but you can't drink. I could stop by the bakery and get cupcakes..."

"No, let's go to Finn's!" Jasmine says. "I love their fries."

Erica laughs. "Spoken like a true pregnant woman."

We end the work day early and head down the block to Finn's. At the bar, the conversation continues along the same lines as the coffee break this morning. After half an hour, Erica, Lina, and Jasmine leave, and Bree orders another drink. I finish my beer and I'm taking out my wallet to pay when Bree leans close to me. "Does it bother you?" she says.

"What?"

"When they talk about birth." She shudders. "All that stuff about pooping on the table, and getting stitches in your vagina...doesn't it freak you out?"

"Not really," I say. "My aunts are pretty graphic and one of them is an OB, so I've been hearing about birth for a long time. It doesn't sound pleasant, but I figure when the time comes I'll be ready."

"Not me," Bree says. "I would never put myself through that. For what? Being a mom sounds like torture. You hear Erica and Lina talking—all their problems revolve around their kids. They gave up their bodies for sleepless nights and a burden that never goes away. Kids make people stay in bad relationships, they cost time and money, they keep women from following their dreams. Why would I put someone else at the center of my life? That's an insane thing to do."

"You make a good point," I say. "I guess it depends on what you want out of life."

"What would you have done if you had been pregnant that time?"

"I would have kept the baby," I say. "The situation wasn't ideal, but I want to have kids someday, so it would have been an easy choice for me. Why—what would you have done?"

"Abortion, no question. I did it once and I'd do it again."

I'm surprised. "Yeah? What happened?"

"I was sixteen," she says. "I went to one of those stupid high school parties—Everclear and juice in somebody's basement. I wasn't on the pill yet; I'd lost my virginity the month before, to my jerkoff boyfriend who dumped me for another girl. I had a crush on this guy Jason...he was a baseball player, and he was always flirting with me in algebra class. Jason and I got smashed at the party and ended up in one of the bedrooms. It's kind of a blur...I don't remember much. I do remember taking the pregnancy test at my best friend's house, and I remember how she was there for me—she went with me to the clinic and everything."

"Wow."

"At the time, she was the only one who knew about it—her and my sister. I explained everything to my sister and I made her get on the pill, too. I never told Jason." Bree shakes her head. "Jason...he couldn't have handled being a father. He was so spoiled—I bet his mom still does his laundry. He was hot, though; the kid would have been cute."

I'm quiet, thinking this through. How can Bree speak casually about something so traumatizing? The whole situation, not just the abortion, would have been hard for me to get over. "I'm sorry," I say.

"Don't be sorry. Imagine what my life would be like if I had kept it! Forget being a lawyer—I'd probably be working at Walmart right now. And I'd have to spend my free time packing lunches and cleaning up toys...hell no. I'm never having kids."

"Jason was an asshole for sleeping with you when you were drunk."

"Most men are assholes. Even if you find a decent guy, it's always the girl who sacrifices more in relationships. Always the girl who suffers more."

Bree takes another sip of her cocktail. She looks graceful as always, with her stylish clothes and her straight posture and the look of indifference on her face. She must be hurt by what she's been through, even if she doesn't show it. Then again, I can't see things from her perspective. She shares more with me than with the other girls at the office, yet I don't understand her. "Can I ask you something?" I say.

"Sure."

"Why don't you go by your full name? I think it's pretty."

"Brielle?" She makes a sound of disgust in her throat. "My father came up with that name. He got it from a town at the shore, near Point Pleasant..."

"I know it."

"My parents aren't from Brielle—they're not that classy—but that's where they got married, when my mom was five months pregnant with me. Back then, she was working part-time at a hair salon; she didn't go to college, barely made it through high school. My father was running his dad's construction company and doing some shady stuff on the side. They weren't in love—they met at a club in Seaside and fucked a few times—but when my mom got pregnant, their families pushed them to get married. It was a stupid decision, and I hate being named after a mistake."

"Your parents have a bad relationship?" I ask.

"They're not together anymore. My father was in our lives for eight years, long enough to give me a sister and to put my mom through hell. He was cheating on her and she knew it, but she wouldn't leave him; she was afraid to raise two kids by herself, especially because he was the one bringing in the money. Then he went to work one day and didn't come back. We never heard from him again. Never got a dime of child support."

"That's horrible."

"My mom says it's the best thing that ever happened to her," Bree says. "When my father left, she had to rely on herself, and she realized she didn't need anybody. She got her associate's degree and started making a steady salary as a radiology tech. She pushed me and my sister to do well in school and sent both of us to college. She used to say, 'Girls, you get a good education and a good job and you'll never depend on anyone for anything.' I listened; my sister, not so much. She quit college after a year and became a bartender. She makes good money, though...she's got big fake boobs...doing well for herself." Bree laughs. "I have to call her—I miss her. My mom too."

Bree and I talk for a little while longer. Now that I've heard about her father, her attitude toward men makes more sense. It's sad that she grew up without any examples of a healthy relationship. Still, I admire her determination to become a lawyer, and I like hanging out with her; she makes me look at the world differently.

After the bar, I drive to Luke's place. It takes him a while to answer the door; when he does, he looks stressed. "Hey baby," he says. "I'm in the middle of something for work—I have to deliver it today and they sent it at the last minute—"

"No worries." I glance around the room. "Where's Scotty?"

"Shit, he's still sleeping. Could you get him?"

I love waking Scotty up from his naps; he's always extra snuggly when he's drowsy. The two of us curl up on the couch and start reading a book. I try to get Nate interested in the book too, but he's hovering around Luke, telling him a story.

"Then Indigo lost his magic," Nate says. "He couldn't breathe fire anymore. And he couldn't fly! And Orangey tried to help him—"

"Not now, buddy," Luke says, without looking up from his laptop. "I'm working."

"But Orangey didn't know how to help. So they went to ask a wizard, but it was a bad wizard! He trapped all the dragons in his castle—"

"I'll listen to you when I'm done," Luke says.

"Come tell me the story, Nate," I say.

Nate ignores me. "But the dragons didn't know how to get out! Then Orangey found the door to a secret room—"

"Nate, what the fuck?" Luke snaps. "I told you—I'm working!"

Nate's face falls. "That's not a nice word, Daddy."

I get up from the couch and take Nate's hand. "Let's go into the kitchen and let Daddy concentrate," I say. "You can talk to me about the dragons."

I sit on the kitchen floor, stacking Tupperwares with Scotty and listening to the chronicles of Orangey and Indigo. Luke and I planned to make balsamic chicken tonight, but I can see that's not going to happen, so I boil water for pasta instead. When Luke comes into the kitchen half an hour later, a pot of penne with pesto is ready on the stove, Nate is playing with a sticker book, and Scotty and I are drumming on the Tupperwares using various utensils. "You're amazing," Luke says to me.

"It's no big deal."

"I have to give you something...hang on..." Luke leaves the room, then comes back and hands me a key. "I got this made for you."

"The key to the apartment?" I'm in awe. "Really?"

"What?" His face starts turning red. "I figured...you're always here..."

"But this is a big step in a relationship, right? It means you trust me."

"Of course I trust you. You think I'd have you around my kids all the time if I didn't?"

"That's true." I kiss him. I can't help myself; holding his key makes me giddy. "Still, it feels special."

"It's too easy to make you happy," he says.

"Let me see," Nate says. He takes the key from my hand and sticks a green smiley face on it. "There. Because you like green."

"Thank you, Nate! This makes it extra special," I say.

"Let's eat," Luke says. "It's getting late..."

Dinner is a painful experience. The kids are tired, and they spend more time whining than eating. When Nate knocks over his cup of water for the second time, Luke gets exasperated. "Dinner is over," he says. He cleans Nate's hands and mouth and points him toward his bedroom. "Put on your pajamas. Scotty, let me see your hands..."

A moment later, Nate is back. "There are no pajamas, Daddy."

"They must all be in the wash," Luke says. "I only did one load of laundry today. You can sleep in your sweatpants—they're comfy."

"I want my race car pajamas," Nate says.

"They're dirty," Luke says. "You can wear them tomorrow."

"That's not fair!"

A fit of coughing interrupts Luke and Nate's conversation. Scotty is hacking and can't seem to stop. "Take it easy, buddy," Luke says, reaching out to unclip the straps on Scotty's chest. Scotty coughs harder, gags, and pukes all over himself and Luke's arm. Then he starts to cry. "Everybody shut up for a second," Luke says, closing his eyes. "One second, please..."

Nate stomps his foot. "I can't go to sleep without my race car pajamas!"

"Enough, Nate!" I say. Normally I don't get involved in disciplining the kids, but Luke seems overwhelmed and I want to help. "We don't have any pajamas. Go to the bathroom and pee before bed."

Nate looks startled by my tone of voice. Then he crosses his arms over his chest. "I don't have to listen to you."

"Yes you do," Luke says. "Do what Gemma said and go pee."

Nate complains the whole way to the bathroom. I turn to Luke, wanting to thank him for giving me authority, but he's pulling off Scotty's vomit-soaked shirt and rubbing the baby's back. "It's okay, Scotty," he says. "I know, that was scary...you're okay..."

It takes us a while to get the kids to bed; we have to empty and refill the humidifiers in both rooms and calm Scotty down. Once the boys are asleep, Luke and I get to work on the mess. We clean up dinner and vomit and throw the clean clothes in the dryer. We work silently; we're too exhausted to talk. When everything is finished, we both collapse on the mattress.

"Too much noise," Luke says. "The kids create so much noise in my head...I can't think..."

"It's quiet now," I say. "You can rest."

Luke lays his head on my stomach; his body is still and heavy. I'm almost asleep when he speaks again. "How are you, baby? How was your day?"

"It was good. Jasmine told us she's pregnant."

We hear a burst of coughing from Scotty's room, then another from Nate's. Luke and I wait a few minutes, but neither sound lets up. "Good for her," Luke says. "She'll never sleep again."

"Which kid should I take?" I ask.

"Stay here and relax."

"I'll get Scotty."

We get out of bed and head to opposite sides of the apartment.

Chapter Eleven

Nate and Scotty are feeling better by the day of Michela's birthday party. We're hosting the party in my backyard; Luke comes over early with the kids to help me, my dad, and Aunt Soph set up. We've had many parties in our yard over the years. Though our house is small, the backyard is larger than the others on our block, and it wraps around one side of the house. According to my dad, my mom fell in love with this yard when they were shopping for houses; she imagined summer barbecues and toddlers on swings and packs of kids throwing snowballs at each other. All those visions came true, though they happened when she was already gone. I have a bittersweet fondness for my yard; I have great memories here, but I'm sad my mom wasn't part of them.

Aunt Soph keeps thanking my dad for letting her use the yard. "This is such a big help," she says for the third time today. "I really appreciate it. We have no space in the apartment and when I looked at places to rent..."

"It's nothing, Soph," my dad says. "Happy to do it. When is the bounce house getting here?"

"I think a truck just pulled up," I say.

The guests—including my family members and Michela's friends—start arriving, and Scotty has his usual meltdown. Luke walks with him around the edge of the yard. I'm watching Nate play with the other kids when Aunt Soph comes up to me. "Look at this," she says, showing me the purple stain on her shirt. "Look at this shit Michela spilled on me. I told her to be careful with the juice box..."

"It won't come out?" I say.

"Scrubbing made it worse." Aunt Soph glances at a group of Michela's friends' moms, who are chatting on the other side of the lawn. "It's bad enough that I look like an old lady compared to these other moms—"

"No you don't."

"And now I have to walk around with grape juice on my shirt. Why doesn't this happen to other people? Look at Evelyn." Aunt Soph nods toward a pretty woman holding a baby. "I hate her. I hate anyone who makes motherhood look easy. She has three kids and she's dressed like a fucking supermodel every time I see her. How does she do it?"

Evelyn moves into the center of the group, catching the sunlight in her blonde hair. Her clothes are fashionable and neat and they flatter her figure; a designer purse is slung over her shoulder. She's wearing lots of jewelry, unlike most moms with small children, and she somehow manages to keep her long, loose hair away from her baby's grubby fingers. I can see Aunt Soph's point—Evelyn is the kind of woman I couldn't imagine sweating, let alone spreading her legs and pushing a bloody, squirming human into the world. Yet she did it—three times! And if she loves her kids, that's something she has in common with Aunt Soph. "I'm sure she has her moments," I say. "You just haven't seen them yet."

"No, she's perfect. We went to her daughter's party last week—it was straight out of Pinterest. Everything coordinated, down to the plastic utensils. The cake could have won a decorating contest—it was fancier than a wedding cake! And there wasn't a single thing out of place at her house. Where does she put all the toys?"

"She was having a party," I say. "So she probably spent extra time straightening up."

"Her house always looks like that; I've been there for play dates before. Meanwhile my apartment is a disaster and I only have one kid. I must be doing something wrong."

"Maybe that's what Evelyn likes," I say. "Some women enjoy looking beautiful and having a beautiful house. You enjoy other things, like taking care of your patients..."

"Being a doctor is no excuse."

I shrug. I don't know what else to say to Aunt Soph; sometimes she's determined to be negative. I think she would be happier if she had close friends who were moms, like the women at the office do. Instead she only confides in me or her sisters; my aunts give her great advice, but they're in a different stage of life since their kids are adults. Aunt Soph should be friends with the moms of Michela's friends. "Go upstairs and put on one of my shirts," I say.

Her face brightens a little. "That black one with the scoop neck?"

"Sure. But you have to promise you'll strike up a conversation with Evelyn today. I bet if you get to know her, you'll see she's going through the same shit you are."

"Deal."

Luke walks up to us; Scotty is still whining in his arms. "Need a break?" I ask.

"Just for a minute. I wanted to get something to eat."

"Take your time—I'm not hungry yet." I hold out my arms for Scotty. "Come here, cutie."

"Hemma," Scotty says. "Hemma take you."

"Yup, I'll take you."

Scotty has been talking more now, and it's adorable to hear him communicate in his little voice. We stroll around the yard, chatting about what we see. "Look at that dog playing next door," I say.

"Ball!" Scotty says.

"Right! He's chasing the ball."

Eventually, we ease our way closer to the party. Most of the kids, including Nate, are jumping around in the bounce house. Luke is standing near the bounce house next to Michela and Aunt Soph; Michela is on the verge of tears. "You told me to rent the unicorn bounce house and I did," Aunt Soph is saying to her. "Now go in and play with the other kids."

"I don't want to," Michela says.

"But it's fun!" Aunt Soph says. "Everybody else is having fun, and you're missing out." Michela starts to cry. "Why are you crying? Kids are supposed to like this stuff!"

"I don't want to go," Michela wails.

Luke crouches down next to Michela. "Are you scared?" he asks. She nods. "I get it—the bounce house is big and loud, and maybe you've never been in one before! But I promise it's safe."

"What if I get stuck?" Michela asks.

"You won't—this flap never closes. And if you did get stuck, I would come and get you. Or Mommy would, or Aunt Gemma. You can come right back out if you don't like it."

Luke and Michela talk for a few more minutes, and Michela gets into the bounce house. Luke straightens up and turns to me. "I'll take Scotty now," he says. "I had lunch."

"Don't walk away with him—he seems to be warming up," I say. "Maybe he'll interact with people for once."

"I can sit with him on the deck," Luke says. "There's another baby over there. I'll see if I can get some food in him..."

Luke heads to the deck with Scotty. "Luke is quite a guy," Aunt Soph says to me. "He's better with my kid than I am."

Her voice is bitter, and I know there's something on her mind other than this party. A grape juice stain and some tears from Michela shouldn't put her in such a bad mood. "What's the matter, Aunt Soph? I ask. "What's bothering you?"

"I'm sorry," she says. "It's nothing against Luke—I'm glad he got her in the bounce house—"

"I know."

"It's just that I ran into Donovan at the hospital yesterday and I've been feeling like a piece of trash since then."

106

I didn't expect this; Aunt Soph hasn't mentioned Michela's father in years. "Why? What happened?"

She sighs. "I tried to avoid him, but he walked up to me. He looked me up and down—with those eyes that are so cruel, so mocking—and said, 'Hey Sophia. How's your daughter?' He knows. He knows Michela is his and he can use that to torment me whenever he wants. What's wrong with me, Gemma? Why did I sleep with someone like that? For a moment of pleasure I gave him power over me—power to take away my dignity even at work, the only place I feel competent. I know I'm a shitty mother but I thought at least I was a good doctor..."

"You're not a shitty mother," I say.

"I am, and now I'm ashamed of myself at work too. The worst part is, I'm going to have to tell Michela the truth someday. She's going to realize she had a father and she'll want to know about him, and what am I supposed to say? That I knew he was evil and I fucked him anyway? I want her to respect herself around guys, but that's the opposite of what I did."

"Tell her it was a mistake," I say. "And she'll learn not to do the same thing."

"She won't trust my judgment once she hears that story. She won't admire me the way she does now; she'll think I'm an idiot, which I am."

"Don't talk about yourself like that." I say. I think back to what Luke said about his relationship with Sylvie—how the kids were the only good thing that came out of their marriage. "Maybe you should frame the situation differently. It was a bad idea to sleep with Donovan, but if you hadn't done it, Michela wouldn't exist. That shows that wonderful things can come from our mistakes. Teach Michela to focus on the good in life instead of the bad."

"I guess."

"And Michela is always going to admire you. You're her hero! She'll love you no matter what."

"Mommy!" Michela runs up to us and throws her arms around Aunt Soph. "Did you see? I went in the bounce house!"

"That's great, my love!" Aunt Soph blinks tears from her eyes and kisses Michela. "I'm proud of you. You're so brave!"

After a while, the kids gather on the deck to eat, and I grab a plate of food and sit with Luke and some of the adults. Scotty is playing with balloons with my dad, and he's so fascinated by the game that he's not crying for me or Luke. It's nice to eat without a toddler at the table—I can relax and listen to the conversation around me. The mom of one of Michela's friends is telling everyone about the trip she took to Italy this past month.

"The Amalfi Coast was beautiful," she's saying. "Though I was surprised that most of the beaches were rocky, not like the white sand beaches you see in Florida or the Caribbean. One morning we saw packs of teenagers jumping off cliffs into the water, and my husband wanted to follow them. 'Let's try it,' he said to me. 'Leave the kids with your parents for a minute.' I was like, 'Are you crazy? Jump off a cliff? We have two kids to live for!' But these teenagers were jumping over and over like it was nothing."

"It's not that dangerous if you go to the right places," I say. "I went cliff jumping when I was in Italy."

"On the Amalfi Coast?" the mom asks.

"No, I was in Puglia, way down south," I say. "If you look at a map of Italy, it's the heel of the boot. I studied in Rome and my roommate was from Puglia; I visited her at her house once. She and her sisters were cliff jumping at the beach, so I tried it."

"Were you scared?" Luke asks.

"A little. But I knew my friend and her sisters did it all the time, and I watched them for a while before I jumped, to figure out the right way to do it."

"You probably like that stuff," the mom says. "Roller coasters and all those thrills..."

"It's not exactly like a roller coaster," I say. "There's a similar drop in your stomach, but on a roller coaster you can feel that you're on a ride. Jumping is like being weightless, suspended in time for a moment—and then there's the rush of relief when you hit the water."

"Hey, Gio," Aunt Dee says to my dad. He's approaching the deck with Scotty, who seems upset. "Did you know your daughter was jumping off cliffs when she was in Italy?"

"I found out after the fact," my dad says. "Luke, he's looking for you."

Luke takes Scotty and starts playing with him in the grass. "Do you speak Italian?" Evelyn asks me.

"I do."

"Are you going to teach your sons Italian?"

"My...? Oh." I feel hot all over. "No, they're not my sons—they're Luke's. He's my boyfriend."

"You should teach them, though," Evelyn says. "They say kids are sponges at this age. My nanny speaks French, and you wouldn't believe what my kids have learned..."

Evelyn goes on bragging about her nanny, and I take the first opportunity to excuse myself from the conversation. I walk over to Luke. I wonder if he heard Evelyn calling me Nate and Scotty's mom. People must make that assumption when they see us together, but this is the first time anyone has said it. It makes me feel wistful and also guilty, like I've crossed a line. "Everything okay?" Luke asks.

"Yeah."

"I had a nice conversation with your aunt Ro earlier."

I clench my teeth. "What did she say?"

"No, it was good. She asked why Scotty wasn't playing with the other kids, so I told her about his stranger anxiety. She said your cousin Louie was like that for three years, and I asked her how she handled it. She gave me a ton of advice."

This is a good sign; Aunt Ro wouldn't bestow her wisdom on someone she disliked. "Sounds like you're in," I say.

"She seems like a warm person—all your aunts do. They're easy to talk to."

I feel a pang of envy. I wish I got along with Nora the way Luke gets along with my aunts. Still, I want him to fit in with my family; I push the thought away and smile. "I knew they would like you."

Luke smiles back and puts his hand on my cheek. His gaze is soft and adoring and it steals the breath out of my chest. "Why are you looking at me like that?" I ask.

"You're beautiful. How am I supposed to look at you?"

I kiss his hand. I want to shower him with kisses but I know other people are watching. "I'm crazy about you too, Luke."

The rest of the party goes well. Luke and the kids leave along with the other guests, and I tell him I'll be over after dinner. My dad and I end up eating late and chatting for a while, so it's close to ten when I head to Luke's apartment.

When I open the door, I find Luke sitting on the floor, playing his electric guitar and singing to himself. Both his guitar and his headphones are plugged into an amp, so I can't hear the music; I watch him for a moment before he notices me. "Hey, baby." He grins and pulls off the headphones. "I didn't hear you come in..."

"Are you working?" I say. "I don't want to interrupt."

"No, I always want to see you."

I sit down next to him. A notebook is open on the floor, and I recognize his handwriting. "What's this?" I say. "Can I see?"

"Sure. I write lyrics in there, drafts of lyrics...or just ideas. If I hear something I like, words or phrases that sound good together, I write them down. Sometimes I find titles or a lyric that way, or I just use the words as a starting point to get me thinking."

I look at the book. Luke's handwriting fits him well; he leaves very little space between words, as if they all came out of him in one breath. The dots on his *i*'s are slashes that morph into subsequent letters. He must write quickly, but he presses hard; I can feel the indent of his words on the other side of the page. Through the scribbles I make out some phrases about fear and risks. "Is this a new song?" I ask.

"Not exactly new...I started it a long time ago, before Scotty was born, and never finished it. I had the verses mostly done, and I had a chorus that was catchy but didn't fit the feeling; I ended up using that chorus in a different song and putting this one aside. Then what you said today about jumping off the cliff made me want to go back to it. I could hear the stillness you described, and the relief...here, listen." He

110

puts his headphones on me and plays the guitar again. The music builds, then pauses—a pause that holds me in a tense grip—and ends in a satisfying crash. "That," Luke says. "That's what you meant, right?"

I'm stunned. "I made you think of that?"

"Yeah. The way you describe your experiences is evocative; I can feel what you felt even if I haven't gone through it myself. Give me more words." He pulls the notebook toward him. "Where was the place you jumped?"

I tell him the name of the beach and talk about jumping in more detail. Luke jots everything down. It pains me to look at his hands; there are raw patches around his nails where he gnawed the skin away. He finishes writing and meets my eyes. "What's the matter?"

"Your fingers," I say. "You have to stop biting them."

"I've been good lately—I haven't done it in over a month. It was just this morning, thinking about the party and meeting everyone..."

"We need to find some other outlet for you when you're nervous. You're ruining your hands. And they must hurt!"

"It's not a big deal. I've had worse habits."

This thought fills me with dread. "Like what?"

"Well..." Luke's shoulders tense. "I used to wash my hands so much that they would bleed."

"Really?"

"I was seven—scared of germs. Anytime I might have touched something dirty I washed them; this happened multiple times an hour. I would turn the water on scalding hot and scrub and scrub with soap until my hands were bright red. My skin was so dry that there were bloody cracks all over my hands and wrists. My mom tried everything to get me to stop—bribery and punishments and hiding the soap—but nothing worked. I couldn't stop. The only thing that made me change was playing guitar."

His last sentence leaves me bewildered. "What? Guitar?"

"My father bought me my first guitar at that time," he says. "He wasn't around enough to teach me but he showed me some basic chords, and when my mom saw I liked it, she got me lessons. When I was playing, I could go for hours without washing my hands—without even thinking about washing them. Music interrupted the thoughts I was stuck on; I started hearing a loop of melodies instead of a loop of worries. It was like my brain had something to do other than repeat all the bad things that could happen to me. The more I played the better I felt...and that broke the habit."

"Wow."

"Making music is my natural state; it's when my mind is at its best. I can't be scared when I'm writing or playing because I'm focused; I'm caught up in the flow of music."

"I know the feeling," I say. "When I'm immersed in writing, I don't think of anything else. So you never went back to washing your hands?"

"I did, twice. The first time, I was a senior in high school and applying to colleges; once I got into Berklee I was able to stop. And when Nate was born, I started again. That time was the worst—even worse than when I was a kid."

"Why?"

"Because I wasn't worried about me getting sick anymore—I was worried about Nate."

I feel the gravity in his words. I know Luke loves his kids, but I didn't give much thought to the other side of that love—didn't realize that when you love someone more than yourself, you have more to fear. "How did you stop?" I ask.

"I went to therapy. It was once a week for a year; it was expensive, but I needed it. I'm not exaggerating when I say it changed my life. Adam worked with me on cognitive behavioral stuff...changing my thought patterns, changing how I respond to being nervous. He showed me that my rituals—washing my hands or asking other people for reassurance—weren't protecting anyone. They were digging me into a deeper hole, and harming Nate's quality of life too. When I stopped giving in to those behaviors the world didn't end and that was empowering. I learned to stop toxic thoughts in their tracks and redirect myself, and to write down my fears so I could see which ones were irrational. I'm not perfect." He glances at his fingers. "But I have tools to deal with my anxiety now; I don't let it get out of control."

I nod. My mind is racing to process this information. I have no experience of mental health issues other than my dad's drinking, and I want to understand what Luke has been through so I can help him. "Do you take medicine?" I ask.

"No. I never did. Adam left the choice up to me; he said medicine would make the work we were doing easier, but I could still get better without it. I'm not against medicine—if it had been more widespread back in the day, my grandma definitely could have used it. We all learned to dance around her anxiety...line up our shoes the right way...never say anything that would make her worry. And Bella has been taking an SSRI since high school and it's really helped her. But medicine is not for me. I don't want to get rid of my nervous energy because not all of it is bad. Some of it..." He searches for the right words. "Some of it is fuel."

"Fuel?"

"That's how I make music, by hearing melodies over and over, by working on a song until I get it right, no matter how many iterations it takes. That's the strength of my process, the repetition. Obsessive thoughts hurt when they're worries but they're useful when they're ideas; they help me create. I'm okay without medicine—I've learned to work with my brain the way it is, the good parts along with the madness. Do you think I'm okay?" He looks apprehensive. "Or is this freaking you out? I'm not crazy."

"I know." I rub his arm. "You're not going to scare me away—you can tell me anything."

"Yeah?"

"Yeah, because..." I hesitate. I know what I want to say and I know I mean it, but now that I'm on the brink of that sentence, I'm terrified. I've only ever used it with Nico, and he said it first so it didn't feel risky. Maybe it's too soon...maybe Luke isn't ready and if I rush things I'll ruin the dynamic between us. "Never mind."

"What?"

"Forget it."

"Please tell me."

His voice is serious, quiet; he's hanging on my next words. It would be dishonest not to say it, when he shares everything with me, when he lays his soul bare all the time. And I want him to know how he makes me feel—I want him to know I'll do anything for him and that there's no greater joy in the world than looking into his eyes. "Because," I say. "Because I love you, so…"

Then he's kissing me, kissing me like he wants to devour me, tilting my head backwards, grazing my lips with his teeth. "I love you too," he says. My heart is bursting; it's overflowing. "I love you, I love you…Gemma, I've been waiting for something to ruin this feeling, I've been waiting to see the darkness in you but there is no darkness, you keep getting more wonderful. And we fit together—this is how love is supposed to feel, like a partnership, like we can count on each other. But are you happy?" He grasps both my hands. "You've taken on a lot, with me and the kids and what we deal with every day…do I really make you happy?"

How could I not be happy, knowing that he loves me, feeling his warm hands wrapped around mine? "Of course I'm happy," I say. "Look, our life is stressful and I wish we had more time alone, but I love the kids too, and I have fun when we're all together. Plus I've always wanted to be part of something bigger than myself…and now I am."

"You're an angel." He leans his forehead against mine. "I'm so lucky you chose me. I love you so much."

As the days go on, Luke tells me he loves me constantly. It gives me a thrill every time, but I can see how other people might find it excessive; Nate is always annoyed by it. On Wednesday, I go to Luke's place after work and find him giving Scotty a snack in his high chair while Nate watches TV. "Hi, Nate!" I say. "Hi, Scotty! What are you eating?" As I get closer to the high chair, Luke grabs me and lands a storm of kisses on my stomach. "I love you," he says.

"I love you too."

"Why do you keep saying that to her?" Nate grumbles.

"Because it's true," Luke says. "I love Gemma. And I love you and Scotty."

"Who do you love the most?" Nate asks.

"Love isn't a contest."

"I think I should be your favorite because I was here first," Nate says.

"You're all my favorite," Luke says. "Spiky, on the other hand, has one favorite to battle with..."

"Not Spiky!"

Luke jumps up from his chair and tackles Nate to the floor. They wrestle for a while, yelling about the dragons. "We'll always be best buddies, all right?" Luke tells him. Nate responds by kicking Luke square in the nose. "Ow! Don't be an asshole!"

"That's not a nice word, Daddy," Nate says between giggles.

Chapter Twelve

Jasmine is close to the end of her first trimester, and she's miserable. She's thrown up several times at the office, and she's always tired. Though she's getting her work done, she's usually in a bad mood; this morning is no exception. She walks out of her office, grimacing and rubbing her temples, and heads to my desk. "Are my documents ready?" she asks me.

"Almost," I say, showing her the stack of papers on my desk. "I'm waiting for one more page...this printer has been giving me trouble."

An error message flashes on the printer for the third time this morning. Jasmine bangs her hand on the machine. "What the fuck?"

"I'll send it to the other printer," I say. "It should come out as soon as Bree is done."

"Why is it always my documents that get stuck?" Jasmine says. "I can't take this anymore...I have such a headache..."

"I'm sorry, Jazz," Lina says. She's refilling her water bottle at the cooler. "Pregnancy sucks sometimes."

"It sucks all the time. And I got into a fight with Mark this morning..." Jasmine hits the printer again, to no avail. "Can we have a coffee break?"

We all gather on the couches. We haven't been making coffee because the smell makes Jasmine nauseous, but we still get together to talk. Jasmine sinks into the pillows at one end of the couch. "I just want to feel better," she says. "When am I going to feel better?"

"Soon," Erica says.

"And Mark has been such an asshole! He's mad at me because we haven't had sex for a month. I told him I feel like shit and he keeps pushing for it anyway. He's like, 'But you're so beautiful like this, you're so sexy, I want you more than ever and I'm suffering.' I'm the one who's suffering! I'm sorry I'm too busy making his child to service him."

"Yikes," Lina says.

"I get that my boobs are big and that's a turnon, but they also hurt like hell and I don't want him touching them! I just want to sleep. It's depressing." Jasmine sighs. "I thought Mark and I had a great relationship, but now that we're not having sex, we keep fighting. Maybe our love is based on physical attraction after all. Maybe there was never anything more to it than sex."

"That's not true," Erica says. "You and Mark adore each other."

"It doesn't feel that way lately," Jasmine says. "It has me thinking—how important is sex in a relationship? Can you have a happy relationship if you don't have sex?"

"You mean never?" Lina says. "I don't think never is good. But the frequency can change depending on what you're going through..."

"Artie and I rarely had sex when Zoe was a baby," Erica says. "We were too stressed. Once we got used to the chaos, we went back to doing it a few times a week. Our sex life is better now than it's ever been—better than when we were younger. Who would have thought, four kids later..."

"Maybe Artie can give Roger some tips," Lina says, and they both laugh.

"That proves my point," Jasmine says. "A happy marriage is about finding someone you want to fuck for the long term."

"No, no, honey, no," Erica says. "There's much more to it than that.

You need respect—"

"Good communication," Lina adds.

"Mutual goals and interests—"

"The willingness to adapt—"

"But all of that won't carry you through if you don't have chemistry, too," Erica says.

"How do you define chemistry?" I ask.

"You know chemistry," Bree says. "You must have it with Luke."

"I want to hear their take on it," I say.

"Chemistry is a powerful attraction that doesn't fade," Erica says. "It keeps getting reinforced because the two of you are on the same wavelength—you're playing the same song. You meet each other's needs instinctively…"

"Sounds like sex to me," Jasmine says.

"It's related to sex, but you can have sex without chemistry, and chemistry without sex," Erica says. "If you sleep with someone and there's no chemistry, you can feel the difference. I think you can tell early in a relationship—before sex—if the chemistry is there. And if it's not, there's no way to force it. I remember back in law school, Lina was dating this guy…what was his name, Greg?"

"Craig," Lina says.

"Oh yeah, Craig. And he was good-looking and nice, but Lina wasn't feeling it, and she kept trying to convince herself that she was. She said, 'He's smart, he has a great job, blah blah blah.' I said, 'But honey, you don't like him. You should be with someone you like, and he deserves someone who likes him too.' So they broke up. And I kid you not, the next day we were at a bar and Roger walked over and started hitting on Lina…"

"He was so hot back then," Lina says.

"From the first date, they were crazy about each other," Erica says. "Remember, Lina? You were like, 'I can't help it, every time we're alone in a room I want to jump on him…'"

"And now he's fat and going bald," Lina says.

"But you still want to jump on him," Erica says.

"Well...yeah." Lina grins. "He gives me this smile sometimes..."

"Like I said—chemistry," Erica says.

"Roger is also my best friend," Lina says. "There's trust in chemistry too, not just passion. You have to enjoy making the other person happy; it's emotional as well as sexual."

"So you think two virgins can have chemistry?" Jasmine asks.

"Absolutely," Erica says.

"I agree with that," I say. "I had great chemistry with my high school boyfriend, and we never did anything more serious than making out."

"And when you get old and sex isn't part of the equation anymore, you can still have chemistry," Erica says. "It just takes the form of cuddling or holding hands."

Jasmine looks tearful. "I don't know if Mark and I are going to make it that far."

"You are," Erica says. "This is just a tough period."

"Mark is wrong for putting pressure on you," Lina says. "But to make him see that, you should talk to him when you're calm. Men tune us out when we yell. Pick a moment when neither one of you is stressed and explain what you're going through."

"Tell him you understand how he feels," Erica says. "Say that you want him all the time too..."

"Yeah, that's good," Lina says.

"But your body is telling you to rest, so you need to rest for you and the baby," Erica says. "He has to make sacrifices for this baby too. And tell him it won't last forever. You'll be feeling better in a couple of weeks, and second trimester sex is awesome—"

The phone rings, and we stay quiet as Bree picks it up. "Callahan and Ramos," she says. Then she looks at Lina. "It's Alice Jeffries, for you."

"I'll take it in my office," Lina says.

We get up from the couches and start heading back to our desks. Erica hugs Jasmine. "You and Mark will get through this," she says. "When you overcome these kinds of problems, it makes your relationship stronger."

"We'll see," Jasmine says. "Thank you for listening."

"Always!"

After work, I head to Luke's place. When I open the door, I'm greeted by the familiar stench of poop. Luke must be changing Scotty in his room, because Nate is alone in the living room, looking glum. "What's up, Nate?" I say.

"We were playing Candy Land, but then Scotty pooped."

"I'll play with you."

Nate and I set up the game again. "You be green," he says. "There's no orange, so I'll be red."

"Awesome," I say. "Candy Land was my favorite game when I was a kid. I used to pretend I was Princess Lolly and my dad was King Kandy, and we would have adventures while we were playing."

"What kinds of adventures?" Nate asks. "Were there dragons?"

"We can pretend there are dragons!"

Nate and I invent a narrative as we're playing. Nate's fantasy games can be exhausting, but sometimes I enjoy them. He's incredibly creative; he plays multiple characters at the same time and surprises me with his plot twists. When I see how much joy it gives Nate to pretend, it reminds me that stories matter—that my own writing, however impractical it may seem, isn't a waste of time. He encourages my imagination while I encourage his.

Luke and Scotty join us after a while, and Luke and I make dinner. Luke seems on edge, but the kids keep hovering around us and it's hard to carry on a conversation. "Is something bothering you?" I ask him before we sit down.

"We'll talk about it when the kids go to sleep."

After dinner, we get the boys ready for bed. We've developed a new routine for this—I put Scotty to bed and Luke takes Nate. This gets the kids to sleep in half the time, and I like taking care of Scotty; it's soothing for me to lie on his floor and tell him a story while he drifts off with his blankie. As Luke and Nate head to Nate's room, I call out after them. "Good night, Nate." I think for a moment, then say the next thought on my mind. "I love you."

I've never said this to the kids before. Nate doesn't say it back, but he runs to me and hugs my leg before going to his room. It's a small gesture, but it means the world to me. I can't stop smiling as I put Scotty down in his crib. "I love you, Scotty," I say.

"Dory," Scotty says. "Hemma dory."

"Of course I'll tell you a story."

Once Scotty is asleep, I find Luke in the kitchen, pouring himself another glass of wine from the bottle we opened at dinner. I get a glass for myself and slip my arm around his waist. "What's up?" I ask.

He kisses me on the forehead. "I was texting with Sylvie earlier. She's taking the kids on August first."

"Wow." I had forgotten about this. "That's a week and a half away!"

"I know. She's landing a few days early, on the thirtieth, and staying with friends in New York. She wants to spend time with the kids here before she brings them to L.A—get them used to her again."

"Makes sense."

"We're going to meet at the park after work next Thursday. Do you want to come?"

I'm startled by the question. Over the past few weeks, I've felt like Sylvie never existed; Luke has been all mine. Now she's creeping back into the picture and I don't know what to expect. What am I supposed to say to her? And how is Luke going to act? It sounds painfully awkward. "You want me there?" I ask.

"Yeah, I think you two should meet. And it would help to have you with me, to keep me calm...I'm having bad anxiety about her taking the kids away. I've been trying not to think about it but now it's here and I'm panicking. I feel better when you're around."

I turn this over in my head. I guess it's good that Luke wants me to meet Sylvie; it would be a red flag if he wanted to be alone with her. I think back to what Jasmine said at the coffee break months ago—that by dating Luke, I was choosing to deal with his ex-wife. I signed up for this and I can't back down. "I'll be there," I say. "Whatever you need."

"Thank you. She'll be cool—she's with somebody new too, so..."

"She knows about me?"

"I told her a while back."

I down the rest of my wine. Luke has put his glass on the counter and is chewing on his fingers; I pull his hand away from his mouth. "It'll be weird," I say. "But we'll handle it."

"You're rock solid, baby."

"I know I am."

I put on a brave face when I'm with Luke, but the truth is I'm nervous about meeting Sylvie. The next day, I share my feelings with the girls at the office and they try to give me advice, but none of them have been through this before. Nobody in my life has dated a divorced guy, let alone a divorced dad; I can't rely on other people's experiences as a guide this time. I have to face the situation myself.

Chapter Thirteen

I wake up on Thursday morning with a headache. Today is the day we're meeting Sylvie at the park; I may have overindulged on the wine last night to ease my worries. I drink a lot of water and go for a run and try to keep my mind occupied, but I'm still out of sorts when I head to Oakfield Park after work.

I don't see Luke's car when I arrive, so I wait in my car, twisting my bracelet around and around my wrist. I've been wearing this bracelet every day since Luke gave it to me last month. We normally don't buy each other gifts and jewelry isn't my thing, but I love this bracelet because of the thought behind it. "It reminded me of you," Luke said when he surprised me with it. "There was a jewelry artist selling her pieces at the library, and this one was turquoise—the stone that has healing powers in your book."

"You remember that?" I said, thinking back to that night in Montclair when I told him about my story.

"Of course!"

I run my fingers over the clasp of the bracelet. Luke loves me, I tell myself. And I love him—that's all that matters. This thought doesn't quiet my fears, but Luke's car has pulled into a spot across the street, so I get out of my car and walk over to him. "Sylvie is in the park," he says. "She just texted me."

"Mama is here!" Nate says.

"That's so exciting, Nate," I say.

We head into the park. Nate spots Sylvie right away and calls out to her, and she stands up from the bench where she was sitting. She's tall, taller than Luke, and her wavy hair is dyed black and red. Both her studded tank top and her jeans are skin-tight, showing off her hourglass figure; a tattoo of a vine climbs up her right arm and blooms into a rose on her shoulder. Her face is gorgeous, the face of a queen—high cheekbones and a slender nose, brown eyes and long lashes made dramatic with makeup. There's something formidable in her presence, and I would be intimidated by her even if I didn't know who she was. "Nate!" she says with a smile. "How are you, buddy?"

Nate throws himself at Sylvie, and she gives him a hug and a kiss. She reaches for Scotty, but the baby lets out a wail and retreats behind Luke's legs. "Take it slow," Luke tells her, putting his hand on Scotty's head. "He needs time to warm up. Um...Gemma, this is Sylvie. Sylvie, Gemma..."

I hold my hand out to Sylvie. "Nice to meet you."

Our handshake is firm and brief. I take note of her red nail polish and many silver rings. "You too," she says.

"Mama!" Nate says. "Watch me climb the rock wall!"

Nate leads Sylvie to the jungle gym. I stand around, feeling unnecessary; Luke is trying to coax Scotty into playing and Nate is delighted to be with his mom, so there's nothing for me to do. Eventually, Luke gets Scotty into a swing, and I hang out next to them. Luke is pushing Scotty, but his eyes are following Nate back and forth across the jungle gym. "If he goes into the tunnel slide, you have to catch him," he calls to Sylvie. She's watching Nate from the ground. "Sylvie! Did you get that?"

Sylvie doesn't answer, so Luke runs to the jungle gym. A moment later, Nate shoots out of the tunnel slide, and Luke catches him. Sylvie and Luke talk for a minute, and then Luke chases Nate up the ramp. Sylvie walks toward me.

I keep pushing Scotty. Out of the corner of my eye, I see Sylvie looking me up and down. Is she trying to decide if she's prettier than me? She is prettier, no contest—her face belongs in movies, and to have a body like that after two babies...but I can't get jealous. I told myself I wouldn't be jealous. "Where are you staying in the city?" I ask her.

"The East Village."

"Cool."

"New York is all right." She shrugs. "Better than here."

"Up," Scotty says. "Up!"

I lift Scotty out of the swing and bump Sylvie with my elbow. She's right next to me—she must have moved closer to pick up Scotty. I feel flustered and shove the baby into her arms. "Oh, sorry. Here you go."

Scotty whimpers and reaches out to me, but Sylvie adjusts him on her hip and starts speaking in a bright voice. "Let's try the slide, buddy!" She walks away. Scotty is crying and I wish I could comfort him, but I know I shouldn't interfere. I join Luke and Nate instead and end up involved in a fantasy game that's too complex for me right now; I can only pretend to pay attention. Luke gives me a quick kiss as we follow Nate across the bridge. "Thank you for doing this," he says. "You okay?"

"I'm fine."

"Watch out for the lava!" Nate yells.

Sylvie and Scotty start playing with us too, and after an hour, Sylvie has to leave. "My bus will be here soon," she says.

Nate bursts into tears. "Don't go, Mama!"

"I'll see you tomorrow!" Sylvie hugs him. "And on Saturday, you're coming to L.A. with me and we'll be together every day!"

"Where do you want to meet tomorrow?" Luke asks her. "It's supposed to rain."

"I'll take them to the mall."

"Okay. I'll meet you there at eleven," Luke says.

"You can just drop them off," Sylvie says. "I can handle my kids at the mall by myself."

"No, I'll be there."

Sylvie's eyes narrow and it looks like she's about to argue, but Nate tugs on her sleeve. "Come home with us, Mama! Please!"

"I'll be back tomorrow," she says. "I love you."

Sylvie kisses the kids goodbye and leaves the park. Nate is crying, so we spend a few minutes calming him down. Then Luke turns to me. "That went all right, I think. What do you think?"

"Could have been worse," I say. It's clear that Luke feels no affection for Sylvie and that's reassuring, but I still felt out of place when she was here; I'm not sure what role to play in this family if the kids' mother is around. "I guess we all have to be polite and get through this."

"Exactly." Luke takes my hand and kisses it. "Do you want to go home now?"

"I promised my dad I'd cook tonight," I say. "He's helping Uncle Vin fix his attic. I'll come over after dinner."

Luke and I put the kids into their car seats, and he drives away. Sylvie is waiting at the bus stop near the entrance of the park; she's smoking and scrolling through her phone. She looks up at me, and I give her a nod as I hurry to my car. "Gemma," she says. "You want a cigarette?"

I freeze. Why would she offer me a cigarette? Are they poisoned? I try to read her face, but she's wearing the same hard, impassive expression she had when we shook hands. "Um..." I say. "I don't smoke."

"That's cute. Come here—I want to talk to you."

I walk over to her, feeling uneasy. We're the only people at the bus stop; if she attacks me there will be no witnesses. But I'm being ridiculous...she only wants to talk. She studies me, takes a long drag off her cigarette. "The kids like you," she says. "Did they like you from the beginning, or did it take a while?"

"It didn't take long," I say. "Luke and I were friends before we started dating, so they were used to me. And my little cousin is close with Nate."

"Interesting. It makes a difference if Nate has somebody to play with. But that's not going to work for me—my boyfriend is never around kids."

"Does your boyfriend live with you?" My fists are clenched. Nate and Scotty might not be my sons, but I love them and I don't want them sleeping in the home of some strange man. "Because if you're bringing the kids there..."

"No, it's not that serious yet. Why—you live with Luke?"

"No."

"Oh." She looks pleased. "I guess I'll wait a few days before I introduce my boyfriend...start with short visits. I don't know how the kids will react to a new man; they're used to being attached at the hip with their father."

Her sarcasm makes me angry. Luke is amazing with his kids; Sylvie can hate him, but she can't insult the way he parents. "I like that he's always with the kids," I say. "That's one of my favorite things about him."

"I figured as much, otherwise how could you stand it? Luke is a good dad, but he's no saint. He can be a stubborn fuck when it comes to the boys. You saw the way he hovered over me at the park, like I couldn't take care of my own kids. He was like that in November, too—I never got a second of quality time with them. And he wanted to stop me from picking them up this month! Did you know that?"

"No."

"It's my right to have them in August—that's in the custody order. But he tried to talk me out of it. 'Wait a few more months,' he kept saying. 'Scotty has stranger anxiety and if you take him away now you'll traumatize him.' Stranger anxiety...I'm not a stranger, I made Scotty! But Luke didn't care how that comment made me feel; my feelings were never a priority once we had kids. It was all about the boys, what he thought was good for the boys—and whatever would ease his latest fear. My God, the fears drove me crazy." She leans closer to me. "'Was this formula bottle open? I think it was open—let's throw it away.' Or 'Nate bumped his head. You think he has a concussion? Should we wake him up at night?' It's unbearable, isn't it?"

I see what Sylvie is saying—Luke's worries can be excessive, and they must have been more annoying when she was caring for an infant at the same time. Still, I love Luke and I'm not going to say anything bad about him. "He's doing better now," I say. "But it must have been a tough time for both of you."

"It was, but because I left, it's like everything I sacrificed for Luke doesn't count. People don't remember all the money we spent on therapy or all the times I picked up the slack while he was washing his hands. I was the one trapped in the house with a screaming baby for a year because Luke didn't like the idea of daycare. He thought I was lucky—imagine, lucky!—because I spent my days covered in shit and spit up while he went to work at a job he didn't like. I would gladly have gone to work, but he had a college degree so he could make more money. He said I should stay home with Nate and that his mother would help me. His mother." She rolls her eyes. "Too bad his mother never liked me."

"She doesn't like me either," I say.

"No? You seem like the kind of woman she would want for Luke— domestic and all. Nurturing."

"I guess not."

"Don't take it personally—she's a bitch. And she's the reason we moved here! I wanted to take Nate to L.A. or Nashville so we could start our music careers, or at least stay in Boston, where I had plenty of friends. But no—we had to live in New Jersey. I hated it here." She pauses, her cigarette close to her mouth, and I see a flash of pain in her face. It's gone in a second but it startles me—it's a crack in her façade, a glimpse at the human underneath. "So I got out, and I don't regret it. But Nate and Scotty are still my sons. Nobody can take that from me."

"I would never come between you and the kids," I say. "That's not my intention at all."

She nods. "We're on the same page, then." The bus pulls up next to us, and Sylvie tosses her cigarette on the ground and crushes it with her foot. "Guess I'll be seeing you around."

"For sure," I say. She gets on the bus, and the doors close behind her. I make my way back to my car.

Later that night, I tell Luke about my conversation with Sylvie.

Though it was awkward, I'm glad Sylvie and I talked—if we're both going to be in the boys' lives, it's best for us to get along. I think Sylvie was wrong to walk out on her family, but I can also see why she was unhappy with Luke. None of what she said changes the fact that I adore Luke and I'll always be honest with him. He listens with wide eyes as I'm talking. "Why would Sylvie tell you all of that?" he says.

"People always talk to me about their problems," I say. "It's been that way my whole life."

"She's trying to turn you against me."

"Nobody could turn me against you."

"You don't know Sylvie," he says. "She always has an agenda."

"She was probably making sure she could take the kids on Saturday—that we wouldn't try to stop her."

"Of course we can't stop her; that's against the law. It's bullshit!" Luke slams his fist on the counter, making me jump. "She didn't want the kids—she left them! I'm the one who does everything for them; they belong with me. But I have to let her take them away and fuck them up—"

"You think she's going to hurt them?"

"Not on purpose. But she's selfish; she does what she wants, and she doesn't think about how the kids feel. You didn't see what Nate was like when she left, crying for his mother every night for weeks, and she couldn't be bothered with a phone call. There's nothing to stop her from breaking his heart again. And she's not careful, Gemma." He runs both his hands through his hair, making it stand on end. "She doesn't watch them the way I do; she gives them too much freedom. I don't even know if her apartment is baby proofed and anything can happen if she's not paying attention..."

"Maybe you can remind her of a few safety things."

"I tried, but she tells me I'm too controlling. I have to control her if she doesn't know what the fuck she's doing! I can't protect the kids when they're with her...and I'm scared."

"I'm sorry, baby," I say. "Sylvie isn't a great parent like you are, but I think the kids will be safe. She took care of them in the past and she must remember what to do." His fingers are in his mouth. "Please stop doing that to your hands—"

"I can't. I can't stop. I don't want to talk about this anymore—let's talk about something else. Let's have another drink."

Wine mellows Luke a little, but not enough. We both end up drinking a lot on Thursday and Friday nights. The boys' flight is at eight A.M. on Saturday morning, so I set my alarm for four forty-five to get ready for the airport. When I wake up, I find Luke on the couch, reading. "You woke up already?" I say.

"I've been up," he says. "I haven't slept."

"All night? Why didn't you wake me—"

"No, it's better that you slept. I'm going to wake Nate; he takes forever to eat breakfast..."

We go through the morning routine with the boys. Luke is a wreck; his eyes are frantic and bloodshot and his hands keep shaking. On our way out the door, he drops the car keys multiple times. "Do you want me to drive?" I ask.

"No, I need to do something with my brain—with my hands."

"Let me drive." I take the keys. "You can control the radio. And I'm sure Nate will give you some pretend character to play..."

Scotty falls asleep on the car ride, but Nate is excited, chattering about what he's going to do with Sylvie. Luke pretends to be enthusiastic while he's gnawing on his fingers. "Mama said there's an ice cream place on her block," Nate says. "We're going to get ice cream today!"

"That's great, buddy!" Luke says.

"And she bought us presents to open on the plane!"

We meet Sylvie at the departures level of the airport. She's wearing big sunglasses on top of her head, which seems incongruous with the rest of her appearance; I wonder if she dresses differently in California. "Are you guys ready to have fun with Mama?" she says.

"Yay!" Nate says.

I kiss each of the kids goodbye while Luke arranges their backpack on top of their rolling suitcase. "I put Scotty's blankie in the front pocket," he tells Sylvie. "He might want it on the plane. And Nate's dinosaurs are there too, and some snacks."

"Sounds good."

"I think I packed everything, but if they're looking for something, let me know and I'll send it..."

"I'm sure it's fine," Sylvie says.

Luke kneels down next to Nate and kisses him for the tenth time today. "I love you," he says. "Listen to Mama, okay? Never walk away from her—stay where she can see you."

"Okay," Nate says.

"Don't go near the street. Or the ocean."

"Okay."

"And look out for your brother; don't let him put things in his mouth." Luke straightens up and turns to Sylvie. "Be careful, please."

"I will," she says. "I love them too, remember?"

Luke gives Scotty a hug and a kiss, and Sylvie picks him up. "Dada." Scotty holds his hand out to Luke. "Dada take you."

"You go with Mama," Luke says. "I'll see you soon."

Scotty starts to cry. "Dada take you! Dada take you!"

"You're all right." Luke's voice is trembling; he kisses Scotty's little fingers. "You're with Mama and Nate! I love you."

Sylvie, Nate, and Scotty walk away. Scotty keeps crying and calling for Luke; Luke grabs my hand and clutches it so hard I think my bones might break. We watch the three of them until they disappear. "Good job," I tell Luke.

Without a word, he turns and speeds toward the exit of the airport. He's still holding my hand and I have to jog to keep up with him. Neither of us speaks until we get to the car.

Luke leans against the passenger door, taking ragged breaths. "It's fucked," he says. "This parenting thing. It's fucked from the start."

"What do you mean?"

"You bring these people into the world—people you love more than anything—who rely on you to keep them safe. You'd die to protect them. But the truth is you're powerless—your kids are in danger all the time and there's nothing you can do about it. They could have cancer lurking inside them and you don't find out until it's too late. They could fall down the stairs and break their necks, or stick their fingers in an outlet or choke or drown. They could go to school and end up getting molested or shot or—"

"Oh God, Luke."

"You hear about these things! There's pain around every corner and your efforts to shield them from it are useless. Once you realize that you can never be at peace again. I'll never be at peace. Still, I let them go." His voice breaks. "I let them go with Sylvie and I don't know what's going to happen..."

"Nothing is going to happen," I say. "She'll take care of them."

He shakes his head and leans into my arms and sobs, sobs with every ounce of violence in his body, and I hold him close and rub his back. I tell him it'll be okay even though it's not okay, even though I can see that all parents are fighting a losing battle. I think of what Bree said about giving up control of your life, and I think of Aunt Soph handing Michela to my aunts and saying, "Get her away from me," and I think that maybe it is a mistake to have kids. Maybe you don't realize it's a mistake until you can't take it back. Maybe parenthood is nothing but a path to heartache, and anyone who understands that would never have a child.

Chapter Fourteen

It's nearly the end of August, and the kids have been gone for weeks. Luke and I miss them, but we're also enjoying our time alone together. It's been a period of mixed emotions.

I love having Luke to myself. I love cooking delicious meals with him and savoring our food and carrying on a conversation without getting interrupted. I love having sex without rushing or worrying about our volume; I love sleeping naked with him and waking up late. I love that we have time for things we couldn't do before, like going to movies and museums and seeing live music and taking day trips to the shore and Philadelphia and New York. We can relax and do what we want without the boys dictating our every move.

One of the benefits of having free time is that Luke and I get to spend hours on music and writing. We sit together and work every Saturday afternoon; he writes songs and I write my novel, and we don't interrupt each other until it's time to make dinner. I wear headphones and I can't hear his music, but I can feel the electricity moving between us—we feed each other's creativity. We're bringing beautiful things to life, and whenever I get stuck, I watch Luke nodding his head and singing to himself, his body moving to the rhythm of what he's playing, and it inspires me. He finds so much joy in the creative process—the process itself, not only its results—and I'm learning to adopt the same approach.

"Some days I hate everything I write," I told him the first Saturday we worked together. I'd had a difficult writing session and was feeling unproductive. "I want to throw my computer against the wall."

"I've been there," he said.

"This book is awful; I don't know why I'm bothering to write it. I'm better off taking a shit on a piece of paper than putting my words on it."

Luke laughed at that, laughed for a while, then pulled me into his arms and kissed me.

"Get back at it tomorrow," he said. "Take a bigger shit."

"Come on."

"I mean it. We all struggle sometimes, but you'll figure it out as long as you keep working. That's where the fun is, anyway—in working."

"The fun?"

"Don't you think it's fun?" he said. "We're blessed to be artists. Try to enjoy it."

I remind myself of this every time I sit down to write. I write because I love it, I tell myself. That makes writing worthwhile, regardless of how the story turns out. There is freedom in working this way, without the hope of success leering over my shoulder; when I'm not worried about my book's audience, I trust my own judgment. I'm critical of my writing—I know which sentences need improvement and which ideas I should throw away—but I've stopped wallowing in self doubt. I get into the zone and work, and like Luke said, it's gratifying to work. I've written more over the past few weeks than I have in months. I have seven chapters written, but there are holes in them; only the first three chapters are at the point where someone else could understand them. I have a clear idea of where the story is headed, though, and I showed it to Luke this past Saturday. "I emailed you something," I told him once we finished working. "It's the first three chapters."

"Of your book?" he said. "Really?"

"Yeah, whenever you have time..."

"I'll read it now!"

He jumped up to grab his laptop, and I felt an attack of insecurity. "I can't watch you read it," I said. "I'll go into the kitchen...I'll start cooking."

I was jittery as I moved around the kitchen, trying not to imagine where Luke was in the story and what he thought of it. As I was stirring the vegetables, he walked into the room behind me, wrapped his arms around my waist, and kissed my neck. "You're brilliant," he said. "And so quiet about it! You've been hiding your talent from me..."

"Stop it," I said. "Don't say nice things because you love me. I want honest feedback."

"This is my honest feedback. I love the book so far. Your descriptions of Arizona are vivid; I can see the landscape clearly in my mind. And the plot is exciting—I can't believe Lydia is playing both sides! When Alana finds out it's going to be a bloodbath..."

"Is there anything you didn't like?" I asked.

He thought for a moment. "Alana was hard to relate to at the beginning. I liked the other characters, but she was too cruel. I only started rooting for her at the end of the third chapter, once I saw how much she loves Linus. Since Alana is the main character, it might turn some people off if they dislike her from the start."

"I could move things around," I said. "Maybe Linus follows Alana to the meeting in the first scene; she told him he was too young to join the rebels, but he shows up and says he wants to fight. Then the reader can meet him right away and see that she's protective of him."

"That's a good idea. People will sympathize with Alana if she shows her human side early on. We all like to see vulnerability in characters...I do, at least. But everything else was awesome. The dialogue was awesome."

My face is burning; I didn't expect so much praise. "Um...thank you for reading it."

"Of course! I can't wait to read more."

"It's going to take me a while."

Luke has started writing a song based on the book, which is too big a compliment for me to wrap my head around. He's written three other songs this month, lyrics and all; he finished the song about the cliff and wrote two new ones. One song, "Above Water," is about me, though he doesn't say my name in it; he told me he never uses people's real names in songs. He sings about how I'm a current running through his life, keeping everything afloat. "I've been trying to get the right image for you," he said. "To describe your strength, and how you make me stronger. Once I had that riff that sounded like water—not the tumult of waves but the steady flow of a river—then it was easy." I love the song because it's about me but also because I enjoy all of Luke's music; his songs are always playing in my head. Luke has recorded the songs on his phone as demos, just him singing and playing guitar. "I have a software on my computer where I can put in the other instruments," he said. "Drums and stuff...but it's not the same as working with musicians and hearing what they bring to the song. I'd rather leave the songs stripped down like this for now. I don't know what I'm going to do with them, but it feels good to make things again." It does feel good to make things, especially when we're together. This month has given me a glimpse of how our relationship would be if, like other couples our age, we had nobody to worry about but ourselves.

Still, life feels empty at times without the kids around. For the first week, I never made a sudden movement without checking to make sure I wouldn't knock down one of the boys; I've gotten used to them standing next to me or behind me. "It's too quiet," Luke keeps saying. "I thought I wanted it quiet, but I don't like this. It's unnerving." It is quiet, and it's strange to see toys in the toy chest instead of scattered everywhere. Luke and I put away all but one toy the day we dropped the kids at the airport. "Leave Fuzzy there," Luke said while we were cleaning. I had been about to take a purple monkey off the couch. "The top of the couch is the tree where he lives. Nate never puts him in the toy chest."

"We have to keep this monkey on the couch?" I said. "Even if the boys aren't here?"

"That's his spot."

"All right." I patted the monkey on the head. "Sorry, Fuzzy."

Luke and I talk about the kids a lot. We talk about Nate's imagination and how proud we are of his stories. We talk about how to handle battles between the boys; now that Scotty is older, the kids play together more, but they also fight more. We talk about Scotty's new rebellious streak and how to discipline him when he breaks the rules. "He's never upset when you yell at him," I tell Luke. "He finds it amusing. He makes that face..." I raise one eyebrow the way Scotty does. "Like he's saying, 'Really, Daddy? You think that's going to stop me?'"

"He's impossible! What about when he's going to do something bad, like stand on the couch or knock over one of Nate's towers, and he smiles at us over his shoulder..." Luke gives me a devious grin, in perfect imitation of Scotty, and we burst out laughing. "It's hilarious," Luke says when he catches his breath. "Life with kids is hilarious. I need to laugh more—that's what's missing..."

Luke video chats with the kids every day, and I've been on several of the calls. The kids look healthy and happy, but it's painful to hear their sweet voices and know they're so far away. Nate tells us about his adventures with Sylvie, but Scotty spends most of the time trying to grab Luke's face through the phone. Luke is always depressed after these calls, and we're both looking forward to getting the kids back on September 3.

Nate starts preschool on September 8; he got a spot in Michela's class. Luke and I went shopping for school supplies and filled up his backpack, which has been sitting by the front door for days. This afternoon we'll pick the kids up from the airport, and Luke keeps fussing over the backpack. "If I get this done now, it's one less thing to worry about once the kids are here," he says. "I want to enjoy these few days with them before school starts. I hate that I have to send Nate away as soon as I get him back."

"School isn't like California," I say. "It's only two days a week. And he'll be home with you at three o'clock."

"I still don't like it." Luke unzips the backpack. "Let me see if the pencil case is here..."

"It's there. You checked three times today." Luke ignores me and looks through the bag again. "You're not going to do this in front of Nate, are you?"

"What do you mean?"

I pull the backpack away from him. "When you're nervous like this, you make me nervous. And the same thing is going to happen to Nate. He's excited about school—don't ruin it for him."

"I'm making sure—"

"No, you're giving in to your anxiety. You know everything is in the bag, right?"

He looks angry for a moment, but then he sighs. "Yeah."

"So don't check again, especially not where Nate is here. If he picks up on how you feel, he'll think school is dangerous—that new situations are dangerous—"

"I don't want that. But I could keep him home—"

"He can't stay home for the rest of his life." I take Luke into my arms. "I'm sorry this is hard for you, but you have to be brave for the boys, like you were at the airport."

"I know. I've been thinking about that quote you told me...'There are wild beasts in every cave...'" He glances at the clock across the room. "Two more hours until we can get the kids."

We head to the airport a little while later. The boys are on the plane with Caitlyn, Luke and Sylvie's friend from Berklee. Caitlyn flies between L.A. and New York frequently, and Sylvie asked her to watch the kids on this trip. This bothers me; I understand why Sylvie wanted to avoid another flight, but I would feel safer if she were with the boys. Luke is wound up, too, so I pretend to be calm as we're waiting at the arrivals gate.

The boys' flight lands, and Luke and I watch travelers walking by for what feels like forever. Then we hear a familiar voice. "Daddy!"

Nate is running toward us at top speed, smiling from ear to ear. Luke kneels down, his face radiant with the kind of love that can only exist between parent and child, and scoops Nate into his arms. "I missed you, buddy!"

"Daddy, they had a movie about dragons on the plane!" Nate says. "Can we watch it at home?"

"Whatever you want," Luke says, nuzzling his face into Nate's chest.

I look up and notice a woman who must be Caitlyn. Scotty is asleep, and she's carrying him with the awkward grip of someone who's not used to holding kids. I rush forward to take him from her arms. "What a flight," she says. "This one cried almost the whole time...he just fell asleep when we landed..."

"Thank you for watching them, Caitlyn. Thank you. Thank you," Luke says.

Scotty stirs, lifts his head off my shoulder, and looks at me. For a moment I'm scared he won't remember me, but he takes the collar of my shirt and starts rubbing it between his fingers. "Hemma," he says. "Hemma take you."

"I love you so much," I say.

"Scotty!" Luke leans over to kiss Scotty. "I missed you!"

Scotty beams and puts his hands on Luke's face. "Dada! Dada!"

"You got so big!" Luke says. "He looks bigger, doesn't he?"

"I got bigger too!" Nate says.

"You did—you're huge!" Luke throws Nate into the air, and he shrieks with joy. "You're as tall as the ceiling! As tall as the clouds!"

Scotty is laughing, and I can't stop smiling as I watch Luke and Nate. The four of us are together again, and all is right in the world.

Chapter Fifteen

It's been a long winter and it's only the first week of January. This New Years' Eve was the first time I stayed up past midnight not to watch the ball drop, but because I was soothing a feverish toddler. Nate loves his preschool, but since September, he's been bringing home every germ imaginable. I can't remember the last time the boys were healthy for more than a week at a time.

"Is this ever going to end?" Luke said on Wednesday night. He was lying on the couch, rubbing his temples, with crumpled tissues all around him. "Or are we going to be sick for the rest of our lives?"

"Spring will be better," I said, with some impatience. I felt awful too, but I was helping Nate with his homework. Luke is useless when he's sick, and I end up taking care of everything at his apartment even if we have the same symptoms. "When the kids can get outside again, they won't catch so many germs."

"This twenty-degree weather has been brutal," Luke said.

"Hemma." Scotty walked up to me, holding the aspirator we use to suck snot out of his nose. "Booga."

"You want to clear your boogers?" I said. "Come here..."

Being sick all the time has been rough, because work has been getting more intense. Jasmine will be on maternity leave starting January 18, and everyone is preparing to have one less lawyer at the office. "I thought you'd take off earlier," Erica said when Jasmine told us her plans. "You're due on February 2, right?"

"I'm saving time for after James is born," Jasmine said. "The women in my family always go past their due dates, and I'll be bored waiting for the baby. Plus Mark will be on a business trip in France until the eighteenth; I don't want to sit at home alone."

Erica and Lina have started taking over Jasmine's clients, and they've passed along more work to me and Bree. We're busy from the start of the work day until the end; we haven't had a coffee break in months. Still, we're all excited for Jasmine. She feels much better than she did in her first trimester, and she's looking forward to being a mom; we had a gender reveal party at the office, and she's been letting us feel the baby kick. "Good morning, James!" Erica says to Jasmine's belly every day. "Are you ready to help Mommy with work?"

Inevitably, a little bump will poke out of Jasmine's stomach and move around under her shirt. "He loves you, Erica," Jasmine says. "He's always kicking when you talk to him."

"He's used to my voice."

On Saturday, I have breakfast with Luke and the kids and then head home to get ready for Jasmine's baby shower. I was worried I'd be sick and would have to miss the party, but luckily I'm feeling better. The shower is forty minutes west of Oakfield, in the town where Jasmine's parents live, so Bree and I are going to carpool; she picks me up outside my house. Bree is wearing a pretty gray sweater dress and her makeup is perfect, but she looks miserable. "I hope this thing doesn't take too long," she says. "I have a ton of reading to do."

"How's law school going?" I ask.

"I don't remember what it was like to sleep, but otherwise, it's good."

"I know that feeling."

"Kids driving you crazy?"

"They're always sick," I say. "When they get over one illness, they catch something else. It's nonstop."

"Give yourself a break," she says. "I know you love the kids, but they're Luke's problem, not yours."

I shrug. I guess she has a point, but I feel guilty when I spend too much time away from the kids. Bree merges onto the highway and we make our way to the shower.

The restaurant is packed with Jasmine's friends and relatives. Jasmine doesn't know about the party, but when she arrives with Mark, she doesn't seem surprised to see us. "I'm happy you're all here!" she says. "But I was expecting this to happen soon. I'm about to pop!"

Jasmine starts mingling with everyone in the room, and Mark walks over to the group of us from the office. According to Jasmine, she and Mark have been getting along; the fighting of the first trimester is long gone. "You ready, Mark?" Erica says, clapping him on the back. "Ready for dirty diapers at three A.M.?"

"I'm ready," he says. "I can't wait to meet the little guy."

"I'm just messing with you—it's the most beautiful thing in the world," Erica says. "You and Jazz are going to be great parents."

The hours pass by as we play games and watch Jasmine open her gifts. When the shower is over, Bree drives me back to Oakfield, and I head to Luke's place.

I find Luke folding laundry on the floor while Nate and Scotty roll their cars around him. I can see they haven't left the house today; all three of them have crowns made of construction paper on their heads, and Luke is wearing one of his threadbare old t-shirts with holes in the collar. "How was the shower?" he asks.

I sit next to him and we talk as we fold. Nate and Scotty push their cars behind a stack of towels. "Hide here," Nate tells Scotty. "There's a monster in the clothes! Uh oh—he's coming this way!"

Nate knocks over the stack of towels, and he and Scotty dive into the heap of laundry to escape. Nate rolls his car into a pile of shirts, which falls as well. "Stop it, guys," I say. "You're messing up the laundry—"

"Roar!" Luke says. He tackles Scotty into the clothes, and Nate climbs on him to fight back. "The monster is here!"

"Luke, seriously," I say. I get up to move the last stack of clothes out of the way, and Luke grabs me around the legs and pulls me down on top of him. "Hey!"

"The monster got Gemma!" Luke shouts.

"I'll save you, Gemma!" Nate says.

I have no choice but to join the wrestling match. After we pummel him with pillows, Luke admits defeat and collapses on his back in the middle of the clothes. "Great work, team," he says. "You beat the monster."

"Yay!" Nate says.

Luke grins at me. It's endearing, watching him play like a kid; he makes a mess, but he and the boys have so much fun that it's hard to get annoyed. "No wonder everything you own is wrinkled," I tell him.

"Monster battles can happen out of nowhere."

The following week is Jasmine's last week before maternity leave, and I'm swamped as usual at work. On Thursday, the office is quiet; Lina is in court, and Erica is working from home because her kids have the flu. I get a lot of work done in the morning because I'm not distracted by clients coming in and out. After lunch, I'm assembling some documents when I hear Jasmine's footsteps in the hallway; she keeps walking back and forth. "What's up?" I ask her.

"Braxton Hicks," she says. "They've been on and off all day."

"Oh. Is there anything I can do to help?"

"I'm okay—I feel better when I'm walking."

I glance at Bree, who is wearing headphones and paying no attention to Jasmine. I go back to work. After an hour, Jasmine is still pacing, and I'm starting to feel concerned. If her contractions aren't stopping, and they're so strong that she can't concentrate on her work... "How many weeks are you, Jazz?" I call after her.

"Thirty-seven."

That's full term; she could be in labor. I get up from my desk and join her in the hallway. "Are you sure they're not labor contractions?"

"Labor?" Her eyes are wide. "Don't say that! They're Braxton-Hicks and they'll go away. Let's get back to work."

Jasmine disappears into her office. A few minutes later, she's pacing the hallway again. I can hear when her contractions start and stop, because she mumbles something under her breath during them. I put my phone in my lap and start timing the contractions. Two hours pass, and the contractions get closer and closer together. When they're four minutes apart—a number that Aunt Soph taught me is significant—I take my phone into the bathroom. My heart is hammering, but my thoughts are clear: I'll text Erica. If she doesn't answer right away, I'll call one of my aunts; they'll know what to do. I explain the situation and send the text.

My phone rings in seconds. It's Erica on FaceTime, and she looks awful. Her eyes are droopy with fatigue and her nose is red. "I got what the kids have," she says in a hoarse voice. "Did Jazz's water break?"

"I don't think so."

"Let me talk to her."

I go back to the reception area. Bree has dropped all pretense of working and looks pale and uneasy as she watches Jasmine from her desk. I try to hand the phone to Jasmine, but she leans over the couch and lets out a long, low moan. "Somebody's in labor," Erica says. "Gemma, you're right—it's time to go to the hospital."

The contraction ends, and Jasmine looks at the phone with tears in her eyes. "I can't be in labor, Erica! I'm not ready! I didn't set up the car seat or the bassinet and Mark is in Paris and I'm alone—"

"You're not alone," Erica says. "We'll figure this out together. Who do you want in the birthing room with you? Do you want to call your mom?"

"God, no—she stresses me out. All my relatives are so overbearing. And my best friend lives two hours away..."

"I would come if it didn't mean bringing the plague," Erica says. "Anyone else?"

Jasmine turns to me. "Will you stay with me? I know it's a lot to ask..."

"Of course," I say. "I'm in."

"Gemma is good—she's a calming presence," Erica says. "Jazz, remember everything we talked about: try to squat and be upright as much as you can. When you're in transition, release the pressure with your voice. And listen to your body when it's time to push. Your body knows which position—"

Jasmine's face changes, and she waves her hand at the phone. She sets off down the hallway again, muttering to herself. "If she needs that much focus, you should go now," Erica says to me. "But first, make her eat something and drink a lot of water. Call me if you need me."

"I'll take care of things at the office," Bree says.

Ten minutes later, Jasmine and I are on our way to the hospital. She's quiet between contractions, but when a contraction comes, she arches her back in pain and repeats some foreign phrases. "Are you speaking a different language?" I ask when the contraction passes.

"It's a poem in Tagalog," she says. "One of my favorites. Those lines are about facing challenges head-on instead of shying away from them. I tried visualization in birth class and it didn't help me, so the teacher told me to pick a mantra. That's my mantra."

"You're a badass," I say. "Quoting poetry in labor..."

"Mark thought I was crazy, but it works." She takes a deep breath. "I never thought I'd have to give birth without Mark. But we've got this, right? Me and you?"

Before I can answer, Jasmine gasps and grabs my hand, her fingernails digging into my palm. I'm nervous—though I've heard plenty of stories, I've never seen anyone in labor before. I wish I had more experience and could be more helpful. At the same time, I'm excited for Jasmine. When this is over—no matter how long it takes—she'll be holding James. I squeeze her hand back and I don't let go even when the contraction is over. "We've got this," I say.

When we get to the hospital, a nurse checks Jasmine's cervix and tells her that she's six centimeters dilated. Jasmine declines an epidural, and we're sent to a labor room, where we meet another nurse. The nurse is around our age, and she gives us a warm smile. "I'm Leslie, and I'm your labor and delivery nurse," she says. "Do you prefer to be called Jasmine, or Mrs. Bryant?"

"Jasmine is fine," Jasmine says. "And this is my friend, Gemma."

"Nice to meet you both," Leslie says. "So you made it to six centimeters at home—that's impressive!"

"I was at the office, actually," Jasmine says.

"The office? Wow!"

"At least my water didn't break there," Jasmine says.

"In all three of my pregnancies, I was terrified my water would break in public," Leslie says. "Even though that's rare. It's been a year since my youngest was born, and I still have nightmares about it happening in the supermarket…"

"Cleanup on aisle five," Jasmine says, and we all laugh. I've decided I like Leslie; she feels like a friend of ours already. Leslie puts a monitor on Jasmine's belly, and Jasmine goes back to walking around the room. Leslie and I encourage her and let her lean on us between contractions. Jasmine is in pain, but she's managing it; she doesn't lose her stamina, even though she vomits once and her contractions are coming more frequently. The three of us are a team, and Leslie and I support her in every way we can.

It's not long before the mood in the room changes. Jasmine's groans turn into a scream and she won't let either of us touch her. "It's coming down!" she shrieks at the ceiling. "It's splitting me open—"

"Keep breathing," Leslie says. "Don't bear down yet—"

"I have to push! I have to push!"

Jasmine's face is twisted with agony and her legs are shaking. I'm shaking too—why is she out of control? Leslie keeps speaking to her in a calm voice. "You're doing great," she says. "Transition is almost over and pushing will feel better…"

"I want to push now!"

Leslie and I look up as a man walks into the room. He introduces himself as Dr. Howell, one of the residents; he seems unfazed by Jasmine's distress. "She's feeling the urge to push," Leslie tells him. "I was about to check her cervix."

"I'll do it," Dr. Howell says. He puts a hand on Jasmine's shoulder. "Mrs. Bryant, if you could lie down—"

"Don't touch me!" Jasmine smacks his hand away. "Get away from me!"

"I need to check your cervix before you can push," Dr. Howell says.

"Let her finish the contraction first," I say.

Dr. Howell sighs. He looks impatient, like Jasmine's labor is an inconvenience, like he would prefer her on her back with her legs up in stirrups. When the contraction is over, Jasmine lets him examine her, and he says she's fully dilated. "We'll tilt up this bed," he tells her. "And you can lie back—"

But Jasmine jumps off the bed, puts her hands on the windowsill across the room, and settles into a squatting position. Her knees are spread far apart and she's grunting like an animal. "Mrs. Bryant," Dr. Howell says. "If you want to deliver this baby—"

At that moment, Aunt Soph walks into the room. She looks shocked to see me, but she recovers quickly and turns to Jasmine. "I'm Dr. Cimino, covering for Dr. Moore—"

"Don't tell me to lie down!" Jasmine yells at her. "I won't lie down!"

"You don't have to," Aunt Soph says. "You tell me how you want to push, okay?"

Jasmine wants to squat, so Leslie finds a squat bar and attaches it to the bed. Jasmine crouches behind it and looks at me. "Stay close," she says.

"I'm here." I put my hand over hers on the bar, and Leslie does the same with her other hand. Jasmine starts to push. Her eyes are squeezed shut and sweat is running down her face; she's giving all of herself with every push. Aunt Soph and Dr. Howell keep counting to ten, but Jasmine doesn't seem to hear them. "One two three four five six seven eight nine ten," they say. "One two three four—"

"Baby is crowning," Leslie says.

"Five six seven eight—"

With a rush of blood and fluid, there's a baby on the bed. Leslie suctions his nose and mouth and he wails at the top of his lungs. "Is he okay?" Jasmine asks. "Is he okay?"

"He's perfect," Aunt Soph says.

Jasmine sinks down onto the bed behind her. "Oh my God."

I stare in awe at the baby—at his little hands as they open and close, at the blue cord protruding from his belly, at the clumps of blood in his thick black hair. I can't believe he just came out of Jasmine—that there's a new life in the room with us. "You did it, Jazz!" I say.

Aunt Soph puts James on Jasmine's chest. She starts crying and kissing him. "I'm your mommy!" she says. "I love you so much! I have to call Mark...somebody find my phone..."

Jasmine and Mark share an emotional FaceTime call, and then Leslie hands James to me while the doctors give Jasmine stitches. The baby is calm now that he's been with Jasmine; his expression is peaceful as he looks up at me. "Welcome to the world, James," I say.

"That was a beautiful birth," Aunt Soph says to Jasmine. "Congratulations. You were so empowered!"

"And it's her first baby, too," Leslie says.

Aunt Soph glances at me. "I hope this doesn't scare you away from giving birth someday, Gemma."

"Not at all," I say, smiling at James.

"Wait, you know each other?" Jasmine says.

"She's my aunt," I say.

"Why didn't you tell me?"

"We were focused on other things," I say. "Aunt Soph, Jasmine and I work together—"

"Work together? We're sisters now," Jasmine says. "Hold my hand—these stitches fucking hurt..."

I stay with Jasmine for another hour, while she gets settled in a postpartum room and starts breastfeeding. Then her mom and aunt arrive; I feel comfortable leaving since I know she won't be alone. I go back to my house to shower and eat. I texted Luke earlier in the day about Jasmine, and since it's close to eleven now, I figure he'll be asleep. When I text him good night, though, he says he's awake. I head to his apartment.

I open the door to find Luke dozing on the couch. He stirs and blinks at me. "Interesting day at the office?"

"I didn't mean to wake you," I say. "Let's hang out tomorrow—"

"No, come here."

He holds his arms out to me, so I join him on the couch. We cuddle and I tell him about Jasmine's labor. "Women are unstoppable," I say. "We can do anything! And it was an amazing feeling, being part of this community that helped her deliver her baby."

"I'm glad things went well," he says. "The birth room is intense."

"How'd you do when you were there?"

"I didn't panic, but I don't think I was much help," he says. "Sylvie mostly wanted me there so she could yell at me, so I served that purpose. But when you see your kid for the first time, when you hear him cry...there's nothing like it."

His words fill me with longing. I've always dreamed of having kids, and Luke is the man I want to raise them with. But maybe he doesn't want another baby; maybe Nate and Scotty are enough for him. "Would you have a baby with me?" I ask.

He looks alarmed. "You want a baby?"

"Not now. I mean in the future, if we got married...would you have more kids, or are you done?"

He smiles. "I'm not done for life, especially if I get to marry you. But I want to wait a few years. When the boys are older, we can have another kid."

"Perfect." I hold him tighter. I love Nate and Scotty with all my heart, but I'd like to experience every stage of motherhood—including pregnancy and raising an infant—from the beginning. I'm glad I can be with Luke and the boys and still get the chance to have a baby someday. "We should stock up on sleep now while we can."

"Good luck with that," Luke says. "Scotty was crying before you got here..."

I don't know if Scotty cries for the rest of the night, because a minute later, I'm asleep. I wake up early in the morning, when the sky is still dark; my body is aching, but there are sentences running through my head. I grab a piece of paper. I write about Jasmine's birth—about her resilience and her joy, about the solidarity between her, me, and Leslie.

My words fall short of capturing the feeling, but I try my best. I save the piece of writing so I can go back to it when it's my turn to join the generations of women who became mothers before me and the generations who will follow. I don't know what my birth will be like, but I believe we can all draw strength from each other's experiences if we pay attention.

Chapter Sixteen

It's Saturday afternoon, and we're in the courtyard of Luke's apartment building, watching Nate and Scotty squirt each other with water guns. Though it's early May, it feels like summer; the sun is beaming and it's close to eighty degrees. "Stay away from that tree," Luke calls out to the boys. "I think there's a wasp nest in there."

"Don't scare them," I say.

"I don't want them to get stung."

I look at the tree Luke mentioned and can't see any wasps, but the sun is so bright that it's making me squint. Luke takes off his sunglasses and puts them on me. "Thanks, baby," I say.

"You always forget your sunglasses."

The rest of the afternoon is peaceful—as peaceful as life can be with two toddlers—but I'm intending to go home before dinner. I wrote for several hours this morning and worked through a scene that was giving me trouble; I'm excited to write more now that I've had a breakthrough. I say goodbye to Luke and the kids, and Nate starts to pout. "You're not supposed to leave," he says. "You're supposed to have dinner with us."

This melts my heart, even though he's whining. "You like when I eat with you?" I say.

"Yeah!"

"Yeah!" Scotty echoes.

I give each of them a hug. I'm overjoyed that they want me around, that I've become a given in their lives. "I love eating with you guys too," I say. "We'll have dinner together tomorrow. And you can help me cook!"

"Will you be here in the morning?" Nate asks. "So I can wake up you and Daddy?"

I glance at Luke, whose eyes are shining. He's been my boyfriend for a year now, but it feels like it's been longer; it's hard to remember a time before I knew him. I can't wait for the day when I can call his home and his family my own. "Not tomorrow," I tell Nate. "I'll come over after breakfast. But someday I'll sleep here every night, and you can wake me up every morning. Someday soon."

Luke follows me to my car. The boys have gone back to their water gun battle; Luke watches them for a moment, then turns to me. "Do you want to live with us?"

My heart starts beating faster. Of course that's what I want, but I didn't expect him to ask me yet. "I would love that," I say.

"Me too. I miss you so much when you're not here. I was worried about how the boys would handle that transition, but they look for you, they ask for you...we all want you around. I know life with kids gets crazy, so if you need some time to think about it..."

I kiss him; his skin smells like the sun. "I'll bring my stuff over tomorrow."

I'm elated as I drive back to my house. Tomorrow I'll be living with Luke! I'm planning to write as soon as I get home, but I get distracted by the sight of my dad sitting on the deck, reading and drinking scotch. I feel a pang of guilt. I hate the idea of leaving my dad alone in this house, with no one to talk to or take care of. His family lives close by, but that's no substitute for having his daughter under the same roof. I'll be ten minutes away, I tell myself. I can visit him every day. Still, I know he'll be lonely. I sit down next to him. "Amazing day, right?" he says. "You can't beat this weather."

I nod and gaze at the backyard. Everything looks the same as it has for years. The hot pink flowers, which come out every summer, have already bloomed on the bushes. The squirrels who try to chew through our garbage cans are running along the top of the fence. The old silver grill is glinting in the sunlight; on the patio below it, there's one broken stone that my cousins and I used to lift up to search for ants. The familiar sights are tinged with loss; it's strange, grieving for a place that's right in front of me. I felt this way when I moved to Arizona, and I ended up yearning for home so much that I came back. This time, though, I won't be coming back. "Dad," I say. "I'm going to move in with Luke."

He looks at me through narrowed eyes. "You think that's a wise idea?"

"Yeah. I love him, and we've been together for a year..."

"A year isn't much when you compare it to spending a lifetime with someone. I would never have dreamed of moving in with your mother before we were married."

I didn't expect this reaction; it seems too old-fashioned for my dad. "Those were different times," I say.

"And better times, in many ways. I was raised to believe that people had to commit to each other if they wanted to live together; they had to take a leap. If you live with Luke now, he'll get all the benefits of having a wife without having to call you his wife. A man could get comfortable in that situation—too comfortable to make any other decisions. I'd like to see him propose to you at least before you move in." He studies my face. "But I know my Gems and you're not listening to a word I'm saying."

"Luke is committed to me—we talk about getting married someday. And we basically live together already; I sleep there most nights, and the kids want me to stay—"

"Have you thought about how this is going to affect them? If you and Luke aren't married, it's easy for you to break up over a small disagreement. Then you'll move out and leave the kids like their mother

153

did. That could be devastating for them."

He has a point; my stomach gets cold at the thought of hurting Nate and Scotty. But that won't happen. Luke and I rarely argue, and when we do, we make up right away. Nothing could come between us. "I would never leave Luke and the kids," I say. "Never."

"You say that now, but living together will test your relationship in new ways. You might not feel head over heels anymore; Luke might not seem so perfect. If you're happy, why are you rushing things? Enjoy what you have and don't put pressure on yourselves. You'll have plenty of years to live together once you're married. And there's no need for you to leave home, financially or otherwise. You have a good situation here, and you can stay as long as you want."

In these words, I hear my dad's real motivation for opposing the move. He wants me at home; he's not ready to let me go. I hug him. "I'm going to miss you too, Dad. But I'll be close by, and the four of us can come over for dinner once a week if that works for you."

He sighs. "You're welcome to come for dinner. But you've made up your mind—you're living with Luke no matter what?"

"I was planning to move in tomorrow."

"Then I have something to give you. Be right back."

He goes inside and heads upstairs. I'm baffled; what does he want to give me? I didn't ask for money or anything. When he returns to the deck, he has a sketch pad in his hands. It must be one of my mom's journals, but I don't recognize it. On the cover, in my mom's messy cursive, are the words: *To Gemma, when you become a mom*. I stare at my name; I've never seen it in her handwriting before. I adore my mom's handwriting—the odd shape of the *G*, the large loopy letters, the sentences slanting on the unlined paper. Reading her journals always made me feel close to her; I discovered her likes and dislikes, her beliefs, the kinds of imagery that struck her. I could imagine how she spoke from the way she formed her sentences. Now, for the first time, I'll get to read something she wrote for me.

"It's the only journal I haven't read," my dad says. "I felt it wasn't my place, since it's addressed to you. If you're going to live with Luke's kids, you're taking on the role of a mom, and you might find something in here that's useful."

I take the journal and run my fingers over my name. Here's a physical reminder of my link to my mom—something I can touch. "Wow. Thank you."

My dad downs the rest of his scotch and attempts a smile. "Should we have dinner?"

"Sure."

Dinner starts out heavy and sad. My dad is trying not to get emotional, and I feel responsible for making him suffer. I want to say something to comfort him, but I know the more I talk about leaving, the worse he will feel. Instead I follow his lead in drinking too much, and by the end of the meal the two of us are laughing over a story Aunt Dee told him earlier. We clean up after dinner, and I take my mom's journal to the couch along with my wine. I figure I can read while my dad is reading, but he never picks up his book; he turns on the TV, which is unlike him, and we make fun of the sitcom that's playing. After a while, the screen gets blurry, and I lay my head against the pillows.

That's how I spend my last night in my childhood home—passed out drunk on the couch, with my dad in his armchair beside me and my mom's journal clutched to my chest.

Chapter Seventeen

It's been three weeks since I moved in with Luke, and the girls at the office are curious about how things are going. "How do you feel now that you're living with Luke?" Erica asks me.

"Tired," I say.

This is the only correct answer. I've never been so tired. In college I would party until dawn and go to class a few hours later, or pull all-nighters to finish a paper; in Tucson I would hike all weekend, wake up at five on Monday morning to write, and power through a long, tough week at work. None of those experiences come close to how exhausting parenthood can be. Before I moved in with Luke, I was rejuvenated by the nights I would spend at my dad's place—nights when I didn't have to cook or clean or entertain the kids, when I could sleep without interruption. Now those nights are gone and the grind is nonstop.

I've taken on more chores than I expected. I change Scotty's diaper sometimes, and I'm always picking up toys, doing laundry, taking out the trash, and sweeping. I used to ignore the mess at Luke's apartment— I figured it wasn't my place to criticize his housekeeping—but now that I live here, I can't stand seeing dirty dishes pile up in the sink while he's watching cartoons with the kids. Luke will clean if I ask him to, but he's never the one who initiates. "Just leave it," he says when he sees me doing housework. "I'll do it when the kids go to sleep. It's not bothering anyone." It is bothering someone—it's bothering me! So I clean up, every time.

Getting to work without running late has also become a struggle. I never get enough time in the bathroom. Nate insists on having privacy when he's on the toilet, but he's usually sitting there singing to himself instead of pooping or peeing. Luke spends forever in the bathroom as well, so I have to organize my morning routine around the two of them. My showers take ten minutes these days and my hair always ends up in a bun. Sometimes I'll go a week without shaving my legs; Luke doesn't mind, but I find it embarrassing. I was never the type to obsess over my appearance, but there are some basic human needs—like the comfort of a long, hot shower—that I've had a hard time giving up. I feel rushed and disheveled every day.

Worse than the chaos and the chores is the fact that I haven't written a word since I moved in with Luke. Scotty wakes up at six A.M. and begs me to play with him, so writing in the morning is impossible. I could ask Luke to take care of Scotty, but Luke is either awake and finishing the work he didn't do for his job the previous day, or he's fast asleep. I feel bad waking him when I'm already awake. I'd like to write on the weekends, but we're so busy with housework and the kids' activities that it seems selfish to ask for an hour to myself. I'm hoping that when Nate's soccer class ends, and when Luke is done with this big project at work, I can fit writing into my routine again.

Though we're living together, it feels like Luke and I get less quality time with each other than we did before. If we manage to have sex after the boys go to bed, we fall asleep afterwards; I'm too tired to stay up talking like we did in the past. Luke wants to spend time with me when I get home from work, but the kids—along with the chores I see as soon as I walk through the door—demand my attention. I have to cook right after work so we can eat at a reasonable time, without keeping the boys up too late. If Luke had his way, he'd chat with me for hours and have dinner with the kids at nine P.M, but I try to keep everyone on a schedule.

On Wednesday, I leave the office late again. Bree switched to full-time law school and is now working part-time at Callahan and Ramos, so the lawyers have given me more responsibilities. I got a raise, which is nice, but the extra work cuts into my time to get things done at home. I feel flustered as soon as I walk into the apartment. Nate and Scotty have made crayon drawings for me and they're excited to tell me every detail of their artwork. I briefly admire the pictures, then go into the kitchen to clear the sink of dirty dishes and start cooking. When I open the dishwasher, the clean dishes are still there. "You didn't empty this?" I say to Luke.

"Sorry—I never got a chance," he says. "So I heard something today—"

"Gemma!" Nate says, waving his picture in my face. "See the frog? I made it green for you!"

"Thank you, Nate—it's beautiful," I say. "Let me start dinner and you can help in a minute."

"There's a position opening up in my company that I could apply for," Luke says. "It would come with a raise, but the problem is I'd have to start going to the office every day. We could use the money, but the reason I took this job was so that I could stay home..."

"Gemma!" Scotty says. He's finally mastered the *G* sound and is speaking well for his age. "I want crayons."

I grab the bucket of crayons off the counter, hand it to Scotty, and go back to the dishes. Luke is still talking. "If I'm paying for preschool and daycare full time, I'd probably break even on the raise," he says. "Which isn't worth it. Then again, I can write childcare expenses off on my taxes..."

"That's my paper!" Nate says. "Gemma! Daddy! Scotty drew on my picture!"

"Give Nate his picture back," I say.

"I don't feel good about it—I like being home. But part of me thinks it's silly to turn down more money. What do you think?" Luke leans closer to me. "Baby? Are you listening?"

"No, I'm not listening," I snap. "You see everything I'm dealing with right now. How am I supposed to listen to you?"

"Forget it," he says. "I'll figure it out myself."

Luke is cold to me for the next hour. I know he wanted my advice, but he picks the worst times to ask for it. Yet I hate when he's mad at me. "I'm sorry I didn't listen before," I say to him at dinner. "But it wasn't a good time to talk..."

"It's never a good time for us to talk," he says. "We have to steal time whenever we can. Look, I appreciate everything you do for me and the boys, but I'm busting my ass too—taking care of the kids is a full time job, and I'm working at the same time. But you don't think about the messes I clean and the fights I break up and everything else I have on my plate; you treat me like one more annoyance to put up with."

"You're right—you handle a lot. I'm just exhausted when I get home from work." I rest my cheek on his hand, which is lying on the table, and he kisses the top of my head. "Do you want to talk now?"

"It's okay—I'm not going to apply for that job. And when you've had a tough day, tell me and we can get takeout. You don't have to cook every night."

"But I like to cook, and I like to eat healthy," I say. "It's a good lesson for the boys."

"You can't do it all, baby. There are only so many hours in a day."

As we're talking, Scotty is lifting the edge of his plate with his fork. The plate flips over and lands on the floor, spilling food everywhere. Anger flares up inside me and I'm about to yell at him, but he looks so stunned that I can't help but smile. "Laugh it off, Soph," I remember Aunt Ro saying years ago. We were at my cousin's wedding, and baby Michela had just pooped all over Aunt Soph's dress. "You gotta laugh, or else you'll cry." I turn to Luke. "At least the floor is eating healthy," I say.

"I'll clean it," he says. "See, Scotty? That's what happens when you play with your food!"

In spite of the frustrations, I'm glad I'm living with Luke. I love him more every day. I love the rise and fall of his chest under my head and his narrow hairy feet with the fourth toes oddly smaller than the pinkies and the way his voice starts out scratchy early in the morning. The smell of his skin turns me on when I'm in the mood and calms my nerves when I'm stressed. He's my favorite person to talk to—when we get a chance to talk—and he showers me with affection. Our souls have curled up together, and I feel entirely safe and entirely loved with him. We have our disagreements, like all couples do, but I wouldn't trade our relationship for any other.

The girls at work have been complaining about their husbands lately, and it's made me appreciate Luke more. Jasmine has been fighting with Mark a lot since James was born; she's back from maternity leave and she's been asking the rest of us for advice. "This is a rough time for everyone," Erica told her yesterday. "Caring for an infant around the clock and running on no sleep. I swear it gets better."

"Until you have baby number two, and then it gets worse," Lina said.

"You're a ray of sunshine, Lina," Erica said.

Erica is usually an optimist, but she's had her share of troubles. She and Artie had work done on their house and spent more money than they anticipated, so they've been cutting back in other areas. "Artie says I spend too much on the kids," she told us. "Can you believe that? I haven't bought anything—anything!—for myself in months, and now he expects me to skimp on the kids' sports equipment. Their activities are expensive, but what am I working for if I can't give my kids everything they need?" I was surprised to hear Erica worrying about her finances; she makes good money and I think Artie does too. I never thought about their spending habits or what kinds of bills they might have.

Luke and I have never fought about money. We take turns paying for groceries and split the other bills in half. At first, Luke was reluctant to let me contribute as much as I do. "How much is our rent?" I asked the day I moved in. "I can write you a check every month."

"You don't have to pay anything," he said. "I just want you with us."

"I'm not going to live here for free! Tell me what it is and I'll pay half."

"No."

I was exasperated. "Luke, if you're not going to treat me like a partner, I'll go back to my dad's place."

"Fine. It's eighteen hundred."

"What about electric, cable..."

Luke explained the bills and how much Sylvie pays him in child support, and we came to a final number. "I feel guilty having you pay half," he said. "There are three of us and only one of you..."

"That doesn't matter," I said. "We're a team." Luke and I were both careful with money before we moved in together, and that hasn't changed; we have inexpensive cars and phones and rarely buy anything other than necessities. I know our finances will get more complicated in the future—I'd like to buy a house, and Nate and Scotty will want to go to college—but for now, we're living within our means and saving a little on the side.

After Luke cleans up the food Scotty dropped on the floor, we finish dinner and put the kids to bed. I fall asleep as soon as my head hits the pillow.

I wake up in the middle of the night with a jolt. Luke has grabbed me around the waist and is gasping for breath. "What's the matter?" I say. His grip is tight, but he's half awake; he must have seen something in his sleep. "It's okay," I say. "You're okay. You're okay." I stroke his hair, and his breathing returns to normal. "You had a bad dream?"

"I was choking." He sits up; he's fully awake now. "There was something stuck in my throat and I was struggling to breathe. You were there, and you saw what was happening; I tried to call out to you but I couldn't make a sound. Then you turned and walked away...you left me..."

"That's horrible."

He's trembling. "Baby, do you like living with me? Or do you regret moving in?"

"Why would you say that?"

"I know you're stressed—way more stressed than you were in the past. The kids and I are pushing you too much..."

"I'm fine." I put my arms around him. "I'm adjusting to this lifestyle, and that takes time. But I want to be here—I love you more than anything."

"I love you too. You make me so happy—too happy—this has been so good for so long and I'm scared I'll fuck it up—"

"You won't," I say. I can see why he's nervous—living together is a big step, and he must have scars from what happened with Sylvie. But he can count on me to stay by his side. "We're going to have ups and downs, but we'll get through them. I'm not going anywhere."

He kisses my neck, then my cheek, then my lips. "I'm sorry I woke you up."

"It's all right. Let's try to relax..."

We lie back down, and I rest my head on his chest and close my eyes.

Chapter Eighteen

We're on the way home from the pediatrician's office with a screaming kid in the back seat and Sylvie's voice on the radio. Nate hates going to the doctor, and his five-year-old checkup today was no exception. "You shouldn't have told him he wouldn't get a shot," I say to Luke.

"I thought he was done! How many shots are there?"

I look out the window, feeling grateful that Scotty is at his grandparents' house instead of here adding to the drama. I can hear Sylvie singing despite Nate's wails; her song, which is her first single as far as I know, tells the story of a man who broke her heart. I wonder if it's about Luke. I haven't asked him; the song has been on the radio constantly this week, but this is the first time we've heard it together. Sylvie has an amazing voice—it's rich and resonant even on the high notes and has eerie girlish undertones in the soft parts of the song. "Sylvie sounds great," I say to Luke.

"Yeah, phenomenal." There is a bitter edge to his voice; he switches the radio to another station. "Nate, stop crying!"

"It hurts!" Nate says.

"It was just a shot, and it was ten minutes ago! Get over it!"

Nate looks shocked; Luke usually has more patience with him. Still, his tantrum is over, and I take the opportunity to lift his mood. "When we get home, let's open that LEGO set you got for your birthday," I say.

"Okay!"

I steal a glance at Luke, who is grinding his teeth as he drives. It must be strange for him, seeing his ex rise to fame; it feels surreal to me and I barely know her. Earlier in our relationship, I might have been plagued by doubts in this situation: Does Luke miss Sylvie when he hears her song? Does he long to be married to an up-and-coming artist? But those thoughts have no power over me anymore; I'm certain Luke loves me and no one else. I take his hand. "Want to have stuffed peppers for dinner?" I ask. "Since I'm off today, I can get started early..."

"Whatever you want."

The day is uneventful; I have a doctor's appointment too, and then I spend time playing with Nate and Scotty. When Luke is done with work, he joins me in the kitchen to help me cook. We're in the middle of a conversation when Nate interrupts us. "Daddy," he says. His arms are overflowing with toy cars; two of them fall onto the kitchen floor. "When is my car track coming? Mama said she would buy it."

"It should be here soon," Luke says. "Things take a while to come in the mail."

"When? Tomorrow?"

"Maybe," Luke says. "You got a million presents for your birthday; why don't you play with another toy?"

"I want to call Mama and ask about the car track."

"Not now," Luke says. "Go play with your brother." Nate leaves the kitchen, and Luke turns to me. "I hope Sylvie sent the damn thing."

"Me too."

"If it doesn't come by the end of the week I'll have to text her."

He rubs his temples. I remember his reaction in the car earlier and I figure it's time to bring up Sylvie's music. "It's weird, right?" I say. "Hearing her song? It's okay if it feels weird..."

"It's fucking weird, and I'm jealous! I wish it were my voice on the radio instead. It's not fair that Sylvie gets to have both and I don't."

"Both of what?"

He sighs. "She gets to have a career in music, which is what I want, but I gave up on that dream because of the kids. She didn't have to give up anything; she left them to become a star, and they still love her. They have more fun with her than they do with me."

I'm taken aback. "That's not true."

"It is. All Sylvie does is buy them presents and take them to amusement parks; it's a big party when they're with Mama. I'm the one who makes them do homework and take naps and eat vegetables, the one who says no to things and punishes them. They don't understand that I do it out of love; they don't appreciate how hard I'm working..."

"Luke." I touch his face. "Of course they don't appreciate it—they're little kids. But they love you more than Sylvie, more than anybody. Don't doubt that for a second."

"There's so little reward in parenthood...so little gratification..."

"It's mostly sacrifice at this point. But someday..."

"Dada." Scotty comes into the kitchen with a blue car in his hand. "Blue for you."

"Thank you, buddy." Luke takes the car and kisses him. "I love you."

"I love you."

Scotty goes back to the living room. "See?" I say to Luke. "He got you a car."

Luke turns the car over in his hands. "It's not that I don't recognize how good I have it," he says. "The boys are happy and healthy and that's what matters. I chose this life on purpose; I wouldn't want someone else to raise my kids."

"I know."

"And I get to be with you, Gemma—I never dreamed I would find someone like you. I can trust you with anything; you fill every day with peace and joy and—"

"I'm not that special," I say.

"You are. The thing is...how can I put this? I feel like I could do more with my life—that I was meant for more—and it's only a lack of time that's standing in my way. I know my music would make an impact, because I've seen it on a small scale; people like my songs, they're affected by them, and it's clear I have talent. If I could be satisfied with being mediocre—if I could see music as a hobby and nothing else—then it wouldn't bother me to give it up for years. But it's not a hobby; it's a calling. If I had the freedom to do the work, to put all my energy into music, I could be great. I really believe that."

"I believe it too."

"I'm trying to accept that it will never happen for me—that I'll never play in front of a big audience or reach anyone beyond my circle of acquaintances with my songs. Yet in spite of logic, I feel the impulse to create—the compulsion. You must feel it too. We can smother that part of ourselves but it doesn't die; we can say our art doesn't matter but it does and it always will. At least writing novels, like you do, is something you can fit into the margins of your life. You don't need an instrument and you don't need other people and you can do it any time of the day or night without making noise..."

"But I don't do it," I say. I sympathized with him up until this point, but his new assumption makes me angry. "I haven't written anything since I moved here."

"Really? I thought in the mornings..."

"Scotty gets up at six, and I can't wake up earlier than that. If I don't get enough sleep, I have no patience with the kids."

"I didn't know," Luke says. "I'll take Scotty every morning. If I'm not awake, wake me up."

"Sometimes you're getting things done for work."

"Then he can sit next to me and watch TV. Take that time for yourself."

I smile. I expected to struggle to find time to write, but Luke is giving me my mornings back without hesitation. "That would help," I say. "And maybe we can make time for music and writing on the weekends—you can take an hour on Saturday and I'll take one on Sunday..."

"All right. My songs will probably never leave this apartment, but at least I'll get them out of my head."

I hug him. "I'm sorry. I like listening to your music..."

"And I'm glad I can share it with you. But it's a blow to the ego, knowing that Sylvie is making it and I can't."

"Do you think her song is about you?"

"I doubt it," he says. "She was never one to write her own music. Her voice is incredible and she's the most driven person I've ever met, but she's a performer; she doesn't need to create. She would have been happy as an actress or a model instead of a singer as long as she got to be famous. All she wanted was to get out of that backwoods town where she grew up and have everybody screaming her name...and she's getting there."

We hear a crash from the living room, and Nate and Scotty start yelling at each other. "On the other hand," Luke says, "this is what I get to deal with." He strides out of the kitchen to break up the fight.

Chapter Nineteen

Over the next few weeks, I feel more fulfilled than when I first moved in with Luke. Writing in the mornings—even when I only get twenty minutes—puts me in a good mood. I get to experience the flow I crave, the flow only writing can give me; it's easier to handle the frustrations of the day when I've already done something for myself. I'm nearing the end of my novel, and I can't wait to write the climactic scenes I've been brainstorming since the beginning. I'll have a lot of revising to do once the first draft is done, but I'm making progress.

Meanwhile, Sylvie is all over the radio and social media. I checked out her Instagram page and saw that her style is different now than when we first met; her hair is a natural shade of brown and her clothes are glamorous. She looks beautiful and dangerous and has a large following already, and I'm sure this is only the beginning of her success. Luke is managing his envy better since we talked; he congratulates Sylvie on FaceTime when, after weeks of being too busy, she finally makes time to talk to the kids. Nate and Scotty are delighted to chat with her. After they hang up, Luke takes Scotty into his room to change his diaper, and Nate turns to me. "Is your mama in California too?" he asks.

"No," I say.

"I never saw her. Where is she?"

I pause. I'm not sure how Luke wants me to respond. "Um," I say. "My mama...well...my mama died a long time ago."

"Died?" Nate's eyes are wide. "Your mama died?"

"Drop it, Nate," Luke says from the other room. "She doesn't want to talk about this."

"It's all right," I say.

"Why did she die?" Nate asks.

"She was in an accident."

"Where did she go?"

I choose my words carefully. I'm determined to handle this question better than my dad did—to offer a little hope, even if I don't believe in the hope myself. "Nobody knows what happens when you die," I say. "Some people think that you start life again as something else—a plant or an animal or a new person. Some people think that you go to heaven, where you're happy forever and you get to see everyone who died in the past."

"So when I go to heaven, I'll see your mama," Nate says.

"That's what some people believe."

"But I won't see you or Daddy or Scotty anymore?"

"Don't worry, buddy," Luke says. He's joined us in the living room, and there are tears in his eyes. "You're not going to heaven anytime soon. None of us are."

"Why?" Nate says.

"Because there's no better place than where we are now, together." Luke kisses Nate. "As long as you don't do anything dangerous, we'll always be together."

"As long as I don't run in the street," Nate says. "Or touch that thing on the wall where the plugs go in."

"Right."

Nate turns to his brother. "Scotty, listen to Daddy's rules so you don't die!"

The conversation lingers on my mind until later that night, after the boys have gone to sleep. My mom's journal is in the dresser drawer where I left it when I first unpacked; living with Luke and the kids has been so chaotic that I never got a chance to read it. Luke is in the bathroom, so I get into bed and open the journal. On the inside cover, before the first entry, I find a dedication to me:

My sweet beautiful amazing Gemma,

I started writing this journal when I was pregnant with you. Like my other journals, it was a place for me to work through my thoughts and feelings—so not all the entries are happy! I hope you don't think I spent your babyhood complaining about you. You've brought me more joy than anything in the world and I love you more than breathing. But the transition to motherhood isn't easy, and since you're going through it now (a CRAZY concept I can't wrap my head around, as I'm looking at you sleeping in your crib!), I wanted to share my experiences with you. I'm grateful that I had other mothers as friends while you were a baby—your dad's sisters, brash as they can be, were a big help—because it made me feel less alone. Remember that you're not alone, and that everything you're feeling is okay. It's okay to love your children and still be sad and frustrated and angry sometimes. It's okay to be TIRED and to long for the bliss of a life without worries. I promise the wonderful moments in motherhood, even if they're few and far between, will outweigh the pain. You can always talk to me when you need advice, but I'm giving you this journal because I assume that my memories, along with the emotional intensity of these early months, will fade over time. There's nothing so relatable as the raw honest truth scribbled down in the moment! Feel free to ask me about anything you read in these pages. I love you so so much!

Love,

Mom

I read the words over and over, imagining my mom sitting next to my crib as she wrote. It pains me to see the sentence: *Feel free to ask me about anything you read in these pages.* My mom thought she would be here to talk about her experiences, that this journal would be the starting point of our conversation. But the journal is all I have. I read the dedication once more, and I see that it has a date in October 1989, when

I was eight months old. I move on to the first journal entry, which is dated more than a year earlier, when my mom found out she was pregnant with me.

There are several entries scattered throughout the months of my mom's pregnancy. She writes about her body changing, about feeling me move, about her fear of birth and her excitement to meet me. She describes how becoming a mother is making her grieve for her own mother again. *Mom, you were my guide through everything while I was growing up,* she writes. *I need you now more than ever and you're not here. How am I supposed to figure this out on my own? I wish you could hug me and tell me you love me and make everything better.* I sympathize with my mom—I'm parenting without my mother too—but I'll admit I don't share her feelings. I can't miss my mom's advice because I've never had it; I don't have twenty years of memories to reflect on like she did with her mom. Instead, everything I know about my mom has been pieced together from pictures and writing and other people's stories. I'm sure my grief would be more intense if I could remember her...but maybe it would be less empty and isolating, too. I've always felt that my mom's death was my dad's loss more than mine; I've never been sure how to mourn her. I turn to the next page, to an entry from when my mom was six months pregnant and still working for Elliot Wahl, a theater producer in New York:

When I had lunch with Dana today, she asked if I'd found a daycare for Gemma. I told her we were still figuring things out, and she started singing the praises of some expensive daycare in Brooklyn where she sends her kids. "They potty trained Madelyn for me," Dana said. "And they made David stop sucking his thumb. They're miracle workers." She told me her kids have been in daycare since they were two months old, and I said that must have been tough for her. "It was, but I had to keep working," she said. "And the teachers there are so nurturing, and so good with the parents too. They wanted me to see all the firsts. I remember picking Madelyn up one day, and she pulled herself up on a chair and took two steps toward me. I started crying; I'd never seen her walk before! The teacher said Madelyn had been taking steps for a week, but they hadn't told me because they wanted me to experience it for myself. They think about things like that, about how the moms feel."

My brain stayed stuck on that thought for the rest of the day—Dana missed her daughter's first steps! And the same thing is going to happen to me. I'm the one carrying and protecting and CREATING Gemma, but once she's born, someone else will see her milestones because I'll be at work. At least Gio gets home at four, and his sisters work part time; they'll get quality time with their kids. I don't get home until seven, and I'm exhausted from the commute and Elliot's petty demands. Elliot...he's selfish and arrogant and doesn't value anything I do! If my work were meaningful I might feel differently, but kissing Elliot's ass just to stay in the theater industry is worth nothing in comparison to being with Gemma.

When I got home from work, I broke down sobbing to Gio. He's such a good man—so calm, so supportive. He held me close and said, "If you want to stay home with the baby, stay home. Leave your job." I started rambling about money and he said, "Let's try it the first year and see how it goes. We have money in the savings that your parents left us. We'll tighten up our spending; we won't need to pay for a second car or your commute to the city. I'll tutor over the summer, and I'm bringing home more money now that I run the drama program at school. We'll make it work."

I don't know how it will work, but the fact that Gio is willing to try it gives me hope. I'll go to the office right up until my due date and I swear I won't buy anything except food and diapers as long as I can stay home with Gemma. It would mean the world to me to have the first year at home, even if I have to go back to work after that. I'll be there for her first steps and her first words and I'll spend every day with her without having to rush anywhere. I can't wait to see her little face and to have her next to me, where she belongs.

This last paragraph brings me to tears. My mom didn't get a full year with me; she only made it nine months. Still, she was there for many of the firsts she longed to see—my first word, which was "Mama," and my first steps. My dad saw both of those milestones too; he told me that I started walking early, at eight months old. "You were a strong baby," he said. "You used to put your hands on the floor and push yourself up to standing without holding anything. Your mother said you'd be an athlete." I wish I could remember my mom saying that. I wish I could remember anything about her—the sound of her voice or her facial expressions or the colors she wore. All her love and all the time she spent with me has faded into oblivion, and there's no way to get it back.

Luke comes out of the bathroom, sees my face, and looks startled. "Baby—are you crying?" He wraps his arms around me. "What's wrong?"

I show him the journal and explain how my dad gave it to me. "I've only read a few entries," I say. "But it's hard to get through it, knowing how the story ends..."

"I'm sorry. And I'm sorry if Nate hurt you before. It wasn't right for him to—"

"He's a kid," I say. "He's supposed to ask us those questions. And I want to read this journal—I want to feel these feelings. It's just a lot at once...I'll have to take breaks."

"Is there any way I can help?"

I lean my head against him. I like listening to his voice up close, inside his chest; it's a soothing sound, the way his heartbeat is soothing. "Talk to me," I say.

"About what?"

"About anything. Your voice makes me feel better."

"Okay." He kisses my head. "Well...Nate read a picture book by himself today. It was a new book from the library, not one he'd memorized. He recognized the sight words we've been working on, and he sounded out some tough words..."

For the next week, I try to read one journal entry a day. Sometimes I'll fit it in on my lunch break, if the girls at the office are eating at their desks; sometimes I'll take the journal into the kitchen when I'm cooking. I keep it in my purse so it's always close by when I have a few minutes. I never took my mom's other journals out of the house, and I like carrying this one around; it feels like my mom is with me wherever I go. This morning after breakfast, I read about my mom's birth and my parents bringing me home from the hospital. I'm eager to read more, but I'm also expecting the rest of the entries to make me emotional. It'll be hard not to cry when I see the first months of my life through my mom's eyes.

It's Saturday, and Nora and Harry offer to babysit for a few hours. This gives me and Luke the chance to exercise and run errands without the kids in tow. When I get back from the supermarket, I find that the car track, Nate's present from Sylvie, has arrived; it was on backorder for weeks. Nate is ecstatic, and he begs Luke to put it together the moment he gets home. Luke opens the box, and I join Harry and Nora on the couch.

The track is huge and made up of a million brightly colored pieces. Both Scotty and Nate are hovering around Luke, grabbing parts of the track. "Come here, boys," Harry says. "Give Daddy space to work."

"I want to help!" Nate says.

"Here—put stickers on that orange thing," Luke says, handing Nate a sheet of stickers. Luke goes back to trying to connect two pieces that are giving him trouble. "Why won't this—motherfucker!"

"Luke!" Nora snaps.

The kids laugh. Luke is clutching his finger, which is bleeding; it got caught on the jagged edge of the piece he was holding. He gets up, puts the sharp piece on a shelf where the boys can't reach it, and heads to the bathroom. "I'll finish the track in a minute," he says. I follow him.

"I bought bigger Band-Aids," I tell him. "Those flimsy Disney ones don't cover anything." Luke wraps a towel around the gash in his finger. "Wow, you sliced yourself pretty badly..."

"I'm an idiot." He's furious. "Some men fix houses and I can't even put together a toy."

"That doesn't matter." I hand him a Band-Aid. "You're still the greatest man I know."

"Yeah? Why?"

"Because you're all heart. You have an infinite capacity for love; it keeps pouring out of you in everything you do. Your devotion to me and the boys gives us courage—courage to believe in ourselves, to be the best people we can be."

His face is red. "You're giving me too much credit."

"You deserve it." I kiss his injured finger, then his palms. At times my affection for him is so big it feels savage; I'd fight packs of wolves to protect his hands. "My God, I love you so much..."

We both glance up to see Nora standing in the doorway. "Nate is looking for Speedy," she says. "I'm not sure which car that is, but it wasn't in the bucket with the others."

"He had it in the mud yesterday—it's on the kitchen sink," Luke says. "I'll wash it—"

"Don't get your hands wet!" I say. "You just put on a Band-Aid."

"I'll wash it," Nora says. She smiles at us. For once, her smile doesn't seem forced; her eyes are in it, and she's looking at me more kindly than usual. "No worries."

She leaves the room. I glance at Luke, wondering if he noticed his mom's expression, but he's wincing as he adjusts the Band-Aid on his finger. Over the past few months, Nora has made an effort to be friendly to me, but I'm still not comfortable around her; I can't shake the feeling that she's waiting for me to do something wrong. "It's not your fault," Luke said when I brought it up. "That's my mom—scared of everything she can't control. It takes forever for her to trust people, even when they've been nothing but wonderful to her. But that's her problem—it doesn't change how I feel about you—"

"I don't know how you two get along," I said.

"We disagree about a lot of things," he said. "But she loves me—she's always been there for me, no matter what. And she would be there for you if you needed her, because you matter to me. Once you're in her circle, you can count on her; it's just rare for her to let her guard down."

This explanation, though it made sense, was frustrating. I've done enough by now to show I'm worthy of Luke; Nora has no reason not to approve of me. For a while I assumed she would never like me, but her reaction today—in a moment when I was showing my emotions without restraint—changed my mind. Nora isn't a cold person; she adores the kids, and she's never done anything malicious to me. Maybe we will have a good relationship someday.

***

I'm halfway through my mom's journal, and I don't want it to end. Her writing ranges from glowing descriptions of her love for me to rants about how hard it is to be a parent. Some of the entries make me laugh:

Painted my toenails today. Felt almost human.

Some of them are desperate:

Now that I'm a mom, it's like my feelings have ceased to exist. All people want to talk about is Gemma. "How's the baby?" they ask. "Is she eating? Is she sleeping? Is she rolling over yet, or trying to hold things?" Is anybody going to ask if I'm okay? Anybody?

Some of them are so relatable I could have written them myself:

I know it's selfish, but I miss writing. I'm a shell of myself without it. I used to think I'd have more time to write once I left my job—what a ridiculous assumption! It's infinitely easier to write on the train or on a lunch break at work than to get five minutes to do ANYTHING with a baby around. Gemma and her unpredictable routines (Why won't she nap on schedule? Why?) control every moment of my life. When she does fall asleep, I can't waste time writing—there are bottles to boil and clothes to wash and messes to clean. Some days I don't get time to shower, let alone craft beautiful sentences.

I have no right to complain, because I'm lucky I get to be home with Gemma. We've sacrificed a lot to support this family with one income, and I'm grateful I don't have to go to work. Still, it's been a tough adjustment. I've lost my identity; I don't even know how to speak to adults anymore. Thank God Dee comes over on Mondays with baby Ant, otherwise I'd have no connection to the outside world other than Gio—and Gio makes my life harder, not easier. He burdens me with his problems at school and expects sex when I'm not in the mood. He tries to help with Gemma but has no common sense—he'll get her riled up and laughing before bedtime and then she'll refuse to fall asleep! I love Gio, but staying in love with him is work; it never felt like work before. And he loves me, but the problem is he wants all of me all the time. Everyone wants all of me and there's nothing left to save for myself.

I hold onto that phrase: *Everyone wants all of me*. It captures how I feel. I love Luke and the kids and I know they love me, but they can be a drain; I give and give and they always need more. I used to feel guilty for not having enough energy—for losing patience with Luke or sleeping late instead of writing or saying no at times when the kids ask me to play. Now I realize there's nothing wrong with me; other parents are exhausted too. All the love in the world can't make me a superhero.

I read one more entry, since the next one is short. My mom starts by speaking directly to me:

Gemma, I've decided that I'm going to share this journal with you someday. I never got started on that baby book, but I've recorded enough milestones in here to replace that. I have so much advice I want to give you...

She goes on to mention what she's learned from feeding me solid foods. When I finish the entry, I turn off the oven. Dinner is ready; I head to the living room to get Luke and the kids.

Chapter Twenty

It's the morning of Nate's preschool graduation. Despite a battle over the bathroom and the cereal that Scotty spilled on the floor, we manage to get everyone out the door on time. The preschool backyard is decorated with banners and balloons and the kids are wearing caps and gowns. Luke, Scotty, and I take seats next to Aunt Soph. The ceremony is adorable; the kids sing songs and dance. Nate keeps breaking away from the line of kids and waving to us, his dark curls poking out from under his hat. After the teachers give out diplomas, they invite everyone to stay for refreshments. Scotty takes off running around the yard and Luke chases him, and I join Nate and his friends near a table of desserts. A bubbly woman with a big smile turns to me. "Hi!" she says. "I'm Liz, Dennis's mom. You must be Nate's mom!"

"She's not my mom," Nate says through a mouthful of cupcake. "She's my Gemma."

He states this as a fact, not an insult, but it stings. "Um," I say. "Yeah, um...I'm his dad's girlfriend."

"Oh," Liz says. "I was wondering why I'd never seen...anyway." She recovers her enthusiasm. "We should get the kids together for a play date this summer! Do you want to exchange numbers?"

I start chatting with Liz, but my heart isn't in it. I should have explained my situation better; I should have made it clear that I'm responsible for Nate. Instead I shortchanged myself in front of her and the parents around us by using the word "girlfriend." I might as well have said, "Don't mind me, I'm just some chick who's having sex with Nate's dad." None of these people understand that I live with the kids and take care of them; I'm essentially a parent but I don't get the title. I'm embarrassed and looking for a way out of the conversation when Luke comes up to me. "Check it out," he says, handing me Nate's report card. "We've got a genius on our hands."

I look at the report card. Nate's marks are high in every category, and his teacher wrote comments at the end:

Nate has exceptional verbal ability. His speaking is advanced and he has begun to read independently. He is also skilled in math, art, and music and is well behaved. Early in the year he struggled to make friends; he preferred talking to adults and didn't know how to join other children's games. However, he has greatly improved in this area and I'm sure he will do well in kindergarten.

These words lift my mood. I'm proud of Nate for succeeding in school, and his report card feels like a compliment; Luke and I must be doing something right if Nate is achieving. "Great job, buddy," I say to Nate. "Your grades in school are awesome! I bet you're working really hard."

"I do a lot of worksheets," he says. "And I can hold the pencil without the gripper! Can I have another cupcake?"

Later that day, I start making dinner while Luke is playing with the kids. My mom's journal is on the counter where I left it three days ago. I've been putting off reading because there are only two entries left, and I don't want the journal to end; once it's over, I'll never hear anything new from my mom again. Still, I'm curious about what the entries say. I keep glancing at the journal as I'm cooking, and eventually I open it up.

The next entry leaves me feeling torn. My mom's words would be inspiring under other circumstances, but because she died soon after writing them, they seem hollow. I read the entry several times and feel more and more hopeless. The washing machine beeps, and Luke comes into the kitchen to switch the clothes to the dryer. He glances at me. "What's the matter?"

He reads me so well. "Something from my mom's journal," I say.

"Do you want to talk about it?"

I hand him the journal. It might be a relief to share my thoughts. "Yeah. Read this entry."

I watch Luke's eyes scanning the passage:

Here's my most important piece of advice, Gemma: Find the activity that soothes your soul and never stop doing it. I gave up writing when I became a mom, telling myself it was a useless indulgence—that housework was more important. But the chores never end, and no matter how much I get done, I never feel accomplished. I've been resentful of you not because I don't love you—my heart swells with joy every time you laugh—but because I don't love myself. I was running on empty and telling myself to suck it up; I didn't realize I was heading for a meltdown. Last Sunday, you knocked your bowl of oatmeal onto the floor—without eating a single bite—after I spent precious time making it and mixing in the fruit you like. There was food EVERYWHERE—on you and me and the hardwood floor and the rug—and I lost it. I screamed every curse word in the book and started throwing things across the room. You cried, of course, and that made me yell more, because I was angry with myself. Gio came in and I lashed out at him and he told me to go upstairs and take a break. I got into bed and sobbed because I was a failure, because I had given up everything to be a good mother and I was a terrible mother. I was desperate for comfort—for any escape from my self-loathing—and there was one place in my mind that had always brought me peace. I started writing my novel again. I wrote for FORTY-FIVE MINUTES. And that gave me the strength to go back downstairs. That afternoon, I actually enjoyed playing with you; I wasn't counting the hours until your next nap. Doing creative work made all the difference.

I talked to Gio, and we figured out a way to fit writing back into my life. The moment he gets home from work, he takes care of you by himself for half an hour, and I get to write. He knows not to interrupt me for ANYTHING during those thirty minutes. We've been sticking to this routine for a week and it's made me feel much better. Usually I come downstairs to find you in a food-stained onesie with your hair disheveled, but who cares? You're happy, and I'm writing again. Progress is slow...I can't get much done in thirty minutes...but that doesn't bother me. I'll finish my novel eventually, even if it takes years. The important thing is to keep working, to keep writing alive in me.

Gemma, whatever it is that you love, it is worth doing. Pursuing your passion isn't selfish; in fact, it will make you a BETTER mom and wife and human. That's worth more than a load of laundry or a clean house, I promise.

"This is great advice," Luke says. "Do you feel this way too—like you need more time to write?"

"It's not that," I say. "My mom died two weeks after writing this entry. She thought she'd have years to write her novel; she was working towards a future she never got. She didn't realize her new routine was useless, that she wouldn't accomplish anything she set out to do..."

"Anything?"

"She never finished the novel; she had a few scenes written when she died, and no outline. Nobody will ever know what was inside her head. And her sacrifices for me—how she gave up everything to be a good mother, like she wrote—went unrecognized too. I don't remember her."

"Memories aren't all that matters," Luke says. "If we died today, Scotty wouldn't remember us when he was an adult, and Nate would have vague memories at best. But they'd carry the love we gave them throughout their lives. The time we spend with our kids shapes who they become, even if they don't remember what we did. And you turned out to be an amazing person—"

"But she didn't get to see that!" The words burst out of me. "She was supposed to watch me grow up—that's what every parent deserves! She should have been there to take me to school and hockey games, to teach me how to read and ride a bike, to go on vacation with me and see me graduate from college. But she didn't have any of those experiences. She never even heard me saying I loved her. All she got out of motherhood was suffering, no satisfaction."

"It couldn't all have been suffering, if she loved you so much…"

"You don't know that. Don't oversimplify things when you don't know how she felt."

Luke is quiet; he knows there's nothing else he can say. He hugs me. "I'm sorry, baby."

I'm shaking with anger. There's no way to justify my mom's death—no way to accept it. The pain feels more acute now that I've read what she wrote to me; I want to defend her the way I would a close friend. But I can't change what happened to her. Luke's arms are solid and comforting around me; in spite of everything, I feel my body relax. "It's unfair," I say.

"It is."

I hear little footsteps coming into the kitchen. "Daddy," Nate says. "I'm hungry."

"Not now, buddy," Luke says. "Give us a minute."

I pull away from Luke. There's no use talking anymore; I've said what I had to say, and the kids need us. "Do you want eggs or mac and cheese?" I ask Nate. "I know you won't eat the fish I made…"

I feel unsettled for the next few hours, especially once the kids are in bed; when they're not distracting me, my thoughts return to my mom. Luke falls asleep before I do, which is rare, and that makes it harder for me to sleep. I toss and turn for an hour, but I can't stop thinking about what I read. I get out of bed and head to the kitchen. Being awake and on edge makes me reckless—I'm going to finish my mom's journal, finish it now, no matter how much it upsets me. I'm prepared to lose sleep for the rest of the night. I open the journal. The last entry is dated November 14, a few days before my mom died:

The joy is in the little things. The frustration is in the little things, too—the diaper explosions and spilled formula and that last strawberry I wanted to eat but gave to you instead. Once kids are in the picture, every grand love story—including mine and Gio's—gets reduced to petty arguments over laundry. But the joys, though they're little, are overwhelming. It's three A.M., and you were up for the past hour with a fever. Tylenol brought it down but you were cranky, so I rocked and rocked you to try to get you to sleep. Eventually I got tired and stretched out on the floor with you, and you climbed onto my stomach, grabbed my face, and pressed your mouth to my cheek. It's the first time you've kissed me and though it was a slobbery mess, my heart was brimming over with love. You said, "Mama," and curled up next to me and fell asleep. Now I'm watching you go through a range of emotions in your sleep—you knit your eyebrows together like you're about to cry, raise one eyebrow in disbelief, and smile a wide, delighted smile. I wish I knew what you were dreaming. Someday you'll be able to tell me.

I used to think of the future and imagine the grand things I would do: I'd write Broadway plays (yeah, right) and travel the world (not on our budget—these days I wear ripped sweatpants and only buy groceries that are on sale). But all of that seems extraneous now that I have you. You're my greatest achievement, my greatest love. I want nothing more than a life filled with little joys.

I can barely make out the last sentence because I'm crying so hard. That's it. That's the end. I'm sad, but I'm also grateful—grateful for the time my mom gave me, and grateful that she left me this journal. I can return to it anytime I want to hear her voice, just like I return to the worlds in my favorite books. It's not the same as having her beside me, but it's something to hold onto. I read the last entry one more time, and it frees me from the guilt I felt earlier. My mom was happy with me after all; I wasn't only a burden to her. She knew I loved her, even if I couldn't say it out loud. I search through the kitchen drawers for a pen. I'm going to write back to my mom—to tell her what this journal meant to me. I know she's gone and she won't read it, but I have to get my thoughts on paper like she did. I put today's date in the empty space under the last entry, and then I start to write:

Dear Mom,

Thank you for this journal. Your writing gave voice to many of my feelings—feelings I was ashamed of, or didn't fully explore, until you put them into words. Thank you for making me feel understood, for being honest, for sharing your advice. And thank you for everything you did for me as a baby. I wish you were still here. I wish you'd had enough time...

I pause. What's enough time? Maybe none of us get enough time, no matter how many years we live. A lifetime is always too short when we're surrounded by people we love. I want to be there for every moment of Nate and Scotty's lives—every struggle, every triumph. I don't want to miss a second. And the same goes for Luke; if I spent a million years with him, I would still want more. I go back to writing:

I'm in love with a man named Luke and I'm helping him raise his sons. I love those kids like they're mine, even if they're not. I promise I'll cherish every moment I get with them, the way you did with me. I'll hold this family close to me until my last breath...

I write for a long time, write everything that's on my mind, until my tears stop flowing. I study the spot in the journal where my words follow my mom's. My handwriting is messy like hers, but mine is print, not cursive, with simpler letters and more space between words. I like seeing our writing together on one page, like we're talking to each other. I close the book and hug it to my chest. Then I get up and go to Scotty's room.

I always check on the boys when I'm awake in the middle of the night—not to make sure they're breathing, like Luke does, but because seeing them at peace brings me peace. Scotty is asleep with his thumb in his mouth and his blankie pressed to his cheek. I smooth down his wild hair and give him a kiss. Nate's room is next. He's splayed out across the bed; his arms are flung to the sides and his bedtime toys have fallen to the floor. His brow is furrowed like sleep is hard work that demands all his concentration. I line his toys up around him and I kiss him too.

Then I go back to my bed, back to Luke. He's fast asleep, but the second I lie down, his arm is around me and he's pulling me close to him. I settle into the warmth of his body, the rhythm of his breathing. I kiss the soft hair on his arm and I fall asleep.

Chapter Twenty-One

Ever since I finished my mom's journal, I've been making an effort to enjoy Nate and Scotty. I play with them more often and pay less attention to the housework. It took practice to learn to focus on a pretend game when there are piles of laundry in the room, but now that I can do it, I've found that I'm happier. My mom was right—the housework never ends—so my only goal is to have enough clean clothes and dishes to get through the day. It's liberating to join Luke and the kids on the floor to build with blocks or to squeeze glitter glue all over crafts without worrying about the mess; the mess gets cleaned up somehow, and the kids benefit from the attention. The apartment is still neater than it was before I moved in, and I delegate specific tasks to Luke, which he makes sure to get done. I'm exhausted as always, but I feel more satisfied at the end of each day.

On the other hand, writing has become a source of disappointment. I finished the first draft of my novel, so I've started revising—a process that is frustrating on the best days and soul-crushing on the worst. Nothing hurts the ego more than evaluating work you've put your heart into for hundreds of hours and deciding what to throw away. My novel is nowhere near as good as it seemed when I was writing it; the thrill of creating gave every scene a promising glow that has now disappeared. All I can see are the flaws. The book is too long, and there are plot points that need to be reworked, and I have to cut out a character I love because her storyline is distracting, and the battle scene I thought was so moving is full of cliches, and why am I doing this? Why am I pretending to be a writer when I have no talent? I return to writing every day because it's the only way to finish this book and I need to finish, but every move I make feels futile.

"The task is insurmountable," I told Luke the other day. "It's like I have to give a haircut to an enormous beast—a beast with miles upon miles of fur—and every morning, I cut one hair."

"Then you'll get there eventually," he said.

When the kids leave for L.A, I'll get more time to write, but I'm dreading it now that revising is a struggle. Luke is sad the kids will be gone for the month; he's not as panicked as he was last year, but he has new concerns. Sylvie's latest single is in the top ten of the *Billboard* Hot 100 chart and this achievement, along with her highly publicized breakup with some famous actor, has made her the subject of many magazine and internet articles. "I hope Sylvie can avoid the paparazzi while the kids are there," Luke says. "I don't want them exposed to that shit..."

"There's not much we can do about it," I say. "We should talk to Nate and Scotty beforehand about what might happen."

After we drop the kids to Sylvie at the airport, Luke and I share a quiet, somber morning together. We're both thinking of all the hours stretching between now and September 1, when we can get Nate and Scotty back. The dark mood doesn't lift until we have sex that afternoon, which releases our tension. We cuddle in bed for a long time, enjoying each other's attention. When we get up to make dinner, Luke looks at his phone. "Hey," he says. "Carter bought a house."

It takes me a minute to place the name; finally, I remember the guitarist Luke played with that night at The Garage. "Your friend from Berklee?" I say.

"Yeah. He says he got a place in Montclair, and he's having a housewarming party next week."

"Wow," I say. "Houses in Montclair are expensive!"

"He's loaded—his parents make millions." Luke starts typing a response. "Do you want to go to the party? It should be fun."

"Sure, if you want."

The night of Carter's party is hot and humid, and I'm apprehensive as we drive into Montclair. Luke and I never make time for friends, unless you count the girls at the office; we've had playdates with Nate's preschool friends and chatted with the parents, but we're not close with them. I rarely interact with anyone who isn't a parent and I've forgotten what people my age care about. What is there to talk about other than the kids? Luke is excited for the party, though, so I try to be enthusiastic. We pull up on a side street close to Bloomfield Avenue and head toward Carter's house. It's not a huge house, but it has nice curb appeal, with beautiful bay windows and a porch. I'm trying to guess how much it cost when Carter opens the door.

Inside, we find groups of people gathered in the living room and dining room. Luke and I give Carter his gift, grab a drink, and mingle for a bit. We end up in conversation with Carter and his friends about how they saw some band I've never heard of in concert. Luke knows the band and has a lot to say, but I'm quiet, observing the crowd. Two girls near me are gossiping about a friend of theirs and the sleazy guys she's been dating, and another group is making plans to meet at a microbrewery. Everyone has been nice to us, but it feels like they live in a different world than we do; they're young and carefree and trendy. I glance at my appearance, then at Luke's. Looking cool is mostly about wearing the right shoes, and my cheap rubber flip flops and Luke's old athletic sneakers make it clear that we are not cool. Yet Luke's demeanor changes when he's with Carter; he stands straighter and speaks with an unfamiliar swagger. He's stepped into another version of himself—his stage persona, the front man in a rock band—and I don't like it. I like my raw, sincere, sensitive Luke, who is moved by everything and isn't afraid to show it. When I see him feign confidence with Carter, I can picture the guy who got his first tattoo because his friends were egging him on. I shouldn't complain—Luke's arm is around my waist, and he's showing me plenty of affection as usual—but I'm disillusioned. I never imagined he could be phony.

I'm still uncomfortable when Carter leads me and Luke into his music studio, a room at the back of the house. There is a baby grand piano inside along with a keyboard and several guitars and amps. "Man, fuck you," Luke says, looking around. "Having a room like this in your house..."

"Makes you want to get back out there, right?" Carter says.

Luke picks up one of the guitars, and the two of them start talking about brands and gear. None of it makes sense to me, so I tune them out and think back to a scene from my novel that I was revising earlier today. I've just decided which lines of dialogue I want to cut when the piano interrupts my thoughts. Luke has played a melody that sounds familiar. "You moved this big guy from your parents' house?" he says to Carter.

"Yeah—what a pain in the ass..."

"You play piano?" I ask Luke, feeling bewildered.

"Only a little," he says. "Enough to work out melodies for songs—I can't play Bach or anything. Carter can..."

"I've been playing piano since I was five," Carter says. "I was classically trained for years, then I tried jazz, and then I picked up the guitar in high school. I never stopped playing piano, but I haven't been a pianist in a band in years, until now. I just started a piano rock group." He turns to Luke. "Matt is playing bass, and I met this awesome drummer—my ex Daphne, you remember her, she introduced us..."

Carter goes on to describe his band, and Luke seems fascinated. "I'm hitting a roadblock with lyrics, though," Carter says. "The other guys expect me to write the songs, but I don't like to work alone. Me and you used to come up with some sick shit together..."

"I remember," Luke says.

"I've written plenty of songs, but the lyrics suck; I can't put words together the way you do. Luke is an incredible lyricist," Carter says to me.

"That won't impress her," Luke says. "She's a better writer than I am."

"Yeah?" Carter says. "You write songs?"

"Novels," I say.

"Oh." He looks back at Luke. "Anyway, do you want to be in the band? I have a guitarist but I can get rid of him..."

"You know I don't have time," Luke says.

"Why not? Gemma will watch the kids for you."

This is a presumptuous comment, and I expect Luke to defend me. Instead he nods; he seems deep in thought. "Maybe."

"Don't you want to see him perform again?" Carter asks me.

"I want him to be happy," I say.

"There you go," Carter says to Luke. "Come jam with us on Sunday and see what you think."

We rejoin the rest of the party and spend more time chatting with people I have nothing in common with. I'm grateful when it's time to leave. We get into the car and Luke starts driving home. "You don't mind if I jam with Carter's band this weekend, right?" he says. "We didn't have any plans..."

"Whatever. Do what you want."

"Are you mad at me?"

"No." I take his hand. "I just...didn't like the vibe at that party."

"It's not our usual crowd."

"We don't have a crowd."

"Sure we do," he says. "Spiky, and the other dragons." I smile in spite of myself. "The party was weird but I'm glad we went. Carter's a good friend."

"He seems a little arrogant," I say.

"He is, but he's brilliant. He's taught me a lot. And there's this magic when we play together—we can read each other, and we bring out the best in each other. I've created music with him I couldn't have made on my own."

"I respect that. But I don't like..." I want to say I don't like who he is around Carter, but I have to phrase it in a way that won't be insulting.

"I don't like seeing you pretend…feeling like we have to pretend…"

"Pretend to be cool when we're not?"

"That's exactly it."

He laughs and kisses my hand. "You're so real. I love you so much."

We pull up to a red light, and Luke turns to me. I look into those eyes I adore and feel a pang of loss—like he's slipping away from me. "Don't change," I say.

"Change?"

The light turns green, but Luke keeps his eyes on me. "I like the way you are with me," I say. "The way you truly are. Please stay that way."

"Of course—always."

A car horn beeps behind us, and Luke goes back to driving. "I'm sorry if I upset you," he says. "But trying to fit in at a party doesn't change who I am."

"I get it." I lean my head on his arm. I know I'm overreacting; I can't expect Luke to be wonderful all the time. Still, I have a sinking feeling in my gut about him hanging out with Carter. "Forget I said anything."

***

Luke is elated when he returns from his jam session on Sunday. He tells me about the music he played and the chemistry he had with the other musicians. This is Luke at his best, fully immersed in what he's feeling—his eyes are glowing and the words keep gushing out of him. "Do you think we could make it work?" he asks. "For me to join the band? It's not a huge time commitment—rehearsal on Tuesday nights, and a gig every once in a while…"

I'm torn. We're overwhelmed with responsibilities already, and I can't imagine having Luke away for several hours a week. But how can I deny him the thing he loves most? I can take care of the boys; Luke carved out time for me to write, and I'll do the same for him. "If it's only a few hours," I say. "And you really want to…"

"That would be amazing! Thank you so much."

At first, I'm not bothered by the Tuesday night rehearsal; I hang out with my dad to pass the time. Luke's band, Spare Keys, has two bar gigs before the boys come home, and I go to both shows. Spare Keys' style of music is different from Orange Line's, but they sound great, and I love hearing where the band has taken Luke's songs. The demos that have played in my head many times are fleshed out onstage, made fuller and more powerful with all the instruments. I would prefer to hear the songs in Luke's voice—Carter is the lead singer—but still I enjoy them. Luke is having the time of his life and it's a thrill to see him perform, and to have him find me and grab me after the show. He's always riled up in those moments and can't keep his hands off me; usually I'd tell him to be appropriate in public but I get caught up in the smell of his sweat and the energy pulsing through the room. I don't care what anyone thinks, I want him kissing me and touching me and when we get home I'm going to tear off his clothes...

Soon enough, the kids are back from L.A. and the excitement is over. I can't go to gigs because I'm watching the boys, and one night of rehearsal a week turns into two, and the bedtime routine is exhausting when I handle it by myself. Luke has also started practicing guitar at night, and that cuts into our time together. Falling asleep in his arms has become a thing of the past; he'll hang around long enough to have sex if I'm in the mood, but then it's straight to his music. I know he has to practice somehow, but I miss cuddling with him; I didn't realize how much I relied on him to fall asleep.

Luke's new schedule isn't the only source of stress at home. Nate has started kindergarten and is struggling to adjust. "How was school?" I asked him the first day. "Did you make new friends?"

"No," Nate said. "The kids are mean."

"Mean? What did they do?"

"They don't listen to the teacher. And Devin said my shoes are stupid—that only babies wear light-up shoes."

"That's not true," I said.

"He wouldn't let me play tag with him and the other boys at recess. And Michela is in the other class and all her friends are girls and it's weird to be the only boy playing with girls."

"Then what did you do at recess?" I asked.

"I played by myself."

This made me want to cry. Nate had been excited when we took him to school in the morning; none of us expected him to be lonely. "I'm sorry, buddy," I say. "But it was only the first day—you'll make friends! I'm sure some of the kids in your class are nice."

"I guess."

"And don't worry about what the mean kids say—they're jealous because you're smarter than them."

Over the next few weeks, Nate's social life doesn't improve. Devin keeps making fun of him, and he hasn't made any friends in his class. Luke shared his concerns with Nate's teacher, who seemed indifferent and told him all kids fit in eventually. Luke is livid. "When I meet Devin's parents, I'm going to give them a piece of my mind," he says. "That shithead is ruining everything for Nate, and the teacher can't be bothered to control him. I've never seen his mom or dad at dropoff but when I do..."

"Don't be a helicopter parent," I say. "I'm upset too, but we have to teach Nate to fight his own battles."

"Teach him to kick Devin's ass?" Luke says.

"Not exactly..."

We talk to Nate and share strategies for dealing with Devin. Still, he comes home from school unhappy, and he's started taking his frustration out on his brother. The boys used to play well together, but now Nate shouts at Scotty, yanks toys out of his hand, and refuses to share. Luke is quick to punish Nate every time this happens, which makes Nate more furious and prone to tantrums. Today I get home from work to find Nate screaming because Luke banned him from playing with his dinosaurs. "Keep acting like this," Luke yells over Nate's wails. "And I'll take away every toy you have—"

"You're not helping," I say to Luke. "He's not listening when he's screaming."

"He needs to know his behavior is unacceptable!"

"Wait until he's calm to discipline him," I say.

"He's never calm," Luke says. "You don't get it—you're not dealing with his bullshit for hours every day. He torments me and Scotty from the moment he gets home. I have to be firm with him to end this."

After a while, Nate curls up on the edge of the couch, and Luke takes Scotty to change his diaper. I sit down next to Nate, whose face is streaked with tears. "I'm sorry you're having a tough time at school," I say. "That's not fair. But it isn't Scotty's fault, and you can't be mean to him. When you're mad, you can go into the bathroom and scream. Or punch a pillow, or rip paper into tiny pieces. Or count to ten..."

Nate shakes his head and pulls a blanket over his face. "I hate school."

I'm sick to my stomach, wishing I could fix everything for Nate. I want to rip his classmates limb from limb for daring to hurt him—for being cruel to someone so precious and bright and full of joy. "I love you so much," I tell him. "And so do Daddy and Scotty. No matter what happens at school, you always get to come home to us. Try to make this your happy place."

I rub his back, and he puts his head in my lap. I feel his shallow, angry breathing start to get quiet. Then Luke and Scotty come back into the room and the chaos begins again.

Chapter Twenty-Two

It's six A.M., and I hear little feet approaching. I try to hold onto the sentence I'm writing but Scotty's voice interrupts it. "Gemma," he says. "Play cars?"

"Morning, buddy," I say. "Let me get Daddy."

I lean over to wake Luke, though I know it's futile. He had rehearsal last night, and for the past two weeks, he's been too tired to wake up early after rehearsal or a gig. My writing time has been reduced from seven mornings a week to four and I'm scrambling to make up for the lost hours. "Baby," I say to Luke. "Scotty is awake."

He presses his face into his pillow. "Can you take him, please?"

"I'm writing."

"I'm so exhausted..."

I sigh, save the five minutes of progress that I made, and close my computer. "Which car should I be today?" I ask Scotty. "The race car or the taxi?"

When I get to work, I'm still frustrated about the time I gave up this morning; at this rate, I'll never finish my novel. It's a slow day at the office, so I decide to talk to the girls about it. We gather on the couches for a coffee break and I tell them about Luke's band. "He loves playing music," I say. "And parents should be allowed to spend some time outside the house. But how much is too much?"

"There has to be a balance," Erica says. "Something you both can agree on. Artie golfs with his friends once or twice a month, and that eats up a whole Sunday. But he doesn't do it every week, and if I have something to do, he'll skip it. You take turns in a relationship. It can't always be Luke's turn."

"I'm sorry, but this is ridiculous," Bree snaps. "Those kids aren't yours and Luke has you slaving over them? Who does he think he is?"

"They feel like my kids," I say.

"But they're not, and he has no right to make you watch them so he can dick around with his friends," Bree says. "He doesn't even have the decency to buy you a ring before he turns you into a housewife..."

"That's not the point. Marriage isn't a Band-Aid," Lina says. "Gemma, if he proposes to you to try to fix this, don't say yes."

"I won't," I say.

"You've put up with a ton of shit to be with Luke, and this is going too far," Bree says. "Tell him to leave that band or you're leaving him."

This sentence gives me chills. Leave Luke? I expected to be with him for the rest of my life. Yet hearing Bree mention leaving so flippantly makes it seem like a possibility. I could break up with Luke, if I wanted; there's nothing binding me to him except the fact that I love him. And if that love is changing...I push the thought out of my mind.

"It doesn't need to be so extreme," Jasmine says. "I see what Bree is saying, but you don't have to give him an ultimatum. Just tell him he has to cut down on the time he spends with his band, and that you need a break from the kids sometimes too."

I take Jasmine's advice and bring up the subject that night at dinner. Luke has been texting back and forth with Carter, so this gives me an opening. "I know you're happy to be playing music," I say. "But this band has become a bigger commitment than you said originally."

"I didn't expect us to get a following so fast," he says. "At least gigging is bringing in extra money."

This means nothing to me; the money isn't much, and even if it were, I'd rather have him home. "But it's a lot of time away from me and the kids," I say. "Can you scale back? You could at least do one rehearsal a week instead of two…"

"The second rehearsal is for songwriting, that's the thing. We want to write two more good songs so we have a full set list without playing so many covers. Once those songs are done, I'll go back to one night a week."

"But I need time to write too. When you're up late, you don't help me in the mornings."

"I'm sorry, baby. I'll give you time on Saturday."

Saturday would be fine, except that it's Nate's first soccer game with the kindergarten team, and then we have an engagement party for Luke's cousin Marisa and Luke has a gig at night. I can see the day filling up and leaving no space for me. "Getting time to write is important to me," I say.

We're interrupted by a wail from Nate. "Scotty kicked me!"

"Nate kick me," Scotty says, jabbing his finger at Nate.

"Can't you guys get along for five minutes?" I say.

Luke gets up to separate the boys, and that's the end of our conversation. I made my point, but Luke didn't hear it. For the first time, I feel lonely next to him.

Later that night, when Luke falls asleep, I try to work through my feelings. I get a piece of paper and write what's on my mind:

I don't like how much time and energy Luke is dedicating to this band. I'm frustrated that he expects me to take on extra responsibilities without asking how I feel. Doesn't he care how I feel? He used to bend over backwards to make me happy but now he pays no attention to my needs. I don't know how he got so selfish. I don't know why…

I pause. I do know why—because he's passionate about music. I've been obsessed with writing projects before, and it's a blissful feeling. Your mind zones in on one purpose—one sacred idea—and everything you do is directed towards that goal. You create your best work in that state, but you can also end up blinded to everything else, including the people who need you; they become a useless distraction, an interruption. Making art is essential but it's also essential that we leave space in our minds and hearts for the people we love. Nothing is more important than the people we love...right?

I stare at the paper, then scribble my next thought. *Unless Luke loves music more than he loves me.*

The sentence hurts, but I give it my full consideration. I've always assumed Luke loves the kids more than me—this seems natural and acceptable. But beyond the boys, I thought I was his greatest love. He tells me he loves me a hundred times a day. He leaves cute notes in my purse and buys the right brand of tampons even when I forget to put them on the supermarket list. He listens to me...or at least he did before he joined the band. But maybe that affection doesn't match what he feels when he's playing. Maybe he's willing to sacrifice time with me—and my happiness—to dedicate himself to music. He once said he would be a great musician if he could focus his time and energy on his work, and he's doing that now. For a moment, I imagine that all his dreams have come true—that he's famous like Sylvie. How would I feel about dating a rock star? I would hate it! I wouldn't want Luke on the road for weeks at a time, away from me and the kids, playing wild shows and staying up late with pretty groupies flocking around him. Music is sexy up to a point, but the Luke I love is the one who folds laundry while wearing a construction paper crown; I don't care if he never touches the guitar again. Am I wrong to want him in that domestic role, neglecting the artistic side of himself? Maybe I'm the one who's selfish.

It's not my fault! I write with sudden fury. *I'm not the reason he's stuck at home. He has two kids!*

I think back to what Bree said earlier today. Would I feel less resentful if Nate and Scotty were my sons? If Luke and I had made them together, or at least if we were married and I was their stepmother, I would have justification for my suffering. This family would officially be mine, and the world would be able to see why I've given up so much for them. But that wouldn't solve everything. In that scenario, I'd still want Luke to scale back on music and take on more tasks at home; I'd still ask for time to myself. The division of labor is the problem, not the fact that the kids aren't mine. In my heart, Nate and Scotty are my kids. I've force-fed them medicine and rocked them to sleep, cleaned up their shit and vomit, given them every last drop of my energy when my well was running dry. I love them like my kids, and that will never change as long as I live with Luke.

There's only one difference, I write. I feel so guilty that I almost don't put the next thought into words, but I know it will get bigger and more terrifying if I suppress it. *Because they're not my sons, I have no obligation to them. I can leave.*

I picture life without Luke and the kids—a life with no diapers or messes or toddlers asking me to play at six in the morning, with no fights over how to handle bad behavior or school drama. I'd have no responsibilities other than writing and going to work; I could choose what to do with my time. I could sleep as much as I wanted! What a free, glorious existence. I once lived like that and I could do it again, if I'm willing to walk away. I could leave these burdens behind...

I follow the idea further and my dream falls to pieces. Nate and Scotty would feel abandoned—again—if I left. And Luke...he trusts me completely and I can't betray that trust. I do have an obligation to this family; I chose to live here. The three of them love me and I love them and there must be another solution. There must be families out there who do it all, who balance everyone's needs. Maybe Luke and I can raise happy kids while each pursuing our art and working and staying in shape and keeping the house clean and spending time together...but it seems impossible. There isn't enough time! Somebody has to give something up, and I guess that somebody is me.

It's not the worst thing in the world, I write. *My writing isn't worth much; I've never had success with it. But Luke is talented. I've seen the way his music wakes up a room, how it keeps crowds of people under its spell. He should be the one who gets to create and I should be proud to support him. That's what I'm good at, anyway—supporting other people. It's the role I've always played. I'm Michela's favorite babysitter and Aunt Soph's confidant. I'm my dad's motivation for staying alive. I'm even an assistant at the office, doing small tasks for the lawyers so they can focus on important work. Maybe I'm meant to help brilliant, powerful people achieve their goals, and I should be satisfied with that. Maybe I don't need a voice of my own...*

Luke's legs jerk in his sleep, and he stirs. He blinks up at me, puts his hand on my thigh. "You're awake? Are you okay?"

I put the pen down. I can't tell him what I was thinking—that I was imagining my life without him. I fall back on my default response. "I'm fine," I say. "Everything is fine."

Chapter Twenty-Three

It's a crisp morning in October, and Nate just scored his third goal of the season. Everyone is cheering. Nate beams as he emerges from the pack of kids who were hugging him. "Great shot, Nate!" Luke shouts.

Nate grins at us and goes back to his team. Playing soccer has transformed Nate's social life; the kids on the team are nice to him, and now he has a circle of friends in kindergarten. Devin is still an asshole, but Nate and his friends stick up for each other. It's amazing how sports can unite people—can create camaraderie between kids who might not have been friends otherwise. I'm glad Luke and I pushed Nate to join the team.

"He's really good," Luke says to me. "I don't know where he gets it from. Not from me..."

"He's an athlete for sure." I think back to the years I spent playing hockey and how much I enjoyed the sport; I would love to go back to the rink with the kids. This time I'll be on the other side of the glass, rooting for Nate, with my hands wrapped around a coffee to keep me warm... "We have to get him on skates."

"Skates?" Luke says. "Isn't hockey a recipe for a concussion?"

"I never got a concussion. And you could get injured in any sport. We should expose Nate to everything—you never know what will stick."

"You want to kill me, right?"

"We'll go skating this winter. Scotty can try too." I turn to Scotty, who is sitting in the grass beside us and munching on a snack. "Want to play hockey, Scotty?"

"Yeah!" he says.

"Scotty is two!" Luke says.

"Then he'll be a beast by the time he gets to school."

Luke laughs and shakes his head, and I take his hand. At this moment, I'm happy with him. We're on the soccer field in the sunlight, caught up in the excitement of the game, and it's easy to forget how hard life has been lately. Luke is still spending several nights a week with his band and I struggle to keep the kids and house in order when he's gone. I haven't worked on my novel in weeks; Luke has been staying up late to write songs, and I've given up on trying to wake him in the mornings. Though I've resigned myself to this lifestyle, I have bouts of resentment, and I also miss Luke. I don't know how I can be angry with him and miss him at the same time, but that's how I feel. "Where do you want to go for dinner on Tuesday?" I ask him. "Your mom said we could have a date night."

"I have rehearsal on Tuesday."

"You can't skip it for once? Or move it to a different day?"

"I was going to ask my mom to watch the kids Saturday night instead," he says. "Then you can come to our gig in the city. My father is going to be there."

His father? Luke rarely mentions his father, and I've never met him. "Really?" I say.

"He texted me last night and said he was in town, so I told him to come to the show. We could meet with him on Sunday instead—bring the kids—but Nate has that birthday party in the middle of the day..."

"Whatever you think," I say. I guess I have to meet Luke's father, though I'm not enthusiastic about it. He can't be a very good person if he hasn't seen his son in years. "If the gig is easier..."

"You like coming to shows, right?" He kisses my neck. "It's more fun when you're there."

It used to be fun, but I'd rather have time alone with Luke. Saturday rolls around quickly, and after another soccer victory in the morning, Luke and I make plans for the evening. We leave the kids with Nora and Harry and head to the city. I've never been a fan of New York, and tonight the grimy subway and rude people annoy me more than usual. "You're in a bad mood?" Luke asks as we approach the bar.

"I'm tired," I say.

"We don't have to stay too late..."

Luke meets up with Carter and the rest of Spare Keys, and I reluctantly grab a drink. I don't see Luke's father and I don't have anyone to talk to; the room stinks of sweat and beer and I wish I had stayed home. The band starts playing and though the music sounds great, it means nothing to me. I'm not aroused or captivated as I watch Luke; I'm bored. I find myself wondering if the kids have fallen asleep and imagining how much progress I could have made on my novel if I'd spent this time alone. When the show is over, Luke comes up to me with his band and his father.

Lenny Reddin introduces himself and shakes my hand, then goes back to explaining something to Carter. Lenny has gray hair in a ponytail and the wrinkled, washed out face of a man who has partied too hard for most of his life. His eyes are the same shade of blue as Luke's, but they have none of Luke's frenzy or warmth; his clothes reek of smoke and the tattoos on his arms and neck are turning green. Still, he's thin and muscular and holds himself with the confidence of the handsome man he must have been in the past. I don't like the lazy, self-assured way he talks and I don't like how all the guys, especially Carter, hang on his every word. Lenny and Luke treat each other like fellow music experts, without any affection, and I feel no need to impress Lenny; I don't see why I had to meet him at all. Luke makes a few attempts to include me in the conversation, but I have nothing to say, and I'm glad when he's ready to go home.

We walk down the block and get on the subway. "My father thought the band was great," Luke tells me.

"Cool."

"I know that wasn't interesting for you—all the music talk. But you probably won't see my father again for another two years…"

"I don't know why I had to see him tonight," I say. "I don't think you owe respect to someone who has done nothing for you."

"I wouldn't call it nothing. Look, he's not your father—"

"What's that supposed to mean?"

"Relax—it's a compliment." Luke puts his hand over my clenched fist. "Your father is amazing; he loves you with all his heart and he'll give you anything you need. But not every parent is like that; some people don't have the guts to put their kids ahead of themselves."

"Then those people shouldn't be parents," I say. "Parents are supposed to make their kids their top priority."

"I agree with you. But my father doesn't feel that way, and I'm not going to hate him for it."

We're quiet for a moment. I'm thinking of the time Luke spent with his father each year when he was a kid and how it adds up to less time than Sylvie spends with Nate and Scotty. Yet everyone, including Luke, believes Sylvie is a bad mother. Men can show no interest in their kids and get away with it but a woman who acts the same way is shunned by society; her lack of devotion seems appalling, even criminal, to the rest of the world. I think Sylvie is selfish but Lenny is selfish too and it's not fair that Luke has accepted him. I doubt Nate and Scotty will be this forgiving of their mother when they're older.

"He wasn't much of a father figure," Luke says. "More like a cool uncle who hung out with me sometimes and didn't make me follow rules. He's not half the father my stepdad has been to me, and of course I owe my mom everything. But he's not all bad. When I was with my father, he gave me his attention; he got me started on guitar and took me to concerts and bought me whatever I wanted. He paid half my college tuition and convinced my mom to let me go to Berklee even though she thought it was a waste of money…which, in retrospect, it probably was.

He's not someone I rely on or ask for advice, but he was in my life when he easily could have been absent. I see no reason to cut ties with him."

"I didn't say you should cut ties. It just…took so little for him to earn the title of father."

"Who cares about a title? The relationship is what matters. I would've liked to have a loving relationship, but it is what it is. You saw his personality—he's obsessed with himself."

"Carter seemed to like talking to him," I say. "Probably thinks he's a good connection."

"Maybe, but Carter has lots of connections already. He was in a band a few years back that got signed to a label. They went on tour and released an album, but they broke up after a year because they were fighting. They were good, though; it must have been fun while it lasted."

I hear the longing in Luke's voice and I decide it's time to set the record straight. "I don't know where you think your band is headed," I say. "But you're not going on tour like Carter or your father. The kids and I need you at home, and we can't travel with you because Nate has school and I have a job."

"We don't have those kinds of ambitions," he says. "We're keeping it local."

"I doubt Carter sees it that way. I'm sure he'd take any opportunity to turn Spare Keys into something bigger. If things worked out somehow—if you got the chance to be famous—what would you do?"

"That's not going to happen."

"But if it did, what would you do?"

He blushes. "I mean…that's so unlikely…"

His hesitation is all the answer I need. Luke is going to do what he wants, regardless of how I feel. Everything I believed about him—that his decisions were guided by love, that he would sacrifice anything for me and the kids—isn't true. He acts fake with me the same way he does with Carter. I shrug out from under his arm and slide to the edge of my seat.

The subway jerks to a stop and the lights go out. We hear a series of bangs and Luke wraps his body around mine, pinning me underneath him. "What is it?" I say.

"Don't know."

Panic grips my heart. I can't see; I know nothing but Luke's rapid breathing. I don't want to die—I don't want Luke to die—and then the lights turn on and the subway starts to move again. The sound of normal conversation resumes around us. Luke lifts his chest off me. "Must have been a malfunction," I say.

"Yeah."

His face is chalk white. I'm shaking, and I understand where his mind went. Our generation has witnessed so much violence—from the September 11 terrorist attacks to the mass shootings in the media—that we've learned to expect it. We react to anything unusual with the thought that someone is trying to kill us. People in Europe don't share the same fear, and I was free from it while I lived there, but in the United States, it's not an irrational response. I imagine that Luke, who already sees danger where it doesn't exist, must feel more paralyzed by that fear than I do. Yet his instinct was to protect me. "You okay?" I say. "I love you."

"I love you too."

We're quiet for the rest of the ride, holding hands and leaning close to each other. It's a relief to get home to the apartment.

By the next morning, I'm frustrated with Luke again. I remember our conversation about touring and how he backed away from giving me an answer. It doesn't help that Carter asks to start Thursday's rehearsal at seven instead of nine. "It's only this week," Luke tells me. "Next week we'll go back to normal."

"That means I have to handle dinner by myself too, on top of bedtime," I say.

"Just this once. I can give you time alone on the weekend to make up for it..."

"Whatever," I say. It's not worth negotiating with him anymore. After a long day, I go to bed early, without having sex or cuddling with Luke. I curl up on one side of the mattress and fall into a fitful sleep.

When I get up in the middle of the night to pee, I see that something is wrong. The lights are on in the bathroom; Luke is sitting on the floor and Nate is vomiting into the toilet. "Looks like a stomach bug," Luke says.

"Oh God," I say.

"You go back to sleep—I'll take care of him."

It's useless, because an hour later I'm throwing up and so is Luke. Scotty is the only one who sleeps through the night. The next day passes by in a blur, with the three of us taking turns vomiting. "Stay away from Scotty," I tell Nate, who has joined his brother on the couch.

"Don't bother—Scotty is doomed," Luke says. "He catches everything Nate gets."

We all stay home from work and school for a few days. We're better by Wednesday, but Scotty's symptoms start on Wednesday night. Luke and I take care of him in shifts, and I feel like a zombie at work on Thursday.

Luke is waiting for me as soon as I get home from the office. "I'm going to rehearsal," he says. "Scotty threw up three times. He just had Pedialyte and a few crackers."

"Oh. Okay."

Luke is out the door before I can say anything else. I forgot about the early rehearsal, and I didn't expect Luke to leave me alone under these circumstances. I look around the room and feel overwhelmed. Scotty is in front of the TV holding a plastic bucket, there are toys everywhere, and the plate of cracker crumbs and cup of Pedialyte are in the middle of the floor. "Gemma!" Nate says. "Will you play the monster game with me?"

"In a minute," I say.

I barely have my shoes off when Scotty knocks over his Pedialyte. I clean it up, throw away his plate, and start microwaving chicken nuggets for Nate. I'm also a character in some pretend game and Nate is giving me too many lines. "Gemma!" Nate says. "You're supposed to say you're scared of the monster..."

"Oh, I'm scared, I'm scared," I say in a silly voice. "Go sit down to eat..."

When I get back to the living room, Scotty has thrown up again and half of it missed the bucket. I kneel down to help him, forgetting that I'm still wearing my work clothes, and end up with vomit on my favorite gray pants. "Stop touching me," I say to Scotty. "Let me take off your shirt—"

"Gemma! The monster is invading the castle!" Nate says.

"Scotty! Stop!" I pull Scotty's sticky fingers out of my hair, strip him down to his diaper, and carry him to the kitchen to wash his hands. Then I head to the living room to tackle the rest of the mess. Nate is sitting sideways on his chair, dropping pieces of food everywhere while he eats. "Sit straight," I tell him.

"The princess and the knight have to hide!" Nate says.

"Belly hurts," Scotty says.

"Do you have to throw up again?" I ask him.

"Where can we hide?" Nate says. "Gemma! Gemma! What does the princess do?"

"Shut up!" I snap at Nate. He looks at me in shock, and then he starts to cry. "I'm sorry, buddy—I can't play right now..."

I turn back to Scotty and my stomach drops. He's having a diaper blowout; poop is running down his legs. "No!" I yell. "Scotty, no! No!"

Scotty bursts into tears. I'm in a room that stinks of poop, with two crying children and a bucket of puke in my hand. This is hell. I'm in hell. I want to scream and sob and rip out my hair and I can't stand one more second with these kids. I walk away into the kitchen.

I close my eyes and focus on my breathing. If I'm alone I can find some pocket of calm, some shred of quiet inside me. I can handle this, I tell myself. One thing at a time. "One thing at a time," I say out loud. The sound of my voice steadies me. "I can handle this." I go back to the living room.

Scotty and Nate are still crying. I pick Scotty up. "It's okay, buddy," I say. "We'll change your diaper. Nate, I'll help you next..."

I comfort both boys, clean them up, and get them into bed. It's after nine and I haven't eaten anything; I sit at the table, open a bag of popcorn, and pour myself a teeming glass of wine. The wine is gone in minutes and I pour another glass. It's going straight to my head but I don't care; my nerves are wound too tightly and I'll do anything to relax them. I take a big gulp and look up as Luke comes through the door.

He tosses his jacket on the couch and kicks off his shoes. The shoes land in two different places but he doesn't pick them up. He puts his guitar down in the middle of the toys, kisses me on the forehead, and goes into the kitchen. "Man, I'm starving," he says. "What a long day..."

I watch him in disbelief. He didn't ask me how things went. He didn't offer to clean up the toys or the chicken nugget crumbs all over the floor. He's making himself a sandwich like nothing in the world exists except his needs. I follow him into the kitchen. "Are you going to ask how Scotty is doing?" I say.

"Okay. How is Scotty doing?"

"He threw up again, and he had diarrhea. Thanks for letting me deal with that."

"I'm sorry." He sighs. "I should have stayed home. But I was with him all day and I needed a break..."

"A break—that must be nice! I haven't had a break in months. But why would you care—my feelings don't matter to you—"

"Take it easy."

"I'm sick of being treated like your servant," I say. "You and the kids do whatever you want and I'm the rag cleaning up your messes. I can't take it anymore!"

"Stop yelling at me. We can talk about this like adults."

"I've tried talking to you, but you don't listen! You don't see how much I've sacrificed—how I've run myself into the ground giving you and the boys my time and energy and love. The only thing I had left for myself was writing, and you took that away too so you could play the guitar."

"You said I could join the band." His voice gets stern. "We talked about it, and we agreed—"

"You misrepresented it to me! You said it wouldn't be a big commitment, but it takes up all your time. You get to throw yourself into music and I'm stuck taking care of your kids. Maybe that's what you wanted all along; maybe that's why you asked me to move in—"

"That's bullshit! Now you're just trying to hurt me—"

"You made me this way!" I shout. "You backed me into this corner and I have to get out. I have to get out!" I stride to the dining room table and grab my purse and keys. I'm not in control of myself anymore; I'm riding this wave of anger and it feels good to release everything, to free the tension that has been building in my chest. "I can leave and get my life back—"

"Leave?" The color drains from his face. "You're not leaving."

"Yes I am."

"But I need you—the kids need you—"

"Don't play the guilt card."

"You should feel guilty! You can't join a family and walk away when things get tough!"

"I can do whatever I want."

He comes at me in a rage and I'm scared he's going to hit me, but he rips my purse out of my hand and flings it against the wall. "You want to go? Go. Take all your shit with you because you're not coming back."

I'm at a loss for words. "I..."

"I never want to see you again. Give me your key."

"My...what?"

"Your key to the apartment! Give it back and get out of my life."

I don't recognize Luke like this, towering over me with his teeth clenched and his eyes full of venom; there's no vulnerability in him, no trace of the softness I'm used to curling up against. I fumble with my keyring. The key to the apartment still has the green sticker Nate put there long ago; I look at the smiley face and see everything I'm about to lose. If I leave, I'll never watch Nate score a soccer goal again. I'll never play cars with Scotty or tell him a bedtime story. I'll miss out on Nate's pretend games and Scotty's hugs and all their years of growing up—every birthday and holiday and dinner after dinner after dinner. I won't hear their little voices saying my name. And there will be no Luke—no waking up in his arms, no sharing ideas with him, no making love to him or having him kiss the beauty marks on my thigh. He won't comfort me or inspire me or look at me with love; he'll see me as an enemy, the way he does now. I run my fingers over the key. I want my life back, but there is no life without Luke and the kids anymore; this family has become my life. My vision blurs with tears.

"Give me the fucking key!"

I reach my arms out to Luke. "I didn't mean it—I don't want to leave."

"That's not fair." He shoves my hands away. "Don't do that—it's not fair—"

"But I love you. I love all three of you and...and...I don't want to live in a world where we're not together."

"Gemma." His shoulders droop, and then I'm in his arms, sobbing into his shirt. "I don't want that either, baby. Don't leave."

"I'm sorry."

"No, it's my fault; I've been an asshole. But I'll fix it." He tightens his grip on me; his heart is racing like a hummingbird's against my head. "Don't give up on me—I love you so much."

We stay that way for a while, our chests heaving, clutching each other. Then we hear footsteps and Nate's voice. "Why is everybody yelling?"

I turn around. Nate is standing in his bedroom doorway, trembling and hugging a stuffed animal. Luke holds out an arm to him. "It's okay, buddy—we had a little argument. We're not mad anymore." Nate comes toward us, slowly, and Luke pulls him into our hug. "We love each other, and we love you. Everything is fine."

Nate looks up at me. "Don't cry, Gemma—we love you."

This makes me cry harder. Nate wraps his arms around my legs, and I kiss the top of his head. "I love you too," I say. "I'll feel better in a minute."

"Gemma!" Scotty calls from his room. "Gemma! Water!"

"I'll take Scotty," Luke says.

By the time we get both boys to sleep, I'm so tired I can barely function. Luke goes into the bathroom to brush his teeth and I fall onto the mattress. My eyes are swollen from crying and my muscles are aching; there are pressing thoughts in my head, but I can't make sense of them. I feel Luke getting into bed. "Do you want to talk about what happened?" he asks.

"Not now—I'm exhausted. Let's talk tomorrow."

"Okay." He pauses. "Can I hold you?"

"Yeah, of course."

He puts his arms around me, and I snuggle against his chest. At his touch, my body feels at peace. I'm not done being mad at him, yet there's a shelter in his arms like nothing else I've ever known.

Chapter Twenty-Four

"Baby, you have to wake up. It's getting late."

I feel the hand shaking my shoulder like it's coming from worlds away. "Hmm?" I mumble.

"You slept through your alarms, and you have to go to work..."

I open my eyes to see Luke leaning over me. The apartment is filled with sunlight, and the kids are playing on the floor. In a flash, I remember everything that happened last night—Scotty's stomach bug and our fight. "Scotty okay?" I ask.

"No poop or vomit yet—we might be past it. But you really have to get up..."

It's close to eight, so I race to get ready. Luke wants to talk to me, but there's no time and I haven't decided what I want to say yet. When I'm about to leave, he follows me to the door. I see the bloody wells around his nails and know he must have chewed on his fingers while I was asleep. "We'll talk later?" he says.

"As soon as I get home." I put my hand on his cheek; I hate seeing him suffer. "Try not to worry—we'll figure it out."

On the drive to work, I think about my fight with Luke. I meant

212

most of what I said, even if I got carried away at the end. I'm not happy with the way things are between us and it was time to make that clear. I want to have a rational conversation later, without yelling, and to do that I have to know what I want. What do I want? I don't want to leave him...yet I feel indignant. I deserve a fulfilling life, and I might only be able to get that if I'm alone. I'm still working things out in my head when I get to the office.

All the girls are in the reception area. Jasmine and Erica are greeting their clients, and Lina is discussing something with Bree. I study the lawyers. These are strong, intelligent women who are raising families while pursuing their goals; they take care of themselves and the people they love. I'm sure they have advice for me, and they've always given advice from the heart. When I get to my desk, I send an email to everyone: *Can you guys spare a few minutes for a coffee break today?*

Lina replies first. *I have time at eleven.*

Erica, Jasmine, and Bree respond too, and at eleven, we gather on the couches. "I have a question," I say. "Am I a fool to put the man and kids I love ahead of myself?"

"Yes," Bree says.

"It depends," Erica says. "What's going on?"

I explain last night's fight and everything I've been feeling. "I used to consider myself a feminist," I say. "Yet here I am giving up my identity for a guy and his kids. I always wanted a family, though; I pictured myself as a mom. Maybe that's why I was attracted to Luke in the first place..." I trail off, thinking. "Maybe I wanted to play house with him— try out this parenthood thing without the commitment. Or maybe I saw the hole in his life and I wanted to save him, like I wish somebody had saved my dad; he's been alone since my mom died. Maybe I got into this relationship for the wrong reasons."

"You think so?" Jasmine says.

"I don't know. Still, I love him." My words are vehement; this is the one thing I'm sure of, that I love Luke in spite of what's happened. "It doesn't matter why I started this because we've built something beautiful together. He's good to me, and we're always there for each other. If he were using me it would be different—I would leave. But he's just made mistakes, and this could work if he's willing to fix them."

"Don't stay because you're used to him," Bree says. "Or because you're afraid to be alone."

"I'm not afraid to be alone. I'll be devastated if this is over, but I'll survive; I have my family and my writing and you guys and I've been single for most of my life. It's not fear that's stopping me—it's the feeling that there's so much left to salvage in this relationship...that what I'll lose by leaving is bigger than what I'll gain."

"What do you want Luke to do differently?" Jasmine asks.

"I want him to value my passion as much as I value his," I say. "To consider how I feel when he's making decisions and to recognize when I need a break. I want him to treat me as an equal."

"That's fair," Erica says.

"But realize this: you're not going to fully get your identity back," Lina says. "You may get more time to yourself, and more respect—which you deserve—but you're never going to have the freedom of a single woman again. If you're looking for that freedom you shouldn't stay with Luke, because he can't give it to you; it's not an option for a mom. When we became parents, we chose to act as members of a family instead of individuals—and that change lasts forever. In your case, you can either accept—without resentment—that your world will never be the same, or you can go back to being single and doing what you want. There is no in between."

I'm struck by this statement. Lina clarified the terms of the battle that's been raging inside me. I see why I've been torn, and I understand the choice I have to make. "You're right," I say. "I've been holding onto my past—my life before kids—because it's still close at hand. I didn't have pregnancy or another transition before I was thrown into this madness, and since I'm not married, the option of making a clean break from this family is on the table. But I can't enjoy being a mom if I'm longing for the old days; I have to let them go. I have to stop looking for an escape from whining and laundry and poop and embrace the life I chose. And I do choose it." I speak with certainty now; I know what I want. "I'm going to stay with Luke because this family's love matters more to me than independence. It's worth more than writing or success or free time or sleep. Being with Luke and the kids is fulfilling, and I wouldn't give it up for anything in the world. I just want Luke to give me time and respect, like we said—to be as dedicated to me as I am to him. If he does that, I'll choose love over freedom."

"That was beautiful," Erica says. "Perfectly said. If Luke can be honest with himself like you are, you two will be fine."

"Stick up for yourself," Jasmine says. "Tell Luke what you want and make sure you get it consistently—not for just a few days."

"Don't let him slide no matter how sweet he acts," Bree says.

"Got it." I look around at the four of them. I'm grateful to have them in my life; they bolster me up even in the hardest times. "You guys are the best."

After work, I head home to the apartment and find Luke doing a puzzle with the kids. "We can talk now," I say. "If you want to put on cartoons for the boys…"

Luke turns on the TV and follows me into the kitchen. He stands across from me with his shoulders hunched, gnawing on his thumb, but he's looking into my eyes and I see he's ready to listen. "Go ahead," he says. "Tell me what you're feeling."

I repeat what I said last night, but I speak calmly, without attacking him. "Parenthood is stressful," I add. "I get overwhelmed sometimes, but I could deal with the chaos before because we were a team. Then you joined the band and we stopped working together; you were only thinking about yourself. I tried to be okay with it—I told myself my feelings didn't matter as long as I was supporting you. But it's not fair for me to live that way, and I'm not going to do it anymore. You have to make my needs a priority too."

"I know," he says. "I quit the band, so—"

"I didn't tell you to quit!"

"It's the only thing that makes sense. There's no way to play music casually with Carter—he's giving his heart and soul to Spare Keys and he expects me to do the same. I can't be that obsessed and take care of my family at the same time. And I thought about what you said on the subway—I wouldn't want a life like Sylvie's or my father's, even if I could have it. I would never want to be away from you and the kids. I would miss you!"

"I miss you now," I say.

"I miss you too. But I was having so much fun with this band and I got greedy. I got a taste of another life, the life I could have had, and I wanted more. I wanted it all—you three and the band—and I fooled myself that if you weren't complaining all the time, you were happy. But that was wrong." He leans forward. "Deep down I knew it was wrong, but it was working so I went with it and I'm sorry. I'll never ignore your feelings again. I feel terrible about what you said—that you gave up writing for me. I believe in your writing and I don't want to be the person who puts out that light..."

"If you give up music, it's the same thing," I say. "Either way one of us is making a sacrifice."

"I'm not giving up music—it brings me joy and keeps me sane. I'm giving up the band. I can go back to writing and playing on my own, in the slivers of time I find, without messing up our schedule. Maybe I'll start self-producing my songs and putting them online; there are platforms like Bandcamp where people do that. I don't expect to have a ton of fans, but at least I'll get my music into someone's ears. I don't need to gig and I don't need to be great; I just need to make music, and I need the four of us to be together. Gemma, you've already given me everything I want. You've filled my life with love. You've stood by me through miserable situations and helped me survive them. You've given the boys a happy, stable home—"

"You did that," I say.

"Not like I do it with you. We work as a team to keep things running around the house and you push me to do what's right for the kids even when I'm scared. And above everything else you make me feel like...like..." His voice is shaking; he struggles to compose himself. "Like...no matter what happens, no matter how bad things get, I'll be okay because I have you. I can face anything when we're together. But I saw the way you looked at me earlier, before you left for work—you felt sorry for me, and that's no good. I don't want you to stay here out of pity or nostalgia or because you're worried about the kids or for any other reason unless this is the life you want. If the kids and I can't make you happy, we're headed for a slow death instead of a fast one and I'd rather it be fast..."

"Luke." I put my arms around his waist. "This is the life I want. This is my family now too."

"You're sure?"

"A hundred percent. After what happened last night, I thought everything through—what this family means to me, what dreams I'm putting aside—and I know this is where I belong. I want to be with the three of you forever."

"That's what I want," he says. "Tell me what to do, then. What do I change?"

"I want time to write again—time we build into our schedule so I can write consistently and I don't have to skip it. I want you to spend more nights with me and the kids; that will be easy if you're not performing."

"Of course. What else?"

I could ask for anything at this moment and get it. But I got what I wanted—I got him to listen to me. I stroke his face, my favorite face in the world; his beard is rough under my fingers and there's a glimmer of tears in his eyes. "That's all, baby," I say. "If we stick to that, I'll be happy."

Luke is true to his word—we develop a new routine and we don't stray from it as the weeks go on. I write in the mornings on Sunday through Thursday and he plays music on Friday and Saturday mornings; if we find time on weekend afternoons, we take turns working. There are no more gigs or rehearsals or text conversations with Carter, and we order pizza twice a week so we can talk after work instead of cooking. We go to sleep early together and we wake up early together, and it's enough. We both get enough of what we need.

On January 5, at 6:37 A.M., I finish my novel. The last revisions are complete and I keep scrolling through the document, wanting to keep my hands in it, searching for anything I might have missed. But it's done—it's done! Now I can write the second book. I check my formatting one last time, then close the document and open several new ones. I'll need a brainstorming document, a timeline, and the actual text of chapter one...

Before I leave for the office, I email the manuscript—it's a manuscript now—to Luke. "I sent you my book," I tell him. "If you want to read it at some point..."

"It's done?" he says.

"Yeah, I finished this morning."

He runs to me, lifts me off my feet, and kisses me. "That's amazing! You're amazing!"

"Don't say that until you read it."

When I get home, Luke tells me he got through the first chapter. "I'm going to read more tonight," he says. "It's been a crazy day."

"No rush."

Once the boys are asleep, I start drifting off as well. Luke is in bed next to me with his computer on his lap. I wake up in the middle of the night, wriggle out of Luke's arms, and head to the bathroom. I thought Luke was asleep, but he jumps up and follows me. "Gemma, how could you kill Linus?" he says. "He was the best character!"

"What?" I say. "What time is it?"

"It's three A.M., and I read the whole book. The way you described him falling without his wings..."

"I knew you would like Linus. He has a lot of you in him."

"So you put me in your story and then you killed me?"

I laugh. "It sounds awful when you say it like that...try to take it as a compliment."

Luke goes on gushing about the book. It's a thrill to see him so excited—to hear his perspective on a story that has existed only for me all these months. I'll never get back to sleep if we keep talking, though, and I've learned to prioritize sleep. "I'm glad you liked it," I say. "We can talk more tomorrow."

"When are we going to Arizona?"

"Huh?"

"Now that I've read your book, I have to see the place for myself."

I smile. Luke's enthusiasm never ceases to impress me. "We'll go this year," I say. "The boys can come too. But for now let's get some sleep."

Chapter Twenty-Five

I've spent the past six months working on the second book in my trilogy and querying agents. Writing is going well; querying has been a failure. Out of the thirty agents I've emailed, only three have responded, and they all sent form rejections after reading my work. I'm planning to reach out to more agents, but the process is slow. I can't dedicate too many hours to querying because I need time to write, and on top of that, I've been establishing a social media presence as an author to gain followers before I get published. I'm being pulled in a million different directions; my mornings were more satisfying when I could focus on writing alone. Still, I know the other tasks are necessary, and I'm hoping to query a few more agents before we leave for Arizona.

Luke and I scheduled the trip for the last week of July. The four of us are flying into Phoenix, and at the end of the week, Sylvie is meeting us at the Phoenix airport to take the kids to L.A. with her. When we sat down to make plans, Luke was surprised at how far apart his top destinations were. "That's a ton of driving," he said. "Four hours from Phoenix to the Grand Canyon? And I heard about something cool called the Painted Desert, but that's hours in the other direction..."

"We have to prioritize what we want to see most," I said. "And be realistic about what the kids can handle. If they're miserable, we won't enjoy the trip either."

"I agree. I'd rather go to less places and build in enough downtime. We need a few days in Sedona—that's most important to me."

The trip began to take shape, and we booked a night in Phoenix, two nights in the Grand Canyon, and three nights in Sedona. I've visited all those places before and I'm looking forward to exploring them with Luke and the kids.

On the day of the flight, Nora drops us off at the airport. The kids and I are excited, but Luke and his mom are both nervous. While we're in the security line, Luke keeps checking the front pocket of his backpack; he's wearing the bag on his chest instead of his back. "Are you missing something?" I ask.

"No, I'm just making sure everything is there...my wallet and stuff."

"Nobody is going to steal from you." I watch him unzip the pocket again. "You don't like to fly, huh?"

"How can you tell?"

"I like to fly!" Nate chirps. "Mama says on the plane we get unlimited shows and unlimited snacks!"

"That's a good rule," Luke says.

In spite of Luke's anxiety, he's all right on the plane, and the kids are well behaved. When we land in Phoenix, we pick up our rental car and head to the hotel. There's a line to check in; while we wait, the kids run around the lobby. "Take it easy, boys," I say.

"This is Orangey's cave," Nate says, crawling behind a couch. "Where does Indigo hide?"

"I want to hide with you!" Scotty says.

"Watch out for that flower pot," I say.

There's an older couple in line in front of us, and I notice the woman looking fondly at Nate and Scotty. She's wearing a straw sun hat on top of her gray hair. "God bless you, darlin'," she says to me in a Southern drawl. "Your sons are the cutest little boys I've ever seen!"

I almost respond the way I have in the past—by telling her they're not my sons. Instead I smile. "That's so sweet," I say. "Thank you."

After an afternoon at the playground and an early dinner, we all pass out at the hotel. The next morning, we set out for the Grand Canyon. It's a long drive, with lots of stops along the way for snacks and bathroom breaks. We listen to the kids' favorite music on loop and play characters in Nate's dragon saga. After a while, the boys get quiet. "The sky is so big here," Nate says, looking out at the open highway. "Bigger than at home."

"Wait until you see where we're headed," I say.

We're exhausted when we arrive, but once we get our first glimpse of the Grand Canyon, our energy returns. We marvel at the scenery and take a million pictures. "The canyon almost looks fake," Luke says. "Like a painting. It's too huge—too majestic—for your brain to comprehend it."

"Look at the colors," Nate says. "I want to draw it!"

"Me too!" Scotty says.

Luke has paper and crayons in his backpack, so we find a place to sit while our little artists create their pictures. I'm full of wonder as I watch the kids drawing. Their view of the world is expanding; they're inspired by what they see. "I wish New Jersey looked like Arizona," Nate says.

"That would be nice, right?" Luke says.

We spend two incredible days at the Grand Canyon. We can't do as much sightseeing as I did with my dad—there is no intense hiking and no getting close to the edge of the rim for a picture—but we have a blast. We take a shuttle bus to different overlooks, and we spend hours at the hotel pool and arcade. Then it's time to head to Sedona.

I decide to drive. As we make our way down Route 89A, a winding two-lane road, Luke chats with the kids about our plans. "We're going to hike tonight at sunset," he says. "Right, Gemma? On the trail you never got to hike when you were in Sedona?"

"Yeah, the Airport Loop," I say. "It's supposed to be easy enough for kids and have amazing views."

"We'll have Scotty nap early in the day so that we—" Luke stops mid-sentence and puts his hand on my arm. "Woah."

We've made a sharp turn, and Oak Creek Canyon unfolds before us. Tree-lined cliffs rise high above our heads and stretch into the gorge below. A series of switchbacks brings us deeper into the canyon; every curve in the road reveals more magnificent scenery. "This is a joke, right?" Luke says. "I'm not really seeing this."

"I want to go there!" Scotty says.

"We are here," Luke says.

We find a place to pull over and admire the canyon, and then we continue our descent. After a while, the red rocks of Sedona come into view. We drive past the towering walls of Slide Rock State Park, through Uptown Sedona with its shops and restaurants, and on to the Red Rock Scenic Byway. Bell Rock, Cathedral Rock, and Courthouse Butte are just as stunning as the first time I saw them; I gaze at the smooth layers of stone, the vivid colors, the shape of each rock formation against the blue and white sky. "Let's park at one of the trailheads and take a walk," I say. "Get a little closer, even if we can't hike far..."

Twenty minutes later, we're on the Bell Rock Trail. Nate is ecstatic; he keeps running back and forth, spinning around in circles, and kicking up clouds of orange dirt. Luke is carrying Scotty on his shoulders. "I want to draw this too!" Scotty says.

"You should!" Luke says. "I'm going to write a song about it...something sweeping..."

I can't stop smiling as I watch the three of them—their small figures against the backdrop of Bell Rock, their curly heads turning from side to side. Here I am in the most beautiful place I've ever seen, and I get to share it with my favorite people. I spread my arms wide. I want to embrace everything—this family, the landscape, the fresh, clean air. I feel blessed to be alive.

"Gemma!" Nate holds up a fistful of rocks. "Can I take these? They're my favorite color!"

"No, buddy," I say. "We have to leave nature the way we found it."

By the time we have lunch, the boys are getting cranky; they fall asleep once we get to the hotel. After naps, showers, and snacks, it's time to leave for the Airport Loop trail. We're on our way out of the hotel room when we hear thunder. "Is it raining?" Luke says.

I look out the window. The clouds have gotten dark; a bolt of lightning splits the sky. "Uh oh," I say. "Looks like a thunderstorm."

"You're kidding." Luke's face falls. "That means no sunset hike."

"We can do it tomorrow."

"We have that dinner reservation tomorrow."

"Oh yeah," I say. "We'll do it the final night; no big deal."

Luke is disappointed for the rest of the evening. The storm is still raging when we put the kids to bed, and the thunder is deafening; the kids keep getting up and coming over to our bed. "We're scared," Nate says. "We want to sleep with you."

"The storm can't hurt us," Luke says. "We're safe inside. And we're already sleeping in the same room."

"We want to sleep in your bed," Nate says.

We hear another crash of thunder, and all four of us jump. I lift my head off Luke's chest. The boys can sleep with us; there's enough room in our king-sized bed, and we weren't expecting to have sex on this trip. "What do you think?" I say to Luke. "They could fit..."

Nate scrambles onto the bed, and Scotty follows him. They squeeze between me and Luke, driving us apart. Luke sighs. "This is for tonight only," he says. "Because of the storm. We're not doing this tomorrow, or at home..."

"Okay, Daddy."

We snuggle under the covers. It's surprisingly comfortable in the crowded bed, with Scotty curled up against my chest. "Tell us a story," Nate says.

"You got a story before," Luke says.

"One more."

"I'll tell it," I say. "Once upon a time..."

Halfway through the story, both boys are asleep. I stretch my arm across them and find Luke's hand; he laces his fingers through mine. I let my head sink into my pillow and I close my eyes.

***

Sedona is the highlight of the trip. We fill our days with short walks on hiking trails, delicious meals, and trips to swimming holes. On our last afternoon, we shop for souvenirs and treat the kids to dessert. Luke looks wary as he watches Scotty digging into an enormous cup of ice cream. "We can't let him eat the whole thing," he says. "It's too much."

"Who cares? Let him enjoy it," I say.

I end up paying for this attitude on the drive to the Airport Loop trail. There are too many cars on the road, and the stop-and-go traffic makes Scotty nauseous. I hear him retch and turn to see chocolate-covered vomit pouring from his mouth. "Oh no—pull over!" I say.

Scotty is sobbing; Nate takes one look at him and starts crying too. I take Scotty out of the car and strip him down to his diaper while Luke runs into a shop for soap and paper towels. Scotty is inconsolable; I try to calm him down, but he won't stop wailing. "It's over," I say. "You're all better now!" He's still hysterical when Luke returns. "You comfort Scotty," I say. "Give me the soap."

I get to work on the car. The smell is sickly sweet, and I'm sweating as I clean. You simply have not lived until you've scrubbed puke out of a car seat in the hot Arizona sun. Try as I might, I can't get the grainy bits out of the straps. "I did my best," I tell Luke. "Put an outfit on Scotty and we'll go..."

"I don't have another outfit," Luke says. "I usually keep one in the bag but we used it yesterday when he got wet."

"Damn," I say. "We'll have to stop at the hotel before the hike."

"We'll never make it for sunset if we do that."

"What are we supposed to do, leave Scotty naked?" I turn from Luke, who looks crushed, to the kids with their tear-stained faces. "They don't seem up for hiking anyway..."

"I really want to do that hike," Luke says.

"Me too, baby, but it's not going to happen."

We drive to the hotel. The sky is changing colors outside the car windows; Luke shakes his head. "It's bullshit," he says. "I can't believe this..."

"We've done so many great things on this trip," I say. "Something was bound to go wrong." My phone buzzes in my pocket, telling me I got an email. I open the message and gasp.

"What's the matter?" Luke says.

"No, it's good! An agent emailed me asking for my full manuscript, plus an outline of the rest of the trilogy."

"Awesome!"

I read the email over and over. "I never expected this agent to get back to me," I say. "She's one of my top choices—she's represented a bunch of my favorite authors."

"Your story is going to blow her away," Luke says.

"Do you mind if I respond to her when we get back to the hotel? I have to put together an outline..."

"Of course. Take your time."

I open my laptop the minute we get inside. No other agent has asked me for an outline, so I have to craft one from scratch. I've jotted down key plot points for the rest of the trilogy, but those notes are too disorganized to send to an agent. I have to make the outline perfect—this could be my chance! Luke and the kids watch TV as I work; after a while, I feel Luke's hand on my shoulder. "Sorry to interrupt you, but I'm going to order food from the restaurant downstairs," he says. "What do you want?"

"Would you rather go out for dinner?" I say. "I can finish this later..."

"No, this is important. Do your work."

I plug away at the outline as Luke and the boys eat and get ready for bed. I feel guilty for letting Luke handle bedtime by himself, but my writing is better when I stay in the zone. By the time I send the email, it's close to eleven P.M., the boys are sound asleep, and Luke is reading and drinking wine out of a plastic cup from the bathroom. "Thank you for giving me that time," I say. "This could be a great opportunity."

"I know, baby. I'm happy for you!"

"I need a drink, too...that was stressful..."

I pour myself wine, go back to the desk, and open the box from the restaurant. My dinner is ice cold, but I don't care; my mind is buzzing and I can barely stop talking long enough to chew. "You won't believe who this agent has represented!" I tell Luke. "Remember that time traveling series that got made into movies?"

Luke takes a seat on the edge of the desk as I go on about the agent. Maybe it's silly to get my hopes up, but this is the closest I've come to getting published, and my dream seems like a possibility. I imagine seeing my books in stores and having thousands of people reading my work. I'm so giddy that it takes me a while to notice Luke's demeanor. He's listening, but he's not smiling, and he's chewing on his fingers for the first time in months. "Are you worried about something?" I ask.

"No, no—you can keep talking."

"You look nervous."

"I'm fine."

He's not fine; my heart races as I watch him. "Please tell me what you're thinking," I say. "I can't relax when you're like this."

He drops his hand from his mouth. "If your books get famous, will you still marry me?"

"Who said anything about getting married?"

"I did." He gets off the desk, kneels in front of me, and pulls a box out of his pocket. "Will you marry me?"

He's holding a ring. A ring. Time stops; I can't process what's happening. Then I look into his eyes and feel a rush of joy and I leap out of my seat and kiss him. "Yes! Yes, I'll marry you!"

"For a second you had me scared—"

"Of course it's a yes! Luke..." We're both shaking. "How did you—when did you get a ring?"

"I bought it at home and brought it with me."

"That's why in the airport...oh my God."

"I planned it better than this," he says. "I wanted to propose to you at sunset but we never went on that hike. I was trying to figure out what else to do—how I could make it special—"

"This is special, because I get to marry you. I don't need any bells and whistles; I just want to be together."

"We'll be together forever." He puts the ring on my finger and kisses my hands. I stare at the diamond sparkling against my skin; it seems too beautiful to be real. "I'll always be by your side, loving you more with every heartbeat..."

We're both elated when we get into bed that night. I'm falling asleep in Luke's arms when a thought occurs to me. "I have to fix the manuscript," I say. "And my author accounts—I'll change everything to Gemma Reddin."

He kisses my neck. "I like the sound of that."

***

When I arrive at work the Monday after the trip, everyone in my life knows I got engaged—except the women at the office. I've been waiting to tell them in person. I glance down the hallway and see that all the lawyers' doors are open, meaning nobody has a client. "Coffee break!" I announce. Multiple voices respond at the same time:

"Not now, Gemma—"

"I'm swamped—"

"Can it wait until noon?"

"Coffee break, now!" I shout.

The girls look concerned as they join me in the reception area. "What's wrong?" Lina asks.

"Nothing is wrong. I have something to show you." I hold up my hand.

We scream so loudly that people come running from the offices upstairs to make sure we're okay.

Chapter Twenty-Six

August is a busy month—Luke and I spend a lot of time talking about the wedding. Everyone in our families wants to congratulate us and ask about our plans, and because the kids are in L.A., we have the chance to look at venues. Every place we visit is expensive, and I'm not sold on the idea of having a big wedding. "It's too much money," I tell Luke. "We should get married at city hall and forget about the party. My dad said he'd give us twenty thousand, but we're better off saving that for a house..."

"My parents are going to chip in, too," he says.

"I don't want them to feel obligated. It's awkward for them to pay since...since you've been married before."

"So what?" he says. "They're happy for us and they want to help. This isn't about the past—it's about me and you."

"That's what I'm saying. I just want to be your wife—I don't need the drama—"

"There is no drama."

"And I hate being the center of attention and worrying about how I look."

Luke studies my face. "You want to get married at city hall? Let's do it this week."

"This week?"

"It takes three days for the paperwork to go through. We'll call today and make an appointment."

I hesitate. This is an easy, affordable solution, and I've been telling myself it's what I want. Yet deep down, I'm longing for a traditional wedding. I picture the white dress, my dad walking me down the aisle, the boys in suits that match Luke's and Michela as a flower girl. I'm not ready to give up those dreams, even if a wedding seems like a waste of money. "Maybe I do want the party," I say. "If we can plan something small...not too extravagant..."

"I'm in for whatever you want."

We haven't made plans by the time we pick the boys up at the airport on August 21. Sylvie only kept them for three weeks because of her tour schedule; she's a headliner now and her fan base is huge. Luke and I are glad to get the kids back early. We don't mention anything about the wedding as Nate and Scotty tell us about their time in L.A. We told the kids we were engaged the day after the proposal and they were excited, but I'm not sure they understood what it meant. It might be hard for them to adjust to having a stepmom, and it doesn't help that we handed them over to Sylvie the same day we shared the news. I can't tell what's going through their heads and I have no idea what Sylvie said to them when we weren't around. Part of the reason I can't get excited about the wedding is because I'm worried about how the kids will react; I want to disrupt their world as little as possible. "Mama said we can go to one of her concerts next time we visit," Nate says as we make our way home.

"That would be cool," Luke says.

"And Mama said she's never getting married again."

I jump. I want to see Nate's expression, but I can't turn around because I'm driving. "Yeah?" Luke says.

"Yeah. She didn't like being married. She said it's nice for you guys to get married if you're happy."

"We're very happy," Luke says.

"But she said she's our only mama, not Gemma," Nate says. "Is that true?"

My heart is pounding. I know how to respond to this—Luke and I have talked about it—but it's nerve-wracking. I don't want to damage the bond I have with Nate. "She'll always be your mama," I say. "You'll keep seeing her as much as you do now and she'll love you forever. But I love you and Scotty as my kids too. I'll be your stepmom, which means you get extra love—from Mama and from me, and of course from Daddy."

"I like living with Gemma and Daddy," Scotty says.

"Me too," Nate says. "I like it the best." This fills me with relief. "But I don't want you guys to fight. When Mama and Daddy were married, they were always fighting."

"We won't fight." Luke leans into the back seat to take Nate's hand. "That's not what getting married means. Mama and I fought because we wanted different things, but Gemma and I want the same thing—to be together and to take care of you two. We'll keep getting along and we'll keep spending time with you and Scotty. Everything stays the same except we call each other husband and wife."

"And you have a wedding," Nate says. "What do you do at a wedding?"

"It's a party to celebrate our family," Luke says. "You and Scotty will be with us, and we get to dance and eat cake—"

"Chocolate cake?" Nate asks. "I only like chocolate. I don't like that white one Grandma gets."

"I want chocolate cake!" Scotty says.

"You guys can pick the cake," I say. "You can help with all the plans. It's a special day for you too!"

Nate and Scotty keep asking questions about the wedding over the next few weeks. They want to know where it will be and who will be there and how many days are left until it happens. It's natural for them to be curious, but I'm feeling pressured. At the same time, we're getting Nate ready for first grade and Scotty ready for preschool; we finally managed to toilet train Scotty, and the process was exhausting. I've also been revising my book. The agent I emailed when we were in Sedona rejected me, but she included criticism in her email and I'll admit a lot of it made sense. I was disappointed about the rejection for several days, but now I'm implementing some of the changes she suggested. "It was a good rejection," I tell Luke. "Most people never get feedback about why they were turned down."

"It's okay to be upset," he says.

"I am upset—I thought this would be my big break and now it's back to square one. But I have to keep trying; I'm not giving up on this book."

The Friday of our engagement party rolls around, and I have a productive writing session in the morning; this alleviates some of my anxiety about what will happen tonight. Nora, Harry, and my dad organized the party at a restaurant with a beautiful outdoor patio. The three of them knew about the proposal before it happened—apparently Luke was sweating bullets when he asked my dad for permission—and they're all looking forward to the wedding. The party is a nice gesture, but I'm sure everyone is going to badger me about my plans and I don't have any plans yet. "We don't even have a bridal party," I tell Luke on the drive. "Is that weird?"

"We have the boys as ring bearers, and you asked Michela to be the flower girl," he says. "Is there anyone you want as a bridesmaid?"

"Not really...the women who matter most to me are my aunts and the girls at the office, but they have their own families and I don't want to burden them. Do we need to have bridesmaids and groomsmen?"

"We don't need to do anything," he says. "This is our wedding. I want my three best friends to be there—you, Nate, and Scotty. I was going to invite some dragons, too..." He glances into the back seat. "But I don't think they wear suits."

"Don't invite Spiky!" Nate says. "He'll ruin the wedding!"

When we get to the restaurant, everyone is thrilled to see us. My aunts and cousins have already seen my ring, but I have to show it off to Luke's family as well. Bella and Marisa are excited in particular; Luke asked them for advice when he first started ring shopping. After they admire the diamond, Marisa talks about her experience planning her wedding, a huge bash that's happening next month. "If you need any help, let me know!" she says to me. "I can put you in touch with my DJ and photographer..."

After lots of wedding talk, it's a relief to sit down next to the kids. Scotty finishes his food while everyone else is working on appetizers, and I entertain him with a coloring book. "I want to play there," he says, pointing at the party store next door to the restaurant. There is a giant Halloween display out front filled with pumpkins, bales of hay, and decorative ghosts and witches. "Can we go?"

"Maybe later," I say.

Scotty keeps badgering me about the party store, and when I'm done with dinner, I agree to take him. "I'll be right back," I tell Luke. He's still eating, and Nate is entertaining his grandparents with some elaborate story. "I'm taking Scotty to play next door."

We've barely made it to the display when I hear Nate running up behind us. I turn, expecting to see Luke, but Nora is with Nate. I stiffen. I never know how to act around Nora, and that hasn't changed now that she's soon to be my mother-in-law. We stay quiet and watch the boys climbing on the bales of hay. Nora keeps looking at me like she's about to say something, then dropping her eyes and fiddling with her watch. Finally she speaks. "I know we've never gotten close, but...I wanted to tell you...I'll be proud to have you as a daughter, Gemma."

I'm stunned. "Wow—that means a lot."

"You've done so much for this family—you're a wonderful mother to Nate and Scotty and a steadying force for Luke. I don't know what would have happened to Luke if he hadn't found you. Thank you for being kind and patient and practical...thank you for taking care of them."

"Don't thank me—Luke is the best thing that ever happened to me," I gush. I never expected praise from Nora, and I'm overwhelmed with gratitude. "He's so loving, he makes me so happy...thank you for raising a great man!"

"I made a lot of mistakes." Nora shakes her head. "Luke was a difficult child. Not that he misbehaved—he loved rules and hated disappointing me. But he was too sensitive; the smallest things upset him. Imagine, he would see a child he'd never met crying on the playground and start crying himself. How are you supposed to raise a kid like that, especially a boy? I was harsh at times, wanting him to be tougher, be wiser—be rational, for God's sake, instead of so emotional. But he is who he is, and you understand him. And you're calm." She puts her hand on my arm. "I couldn't help passing my worries along to Luke, but Nate and Scotty will grow up with less fear because of you. You're so good with them."

"I'm trying," I say. "I don't do everything right, but I love them and I'm trying my best..."

"That's all we can do."

We smile at each other. A weight has been lifted off my shoulders— Nora and I can get along after all. I give her a hug. "I'm proud to call you my mom too. I'm so glad to be part of this family."

Later that night, I tell Luke about my conversation with Nora, and he's pleasantly surprised. He also shares ideas for venues that he heard from Marisa. "She looked into some small venues before she decided to go all out and have a big wedding," he says. "Apparently there are restaurants that do weddings for fifty people, and you can still have a dance floor and cocktail hour. She mentioned two places in Morristown, and an Italian restaurant here in Oakfield—that one behind the park—"

"The park?" I grab Luke's arm. "That's where we met! We could have the ceremony outside in the park, then go to the restaurant for the reception..."

"That would be cool."

I think back to my first glimpse of Luke—that cute guy playing with his son on the playground. He was a stranger two and a half years ago and now he's becoming my husband. It's amazing that we ended up together—that one afternoon changed our lives forever. The park is the right place for us to get married. "Let's call the restaurant tomorrow!" I say.

He kisses me. "I like seeing you like this—I like when your eyes light up. You're supposed to be this excited about your wedding..."

"Hopefully the restaurant won't be too expensive and we can still put money aside for a house. We'll need our own place eventually; I don't want to sleep on a mattress on the floor forever."

"We should move Nate into Scotty's room," he says. "They're old enough to share a room without waking each other up. Then you and I can have the other bedroom."

"How luxurious!"

"It's not a house yet, but it's an upgrade from the floor..."

When we move Nate's bed the next day, the boys are ecstatic to be in the same room. They set up their toys and start jumping from one bed to the other. "Someone is going to get hurt," Luke warns them.

"Let them have fun," I say.

"Brothers, brothers, brothers forever," Nate sings, and Scotty joins in. "Always sticking, sticking together..."

"Where's that song from?" Luke asks.

"We made it up!" Scotty says.

Luke turns to me and raises his eyebrows. "Of course they did," I say.

"It's really catchy," Luke says.

"Can we record it on your phone later?" Nate asks. "You can play guitar!"

"Definitely!" Luke says. The boys go on singing and jumping on the beds. Luke puts his arm around my waist. "We have the best kids in the world."

"No question," I say.

Chapter Twenty-Seven

I wake up early on my wedding day—May 12, 2018—and head downstairs to make coffee. The house is quiet, meaning my dad has already gone out for a jog. I slept at my dad's house last night while Luke stayed with the kids at the apartment; we're delaying seeing each other until our first look before the ceremony today. The tradition seemed like a fun idea when we talked about it, but I haven't spent a night away from Luke and the kids in years and I miss them. I take my coffee, a towel, and my laptop out to the deck in the backyard.

The chairs are still wet from last night's rain, as expected. I dry them and look up at the sky. I've been crossing my fingers that we won't have to use the tents we rented for the ceremony, but it's been raining all week and I've nearly given up hope. Today's clouds are white, though, and the sun keeps poking through them; we might get a nice day. I check my email, then open up the documents for the second book of my trilogy.

Two months ago, I signed a contract with Alpha Centauri Publications, a well-established small press that specializes in science fiction and fantasy. They've been around for decades, and a handful of their authors have become bestsellers in the genre. The money is minimal—my advance was two thousand dollars—and they don't have the marketing and distribution power of a Big 5 publisher, but it's exciting to work with people who are passionate about my book. My launch date is set for next summer; I delivered my manuscript a few weeks ago, after the first round of edits, and I'm waiting to hear back from my editor. In the meantime, I'm writing Book Two and jotting down notes for Book Three. My book deal was only for Book One, but my editor thinks it's likely I'll get signed for the rest of the trilogy if the first book does well. I plan to finish the trilogy either way; it grounds me to have something to write during this stressful process. I turn my attention to the sentences on the screen and get to work.

After a while, I hear my dad approaching. He's sweating and guzzling a bottle of water. "Don't worry about rain, Gems," he says. "It's clearing up."

"Awesome! I'm going for a run, too."

After lunch, my aunts and Michela arrive at the house to help me get ready. Aunt Dee is a hairdresser by profession and Aunt Ro has always been good with makeup, so they're in charge of my look for the wedding. I grin as the five of them spread out in my childhood bedroom, lying their dresses across my bed and unloading beauty supplies from their bags. "It's go time!" Aunt Ro says. "I'm so excited—you haven't let me do your makeup since the prom..."

"Keep it light," I say. "I don't want too much."

"That's exactly what she said back then," Aunt Vanna says.

"Trust me, Gems—I know what you like," Aunt Ro says.

"Can we put on music?" Michela asks.

It feels like a party already—we're blasting music on Aunt Soph's phone, telling stories, and laughing. The photographer arrives just as Aunt Vanna is lacing up the back of my dress. "Let me get a detail shot of the shoes and jewelry," she says after she snaps several pictures.

There isn't much jewelry; I'm only wearing my engagement ring, which I never take off, and my mom's garnet ring. I've cherished the garnet ring since my dad gave me all my mom's jewelry when I was a teenager. Her countless bracelets, necklaces, and earrings are in a box on my dresser, but the only piece I wear regularly is this ring. I like garnets because they're earthy and understated, not flashy like other gemstones, and I love the story behind the ring. It was the first gift my dad bought for my mom, on Valentine's Day a month after they started dating. I like imagining my parents back then—nineteen and crazy about each other, embarking on the greatest love story of their lives. I press the ring to my cheek. My mom is the only woman missing from this room; I wish she were standing beside me. I'm honoring her at the ceremony with a chair in the front row covered in flowers and a plaque that reads "In loving memory of Siena Cimino," but wearing her ring is more meaningful to me. Like the journals, it's a personal, private link to my mom that only my dad and I understand.

When my aunts and I are ready, we head to Oakfield Park. The clouds have disappeared, and the ceremony area looks just as I planned—the rows of white chairs, the rustic wooden arch at the altar. Luke and the kids aren't there yet, and the photographer scopes out a location for the first look. "I'm thinking underneath these trees," she says. "We'll have Luke stand near the—"

"Gemma! Gemma!"

I turn to see Nate and Scotty running toward me. They're wearing identical suits and clutching fistfuls of dandelions. I open my arms to them and they barrel into me, leaving streaks of mud across my dress. "We got you flowers!" Nate says.

"I love them!" I say.

"We were going to pick more, but Daddy said to get out of the dirt."

"Daddy was right," I say. "Where is Daddy?"

"Over here."

Luke walks up to me, beaming. His smile is so wide it scrunches up his eyes and he looks handsome and polished in his navy suit. I throw my arms around his neck. "I missed you!"

"You're beautiful!" He kisses me once, twice, three times, runs his hands over my hair and dress. "Baby...you look incredible!"

The photographer takes a bunch of pictures, and then we pose for formal photos by ourselves and with our families in different areas of the park. I stick the dandelions into my bouquet of white calla lilies and the kids toss more dandelions into Michela's basket of petals. "Get those weeds out of your basket," Aunt Soph says.

"I like them!" Michela says.

"She can throw those in the aisle too," I say. "Whatever makes the kids happy."

"It's four fifteen," Aunt Vanna says. "You should take your places before the guests arrive."

The ceremony begins; my dad, Michela, and I hide in the gazebo at one end of the park while Luke and the boys walk down the aisle. Aunt Vanna, who is in charge of giving us our cues, sends Michela out after Nate and Scotty. My dad offers me his arm. "Ready, Gems?"

"Ready!"

Aunt Vanna nods to us, but my dad pauses to kiss me on the forehead. "I love you," he says. "I'm so happy you're happy. That means everything to me."

As we make our way down the aisle, I smile at the faces in the crowd. All my relatives are there, including Aunt Cara and her wife, who made the trip from Europe. I see Nora, Harry, Lenny, and the rest of Luke's family; Carter and his date; and Bree along with the women from the office and their husbands. Then we reach the altar and I join hands with Luke.

Luke and I hired Reverend David DePaolo, the officiant from Marisa's wedding, to lead our ceremony. We were comfortable with him after seeing him perform a simple, heartfelt ceremony infused with some humor. David talks about the nature of love, then invites Bella and Marisa to read a poem together. Once they're done, David explains the sanctity of our marriage vows. The boys, who are standing at the altar with us, start to squirm. "When do we get cake?" Nate asks, interrupting · David.

"I was wondering the same thing," David says. "You've got the right idea, kid."

"The sun is in my eyes," Scotty whines.

"Do you guys want to sit with Grandma?" Luke asks, and the boys run to Nora in the front row. "Um...sorry, Reverend..."

"You got them to wear suits—you're winning as parents," David says. "So, as I was saying..."

Eventually, it's time for us to say our vows. David gives Luke a series of phrases to repeat. I'm trembling as I listen; my joy and anticipation have built to a peak and looking into Luke's bright eyes makes me want to cry. Words tumble over each other in my head: Yes, I take this man with his heart like a hummingbird's and his voice full of gravel and his arms always reaching out to me, always holding me close to him. I take his fears and the ruined skin around his nails and the tattoo that used to have Sylvie's name and every flaw I may find as the days go on. I take it all and love it all, now and forever; Luke is an extension of myself. I take our sons and the men they will become and the years stretching before us, whatever the future brings. As I'm thinking this, David asks me to repeat my vows and I can't get through the first words without crying. Luke takes my face into his hands and kisses the tears on my cheek. "You're not supposed to kiss her yet!" David says.

"But she's crying!" Luke says.

David feigns annoyance and turns to the crowd. "Kids these days don't know how to wait..."

Everyone laughs. Luke and I laugh too, and this puts a stop to my tears. I compose myself and get through the rest of the vows. We exchange rings, and then we get to share a real kiss. When we break apart, we keep our faces close, our noses touching. "My husband," I say.

"Finally," he says.

We leave the altar hand in hand as the crowd cheers. When we arrive at the restaurant for cocktail hour, we're bombarded with hugs from friends and family. We can't eat or drink anything because everywhere we turn, someone wants to congratulate us. When we reach the group of girls from the office, Jasmine hands us two plates piled with food. "None of us ate at our weddings," she says. "Put something in your stomachs now while you can."

I can't take a bite yet; I have to give each of them a hug. "I'm so glad you guys are here!"

"That was a beautiful ceremony," Lina says.

"I love your dress!" Bree says.

"I love the dandelions in your bouquet," Erica says.

"Nate and Scotty's contribution," I say.

Cocktail hour flies by, and then it's time for dancing. Jasmine was right—Luke and I are having too much fun to eat. We dance through dinner and dessert and only stop when Scotty asks Luke to take him to the bathroom. I sink into a chair next to Aunt Soph; it's the first time I've sat down in hours and my feet are killing me. I observe the scene around me. The DJ is playing a slow song, and almost everyone is on the dance floor. It strikes me how many couples are in the room—old couples and young couples, Harry's parents who are in their late eighties and Bella with the guy she just started dating and my cousin Tommy with his pregnant wife. It's heartwarming to witness so much love. Then I glance at the people who are sitting down. Bree is sipping a martini and scrolling through her phone; she's paying no attention to the dancing couples, and I remind myself that she likes being single. My dad is at the next table, leaning forward in his chair to listen to Nate and Michela. I feel a pang of sorrow. My dad is alone and he'll always be alone; that's a sad existence for someone so kind and loyal. I turn to Aunt Soph. "The kids have had your dad's ear for a while," she says. "Michela never stops talking."

"Same with Nate." I put my hand over hers. "Don't end up like my dad, Aunt Soph."

"What?"

"Don't settle for being lonely for the rest of your life. I'm sure there's a man out there who could make you happy if you're willing to look. Maybe you could try one of those dating websites—find someone who's serious and wants to commit, who's intelligent like you and has similar interests. You're an amazing person and you deserve a great partner."

"I don't need a partner." She's insulted. "I'm managing everything on my own. Michela and I are fine—"

"I know that. But love makes life a lot more pleasant."

Her expression softens; she looks at the rings on my hand, then at my dress. "I'm glad you're in love," she says. "You're glowing! And you and Luke are perfect for each other."

"Thank you."

"I still can't believe this is your wedding day! It feels like yesterday you were a kid in sweatpants..."

"I would have worn sweatpants today if it were socially acceptable."

We laugh. Luke and Scotty return from the bathroom; Scotty runs over to the kids, and Luke walks up to us and puts his arm around me. "How's my wife?" he asks.

"Extremely happy."

I rest my head against his. Aunt Soph gets up, presumably to give us time alone, but Luke addresses her. "Michela is brilliant," he says. "I was showing the kids how the chandelier formed rainbows on the wall, and she started telling us about the electromagnetic spectrum and the different wavelengths..."

"She's been into that lately," Aunt Soph says. "We saw a cool exhibit at the science museum and she wanted to know more, so we've been reading books about it."

"It's awesome that you're exposing her to that," Luke says. "She explained the concept really well!"

Aunt Soph looks embarrassed to be caught in the act of good parenting. "I guess," she says. "She likes to learn."

An upbeat song starts to play, and Aunt Soph disappears into a cluster of my aunts. Luke kisses me; for a moment there is nothing in the world but his lips and mine. Then I feel a little hand on my leg. "Gemma," Scotty pouts. "Nate won't let me be a superhero."

"I'm the superhero in this game!" Nate says.

"You can both be superheroes," I say.

"And we'll be the villains," Luke says. "Watch out—we're going to capture you!"

Nate and Scotty bolt away across the dance floor. I give Luke one more kiss before we take off running after the kids.

**

The weather is cold and windy on Bree's last day at Callahan and Ramos. It's October, and Bree will be starting her job at a Big Law firm in New York next week. Though Erica and Lina wanted to keep her on as an associate, I'm sure Bree is looking for more money and prestige than she can get at our cozy estate planning firm. We've known about her plans for a while, but now that the time has come to say goodbye, it feels surreal. After lunch, we gather on the couches for cake and a coffee break.

We're a bigger group now; Erica and Lina recently hired another associate and a legal assistant. Kathleen, who I'm training, is twenty-two, fresh out of college, and full of enthusiasm; Aditi just graduated from law school and is navigating her first serious relationship. Both girls fit in well with our team, and they're fascinated when the rest of us tell stories about our husbands and kids. I feel like one of the wise older women at the office, sharing my advice with the younger girls during coffee breaks. I like Kathleen and Aditi, but I'm going to miss Bree a lot.

The coffee break feels fun and celebratory, but once Bree gets up to finish packing her box of belongings, we grow somber. Even Bree looks like she's ready to cry. "This has been a great job," she says to us. "Thank you for being flexible and supporting me while I got through law school. Thank you for everything you've taught me."

"Of course," Lina says.

"And I don't mean only the legal stuff. I mean..." Tears start running down Bree's cheeks. "Working here is like being part of a family. I'm grateful I had you guys as sisters all these years."

"Honey!" Erica bursts into tears and puts her arms around Bree. "You'll always be part of this family! We love you!"

"Come back and visit us anytime," Jasmine says.

Bree's shoulders are shaking. I've never seen her like this, overtaken by her feelings; I didn't realize she cherished us so much. When Erica lets go of her, she straightens up and dries her eyes. "You've created something amazing here," she says. "Don't ever change the vibe."

"We won't," Erica says.

After multiple rounds of hugs with everyone, Bree picks up her box.

I hold open the door for her. "I'll miss you, Gemma," she says. "When's your book coming out again?"

"July first, 2019."

"Awesome—can't wait to buy it! Text me that day to remind me. And let me know if you want to grab drinks sometime."

"Definitely."

Bree smiles at me, then strides out the door on her high heels.

***

It's my thirtieth birthday, and I'm crouched on the bathroom floor over a white stick. I'm waiting for the screen to load; I chose a digital test this time because those pink lines drive me crazy. This is the same place I took my first pregnancy test nearly four years ago, but this time I'm hoping with all my heart for a positive result.

Once a word comes up on the screen, I head to my childhood bedroom. It's early in the morning, and the winter light peeks tentatively through the window blinds. Luke is asleep in my bed, and Nate and Scotty are passed out on the floor. We're closing on our house—a colonial here in Oakfield—tomorrow, and we've been living with my dad for the past week to avoid paying rent. It's crowded in this tiny room, but our family loves being together. I cover Nate and Scotty with the blanket they kicked aside and I get into bed with Luke.

I kiss him; he stirs and opens his eyes. "Did you take the test?" he asks. "What did it say?"

I hand him the stick. "Honey, here we go…"

ACKNOWLEDGMENTS

As always, I'm grateful to my husband and children for their love, support, and ideas. Thank you to the women I count on for their honest advice—my mom first and foremost, plus the other women in my family and my friends. Special thanks to Ally for her help with my opening paragraph. Thank you to the men in my family too, especially Stevie, who is my proofreader, format fixer, grammar police, and resource on law firms. You probably deserve an editor credit by now.

Thank you to the musicians who shared their wisdom with me: Mary Voutsa, Joanna Sibilia, and Chuck Salamone. "Music is the greatest of all the arts," as Gemma says, and I hope I've done a decent job portraying it. Thank you to Sandra Reddy for all the useful feedback—I can't wait to read your novel when it's finished! Thank you to Donna Norman-Carbone and Lainey Cameron for the enthusiasm and support. And I am grateful to you, readers, for taking this journey with me.

ABOUT THE AUTHOR

Raquel Drosos is the author of the novels *Games of Chance* and *Like a Mom*. She is a member of the Women's Fiction Writers Association (WFWA). Raquel grew up in New Jersey and still lives there with her husband and their two wildly imaginative children.

Find out more on www.raqueldrosos.com, where you can also sign up for her author newsletter, "Make a Mess."

Made in the USA
Middletown, DE
22 February 2025

71584496R00146